KILL SWITCH

A TOM ROLLINS THRILLER

PAUL HEATLEY

INKUBATOR
BOOKS

Published by Inkubator Books
www.inkubatorbooks.com

ISBN (eBook): 978-1-83756-434-7
ISBN (Paperback): 978-1-83756-435-4

For Aidan

PROLOGUE

Orlando Higgs has never been to San Francisco before. This is his first time.

As such, he acquaints himself with the city. He rides the tram, and the bus. He walks up and down the hills. He's learnt that forty-eight of them are named. He can't remember them all, but he knows where they are. He's committed their locations to memory. Everything about the layout of the city, he keeps it in mind.

On one quiet day, Orlando even takes the ferry out to Alcatraz, and strolls around the island with the tourists and the families and the elderly couples. In his chinos and his Hawaiian shirts, to anyone else he'd appear to be just another tourist. But he's not a tourist. He's here for work. And despite how it may appear, as he walks solo through the city, he's not here alone. He's mic'd up, just in case. He wears an earpiece that he conceals beneath a fedora. It's not the kind of hat he'd ordinarily wear, but its wide brim conceals his earpiece. His microphone is concealed in his wristwatch, though he hasn't had any need to use it, and it's rare that anyone from his team contacts him on the radio.

The only reason for him and his team to be here in San Francisco is on an operation. An important operation that, they've been assured, will make them all very wealthy men. Orlando didn't come into this life for the sightseeing; he entered it for the money.

Still, he's enjoyed his time in San Francisco. The weather has been good, and so has the food. He's looked at it like a small vacation, before they get down to business. Orlando can't remember the last time he took a vacation. He joined the Army at twenty-one, and he was kicked out at twenty-nine, and in the ten years since he's worked freelance, running various operations around the globe, both before he acquired his current team, and after. It's the kind of lifestyle that doesn't really accommodate vacations. It's always about moving from one job to the next. It's about keeping on the move so the aftermath of the last job doesn't catch up to them.

It's about staying alive.

He and his team of five reached San Francisco a few weeks earlier than they needed to. Three of them have been exploring the city, taking in the lay of the land, preparing for what is to come. The remaining two, Corey Crewe and Eddie Mitchell, have been hard at work in their own respective field. They're Orlando's computer experts. His techs. They spend their time in the temporary HQ they've set up. It's an old warehouse, long abandoned and fallen to ruin, nestled near to other, still-functional, warehouses. The location is on the water, and at night, when Orlando is on guard duty, he stares out across the bay, careful not to feel himself lulled to sleep by the rhythmic lapping of the waves. This is where Corey and Eddie have been spending all of their time while the others explore. They've been setting up and preparing for what's to come, too, but they've also been searching.

Of course, it isn't all exploration. They're a team, and Orlando knows he needs to keep them sharp. These weeks before they launch their operation, they might be spending them in a pleasant place with pleasant weather, but it's important they don't go soft. Orlando runs daily drills, every morning, keeping his team in top shape. He trusts his men, though. They won't over-indulge. They won't slip up. Just like him, they pride themselves on their professionalism, despite their inauspicious beginnings.

Like Orlando, they're all ex-military. Like him, they were all either booted out of their previous regiments for various infractions – fighting, racketeering, and Josh Chlebek was even participating in the running of a prostitution ring – or serving court martials. Their punishments are how Orlando found them. How he recruited them. They're a motley crew, certainly, but they make it work. He was very specific about the people he chose to recruit.

After one week in the city, when Orlando returns to the warehouse after his daily wanderings, Corey is waiting for him. He's grinning broadly.

"You look in a good mood," Orlando says.

"Because I *am*," Corey says. "And you're gonna be, too."

"You didn't radio."

"It could wait. It wasn't an emergency."

"Okay. Make my day."

Corey holds out a photograph. It's blurred, but next to it is a printout, detailing the subject in the picture. It comes with a clearer shot, too, of a man in Army uniform.

"Picked him up on the facial recognition software we've got set up," Corey says while Orlando reads. "Thoughts?"

Orlando reads to the bottom of the document. He smiles a little. "He hasn't been in the Army for a long time."

"No, he hasn't. Looks like he's been travelling, and getting himself into a lot of trouble."

"I saw that," Orlando says. "I liked it. The trouble works for our profile."

"That's what I thought. Eddie, too, when I showed him."

Orlando looks at the image again, and then hands it back over. "How long has he been in the city?"

"Just over a month."

"That's *also* good. You're right, Corey – this news *has* put me in a good mood. Hell, I was already in a good mood – this has made it *better*."

"I live to serve," Corey says. "You're happy with him? I should get to work on the footage?"

"I'm more than happy," Orlando says. "He's perfect. Get to it. And keep an eye on him – make sure he doesn't decide to suddenly leave the city. I want him under twenty-four-hour surveillance. Let the others know when they get back that we've found our man."

Corey nods, pleased with himself, and hurries back to his station. Orlando smiles to himself as he heads to his cot at the rear of the warehouse. As much as they'd planned and prepared, there was still one piece of the puzzle they were putting together that needed to be found. Seems like Corey has found it for them.

Orlando lies flat on his cot, lacing his fingers together behind his head, eyes turned to the high ceiling. Things are progressing smoothly. They're on track. In just a few short weeks, Mr. Tom Rollins is going to have a very bad time.

1

Tom Rollins has been in San Francisco for just over two months. When he first arrived at the city, he was just passing by when his car's exhaust started to rattle and roar. He'd picked the Ford up in Detroit, and he'd already put a lot of miles on it in the just six months since then. He checked it over himself at the side of the road. It was still driveable. The exhaust was a minor thing to replace, and so instead of dumping the car and finding a replacement, Tom took it to a garage. It was going to take a day for a part to come in. While he waited, he took a stroll down the block and came to a diner with a 'Help Wanted' sign in the window. Shrugging to himself, Tom went inside and interviewed for the job.

And then, before he knows it, two months have passed. Tom is still working as a short-order cook at the diner. He's found himself a small place to stay in the Bayview neighbourhood, not far from where he works. When he has a shift, he tends to walk there.

The diner is called Sam's. A straightforward name, after

its owner. Sam's has been running for twenty-two years. It's open twenty-four hours. Tom is usually put on the night shift. He knows why. His employer and his co-workers have made no secret as to why he's assigned nights, and it has nothing to do with his cooking.

Bayview is not the most dangerous neighbourhood in San Francisco. A higher crime rate than average, but on the streets and in the place he rents, Tom has never had any trouble. After hours though, at midnight and beyond, no matter where you are in the country, that's when the creeps and the dangerous people come out. And that's why Tom works the night shift at Sam's. To keep the till safe and, more importantly, the other staff.

It hadn't taken long for Sam's other employees to see what Tom was capable of. Just five shifts in, and his first night. Up to that point he'd been working days under Sam's supervision. Sam had decided it was time for him to go it alone, unsupervised, and they'd see how he did. That first night shift, everything changed.

Two guys came in, stockings pulled over their faces, waving a gun around. Two skinny white guys, meth mouths clear even through the nylon. The gun was a broken Smith & Wesson Model 10. It wasn't loaded. The two men were desperate, and Tom didn't want to hurt them. He tried talking to them first. Calming them down. He let them know that he knew their gun was empty, and that even if it was loaded it wouldn't be able to fire – with its missing hammer and bent barrel, it was more likely to hurt them than anyone else.

They didn't back down. They got stupid. They swung at him with the revolver. Tom easily disarmed and subdued them. The two waitresses on service were impressed. Word spread through Sam's meagre workforce. From that moment on, Tom worked nights.

He doesn't mind. It's not always so eventful. In fact, it's rare that Tom has to step out from behind the grill. The waitresses tell him that he's given Sam's a reputation – if you come after hours, you come for food and food only. You don't come looking for trouble. Things aren't how they used to be. Sam himself is happy, too. Means he's not losing takings, as scant as they are at this time of the night.

Tom works with a few different waitresses. There are eight employed by Sam's, though only four of them work nights, and only two at a time. The four who work the nights are the younger members of staff. Three of them are college students, and the fourth is an artist who says she's up through the nights anyway.

From the outside, Sam's is a deceptive building. It's much bigger inside than it looks from the front. It appears to be a small box with a low, flat roof, located in between a florist and a craft supplies. Through the door, however, it opens out, the walls lined with booths, and the floorspace filled with eight round tables. At the back of the building is the counter, which has stools in front of it like a bar, and beyond that the kitchen where Tom spends most of his time. Tom keeps the area clean and ordered. Unless someone is ordering food, there isn't much to do, and so he has to find ways to preoccupy himself. He scrubs the grills, or mops the floor. He sharpens the knives and arranges the utensils. He puts away the drying crockery that the day cook put through the machine before he left.

Tonight, the two waitresses are both college students. Mandy and Amira. Mandy studies psychology, and she works on an upcoming essay leaning on the counter next to the till. Amira studies biology, but she's not currently working on any essays. Instead, she's focussing on her job, clearing mugs and plates from a table at the window under the neon 'Open 24hrs' sign that glows pink against the side of her face. It's a quiet night. Tom has grilled four burgers, a steak, and a chicken breast. There have been three tables order food, and two people come to the counter to drink coffee before they headed to their own late shifts. Currently, there is only one customer in, an older man sat by a window in the corner booth and sipping from a diet soda. Only at weekends can they expect Sam's to be busy, when people have been out at bars or clubs and they leave, suddenly finding themselves hungry on the way home. Tonight is Wednesday – technically, since it's after midnight, it's now Thursday morning. Not long until the weekend rush. Tom is working tomorrow night and then he has a couple of days off. There's usually less trouble at the weekends. More customers means more witnesses, and so no one tries anything stupid.

Amira enters the kitchen, the plates stacked up in both hands, the mugs on top of them. She starts rinsing them off in the sink before lining them up on the rack to go through the machine.

"I can do that," Tom says.

"That's okay," Amira says. She flicks a braid out of her face as she turns back to face him over her shoulder. "It's not like I'm rushed off my feet out there. How you holding up back here?"

Tom leans against the counter, arms folded. He shrugs.

Amira laughs. "You know, I don't know why Sam keeps this place twenty-four hours. I think when he first opened people were more likely to come out to eat at all hours, but it's not like that anymore. People don't have to leave their homes after midnight if they're hungry, and they won't. They can just go online and order something to come to them. In fact, I'm surprised he hasn't hired a delivery driver and tried to get in on *that* action. It would make more sense."

"You could always make the suggestion," Tom says.

"He'll never do it. He's too old school. He's got too much nostalgia for the past – that's why we're open all night."

"You don't like the night shift?"

Amira shrugs. "I don't mind it, if I'm honest. It pays better. And plus, the women who don't work it, they've got kids – and grandkids – and I'd feel bad if I forced my way onto days and they didn't get to spend so much time with their families. Working nights is better for my courses, too."

"I'm surprised you're able to do college *and* work nights."

Amira shrugs. She pushes the crockery through the machine and it comes to life, spraying the plates and mugs with hot, soapy water. She doesn't leave the kitchen yet. "It's manageable. If it wasn't, I'd have to find something else."

"When do you sleep?"

"When I can," she says, raising her eyebrows. "My dad says I need to appreciate this kind of energy and this kind of metabolism while I'm young. He says I won't be able to run at this kind of pace when I'm older. How old are you, Tom?"

Tom gives her a look. "I'm thirty-four," he says. "Are you implying I'm past my prime?"

She laughs. "No – my dad's fifty-two. You've still got a way to go."

Amira doesn't live far from where Tom is staying. Mandy always gets picked up after every shift by her boyfriend, and Tom and Amira wait with her, and then Tom walks Amira back to hers. She lives with a couple of other students, all of them on different courses, and they all keep different hours. "We thought living together would be great, a lot of fun," she told him once. "But it turns out we hardly ever see each other."

"Obviously, I'm not gonna be here forever," she says now. "I've got another year on my course, and then after that I'll have to find something that puts the degree to use." She leans against the sink, looking back at Tom. "Do you have plans?"

Tom shrugs. "A life plan? I can't remember the last time I had one of those."

Amira looks surprised. "Oh yeah? You just gonna stay here?"

"Just as long as I need to. And then I'll move on to somewhere else."

Amira regards him silently for a while, as if deliberating what she'll say next. The dishes have come out of the machine, and they leave them to drip dry. "You know, people here wonder about you."

"In what way?"

"Like, who you are. They ask me about you. They know we walk back together, so they think I'm getting your life story every night. They're always disappointed when I tell them that outside of here you're just the same as inside."

"Well, I'm an open book," Tom says. "All anyone has to do is ask."

Amira grins. "That simple, huh?"

"It always is."

"All right. Where'd you come from?"

"Before I came here? Nowhere in particular. I'd been in Mississippi a while, but then I was just driving, state to state.

I didn't stay anywhere for too long. I stopped in to see my dad in New Mexico. He's ill."

"Oh. I'm sorry to hear that. Is it...is it serious?"

"It's cancer," Tom says. "And it's going to kill him, but if you saw him you wouldn't know it. He still looks the same as he ever did, except for when he moves. He winces a lot. Other than that, you can't tell."

Amira looks hesitant to ask anything else. It's clear she feels like she may have crossed a line, learning about his dying father.

"I'm sorry if things suddenly got heavy," Tom says.

"No, no, it's not that." Amira clears her throat. "He lives in New Mexico? Is that where you're from?"

Tom nods.

"Far from home."

"It hasn't been home for a long time. Nowhere has, not really."

"So you just travel? Just drift, state to state, nowhere in mind, like a modern-day beatnik?"

Tom laughs. "I don't think of myself as a beatnik."

"I get that you're living it, but have you read *On The Road*?"

"Yes, I've read it. And you're not the first person to ask me that."

"You read it recently?"

"Long time ago."

"You think maybe it could have inspired your current lifestyle?"

"Maybe. Who knows? Somewhere deep down in my subconscious."

"Is this all you've ever done? Travelled? Where did you learn to fight?"

"I was in the Army."

Amira's eyes go round. "Shit, for real? You know, people have wondered that. Or that maybe you were a cop."

"Well, now you can tell some of them they were right."

Amira starts to say something else, but Mandy interrupts, leaning through the pass. "Uh – *Tom*?"

Tom picks up on her tone. He springs to attention, pulling off his apron and striding through to the front, motioning for Amira to stay where she is. He doesn't dump the apron. He keeps hold of it.

Mandy has her back up against the pass, eyes wide, as far back from the till and the front counter as she can get.

There's a man standing in front of the till. He's wearing a mask and he has a machete.

The remaining customer in the diner presses himself up into the corner of the booth, frozen, too fearful to flee, hoping that if he stays very still and out of the way he won't be seen.

The mask is a balaclava, covering all of the machete wielder's features except for his mouth, nostrils, and eyes. His eyes are not the wide, bugging-out orbs of a desperate junkie. They're narrowed and focussed. More than that. They're malicious. The man has come here wanting something.

It doesn't take long for him to make his wants clear. "Money, motherfucker! Empty out the register!"

Tom steps out from around the counter, both hands raised, the apron bunched up in his right.

The man snorts. "What do you think you're gonna do? Huh? Get your ass back in that kitchen before I cut your motherfucking head off!"

It doesn't take Tom long to assess the situation, nor

how to handle the man with the machete. With the desperate junkies, he can talk them down. Persuade them that what they're doing is wrong, and that this isn't a path they want to go down. There was one time, a young guy came in, so young and scrawny and sickly. He asked for a glass of water and then sat in a booth, and kept looking over his shoulder at the counter, at the till. Tom could see his nervous energy. The way his legs bounced under the table. The hunted, cornered look in his eyes and on his face. Tom sat down opposite him. Told him he'd be making a mistake. That if he tried to rob the register, Tom was going to have to stop him. The kid swallowed. He was desperate. Tom made him a burger and fries, on the house. The kid ate quick, like a ravenous animal. When he was through, Tom told him to come back the next night. Said he'd feed him again, and then he'd drive him to rehab. Tom said he'd pay for it. The kid didn't have to do a thing – he just needed to turn up.

The kid never came back.

Tom doesn't regret trying to help. His only regret would be if he hadn't. He'll never feel bad about trying to help a person, especially if they're vulnerable.

All to say, a soft approach isn't going to work with this masked man. There are two categories – the soft touch, and the hard. This man, and his erratic machete, fall squarely into the latter. He wants the money, and he's willing to cut through Tom and the two waitresses to get to it, no matter how meagre it may be. A man willing to kill for a handful of dollars cannot be reasoned with.

Tom keeps his hands up. He steps lightly to the side, circling the man. The masked man's attention splits between Tom and the till, and Mandy behind it.

"Get your ass back," the man says, spinning on Tom and jabbing at him with the tip of the machete.

"Why don't you just calm down," Tom says, "and put the machete on the ground."

The man glares at him. "I'm already tired of your shit, man," he says. "You got five seconds to get outta my face, or I'm gonna start swinging."

They face off. Silently, Tom counts off the seconds. He gets to seven. "You know how to count, right?"

The man roars, telegraphing what he's about to do. He rears back with the machete and swings down, looking to split Tom in half. Tom is ready, and easily steps to his left, to the outside of the man's slash. He steps through, whipping the apron out so it catches across the front of the man's neck. He grabs the apron at both ends, goes back-to-back with the man, and flips him over his shoulder so he lands on his front. Tom quickly follows up and stamps down on the man's right hand clutching tight to the machete.

The man cries out, his grip broken, and Tom kicks the machete away. He still has the apron wrapped around the man's neck, keeping control of him. He wrenches it tight and slams his knee into the side of the man's head twice, until he falls limp. Tom lets him fall flat on his face.

Mandy and Amira are together behind the counter, watching on.

"We've called the cops," Mandy says.

2

It's twenty minutes before the cops arrive. Tom has bound the man's wrists and ankles with a couple more aprons. He's removed his mask, too, and stuffed it into his mouth to keep him quiet. After he came round, he started cursing loudly, demanding to be released, making derogatory remarks toward both Mandy and Amira. Tom smacked him in the mouth to teach him some manners, and then gagged him with the mask.

The man is sitting on the floor, his back to the booth closest to the door. Tom is in the booth beside him. Since being gagged, he's calmed down. He hasn't been so rowdy. Hasn't tried to break free. Has understood his situation and quietly accepted it.

The cops, when they arrive, are familiar to Tom. Nina Perry and David Remsburg. Nina is smiling when she enters, shaking her head, looking down at the captured man. "Your handiwork?" she says to Tom.

"He wouldn't listen to reason," Tom says.

"He had a machete," Mandy calls from behind the counter.

"That so?" Nina says, though she's still looking at Tom. "And you disarmed him?"

"Somebody had to."

She laughs. It's a pleasant sound. Nina is Black. Her hair is cut short around the sides and back, though sits longer on top. She's a similar height to Tom, when he's standing, and her build is athletic from hours spent in the station's gym, working on her cardio and strength. She's easy on the eye, too, and Tom always finds himself pleased to see her, regardless of the circumstances. "And where is said machete now?" she says.

Tom points. "Left it where he dropped it."

David whistles low as he retrieves the blade. "Someone came to play." David is white, his blond hair cut short to his skull. He's conventionally handsome, square-jawed, and in his uniform looks like a model playing dress-up whilst on a shoot. He takes the machete out to their cruiser.

"I gotta say, Rollins, we're not getting as many calls here as we used to," Nina says. "You've calmed things down."

Tom tilts his head toward the man sitting on the floor nearby. "There's always exceptions. You had a busy night?"

"We were dealing with a domestic dispute when we got the call to come here," she says. "Hence our being a little late."

"I had no expectations for when you'd arrive."

"Maybe not, but I pride myself on my timekeeping. My mom used to always say, if you're not early you're late. Of course, we figured you'd have the situation under control. If every callout was like this our jobs would be a lot easier."

"I'll pass that on," Tom says.

David returns and the cops untie the aprons from the attacker's wrists and ankles, handing them back to Tom. They slap cuffs on him. David escorts him out to the cruiser, but Nina hangs back. "Well," she says. "I guess I'll see you again next time there's an attempted robbery."

"Like you said, that could be a while. It's been getting quieter."

Nina nods. "Sam's isn't as much of a target as it used to be. Before you started, we'd get here just to clean up the mess and take statements. We didn't have any perps to transport to the station."

"I like to make sure you're earning that salary."

Nina laughs. She looks toward the door, through the glass, and sees that David is behind the wheel of the cruiser, waiting for her. "Well," she says. "Until next time."

Tom nods. As she begins to turn, he says, "Unless we happen to bump into each other before then, I suppose."

Nina pauses. She smiles at him. "It's always possible," she says. "You know Harry's Coffee House? Whenever I work nights, I always stop in there before my shift." She shrugs, like it's no big deal. "It's good coffee. Maybe you should give it a try sometime."

"When's your next shift?"

"Tomorrow night, as it happens."

"If I'm passing by, I'll be sure to call in."

"You do that." Still smiling at him, Nina leaves the diner.

Tom watches her go. Sees the cruiser pass by a black Ford van parked to the side a little way down. The van was there when Tom first started his shift. He checks all the parked vehicles when he starts. Force of habit. Some of the cars have gone since he began. Most of them are still there, empty, parked up for the night.

In the distance, the sky is lightening. Soon it will be dawn, and the end of Tom's shift.

When he turns, Mandy and Amira are both behind the counter. They're watching him, and smirking. There's no one else in the diner.

"What?" Tom says.

"Did you just make a date?" Mandy says.

"A date?" Tom says.

"Oh, come *on*," Amira says. "Whenever she walks in, I always see how your little face lights up, so don't go and give us that."

"Y'know," Mandy says, "sometimes I think you're glad when someone tries to rob us, because you know exactly who's going to turn up to take them away."

Tom grins. "You've seen through my ploy." He winks, then takes the aprons through to the kitchen and puts them in the washing machine.

The next couple of hours pass without incident. They serve a few coffees and someone orders pancakes, but their shift is over before the breakfast rush can begin. Amira pokes her head into the kitchen before they need to leave. "I'm not gonna be walking back with you this morning," she says. "I'm gonna get a ride with Mandy and her boyfriend – I need to go to the store and they're passing that way."

"Sure," Tom says.

"Try not to miss me too much," Amira says. "Although, from what we saw earlier, it doesn't seem like you're gonna be lonely at all."

Tom looks at her, amused.

Amira holds up her hands. "Hey, all I'll say is, she's a beautiful woman, and I'm real happy for you both." She winks at him and leaves the kitchen.

Tom's replacement runs late, and Tom leaves the diner ten minutes after his shift ends. He pauses on the sidewalk outside, breathing in the morning air, feeling the warmth of the rising sun on his face and scalp, already settling into the ground beneath him. As he prepares to set off, he pauses, looking to his left. The van is still there. Most of the vehicles around it have moved now, the people who were parked overnight having headed off to work or school or wherever. The few others that remain are cars, and Tom can see through them. Can see that they're empty. The van's rear windows are blacked out. Tom stares at them. His latent paranoia, ever present, comes to the fore. He never ignores it. It's kept him alive on more than one occasion.

There's movement in the van. A slight jostle, as if someone is in the back and has perhaps moved through to the front.

Tom's place is over the road and straight up the hill. He crosses the road, but he heads left, toward the van. He wants to pass by and take a look inside, get a glance at the occupants. As he gets near, the van suddenly roars into life, and pulls out onto the road so abruptly it couldn't have checked its mirrors before merging. Luckily for it, nothing else is coming.

It was a strange and sudden thing for the van to do, as if spooked off by Tom's approach. He watches it go, turning right at the junction and disappearing out of sight. Tom saw its licence plate, though. He keeps it in mind, silently reciting it to himself over and over, then he turns and starts the walk up the hill to his temporary home.

3

Tom's apartment isn't far from the diner. Just a fifteen-minute walk, uphill all the way. Tom keeps in shape, and the hill doesn't affect him. On his days off, he walks down it and runs back up. *That's* when his calves, thighs, and hamstrings begin to ache and burn.

When he reaches his apartment, the van is still on his mind. He doesn't go straight in. He looks the door over, and the front of the building, but there's nothing overtly wrong. He pulls out his key and goes inside. Closing the door behind him, he pauses in the small hallway. He listens. He sniffs the air. There's nothing to hear or smell. He makes his way through the apartment, checking on each room. Everything is where it should be – until he reaches his bedroom.

Whoever has been in his apartment, they were careful. They covered their tracks. They stepped lightly. However, Tom left the drawer on his bedside table open barely half an inch, the gap it would have created at the top covered by the overhang of the top of the table. The drawer has been pushed completely shut, no doubt after being pulled open and searched.

Now that he knows someone has been inside, Tom will go back through the apartment, looking everything over, checking to see if anything has been taken. He starts in his bedroom. Nothing has been taken from the drawer. He goes into the wardrobe. When Tom travels, all he ever takes with him is his backpack. It carries the few clothes he owns, but also the burner phones he carries, his Beretta, his KA-BAR, and a picture of a woman now long dead. A woman he loved, and whom a part of him always will. Alejandra. The backpack is where it should be. Tom unzips it and looks through. Its contents are untouched.

After checking all of the apartment, Tom is convinced that nothing has been taken. In the living room, he goes to the window and peers out at the street. He looks for the van that drove away from him, but whoever was in here was clearly a pro and he doubts they'd sit outside with a vehicle he recognises. Sure enough, the van is nowhere to be seen. He looks over the other vehicles present, but they all appear to be empty. They're familiar to him, too. He recognises them as belonging to his neighbours, or friends of theirs who come to visit. None of the vehicles stand out as unfamiliar.

Ordinarily, when Tom gets back after a night shift, he goes straight to bed and gets some sleep. Right now, there's no chance of rest. Knowing that someone has been here, has looked through his temporary home and his scant possessions, Tom is wide awake. He's wired. He needs answers.

Tom leaves the apartment. He starts walking. Circles the block, looking for anything that might be out of place. He's casual about it. His head isn't on a swivel. If anyone is watching, he doesn't want them to know that he's figured out they broke in. His eyes, however, cut left to right, checking every parked vehicle he passes, and looking at the homes of his neighbours, looking to see if there appear to be any new arrivals on the block.

Tom doesn't see anything that causes alarm. Nothing stands out. He keeps walking. Until he finds something, until he has an answer, he's not going to be able to return to the apartment. He's not going to be able to rest.

4

It's a pleasant day, so Orlando Higgs sits at an outside table of a café. It's his first time at the café. He eats somewhere different every day, every meal time. After three weeks, he's still exploring San Francisco. His time as a tourist, however, is soon drawing to a close, he knows. Just a few days left. His team have been working hard, laying groundwork, preparing for what's to come.

By this point, Orlando's team are a well-oiled machine, and he knows he can leave them to their own devices. He heads out for the day, and trusts them to get the work done. Every night, he returns to the warehouse and they update him on what they've been doing. They would never dream of slacking. Would never do anything to upset him.

Sitting on the sidewalk outside the café isn't exactly like patronizing a Parisian bistro, but Orlando has done that, too, and it wasn't all it was made out to be.

He picks at a pastry and sips from an espresso. Orlando rarely allows sugar and carbs to pass his lips, but seeing as a large part of this mission has been an unofficial vacation, he's allowing himself this one indulgence before it's over. He keeps himself tight. Just as he gets his men to run daily drills, he puts himself through his paces, too. As they're keeping a low profile in San Francisco he hasn't found a gym to visit, but bodyweight exercises in the warehouse are enough for now. The same goes for his men. When Orlando feels the need for some extra weight, he hoists Eddie up onto his shoulders and squats with him.

It's early afternoon, and the café will be closing soon. The sun is still shining, and the front of the café catches a large sunbeam. Orlando feels it upon his face. He closes his eyes and breathes deeply, enjoying the warmth, the light shining red through his eyelids.

His phone rings, vibrating against his thigh. Orlando opens his eyes and takes it from his pocket, checking the caller ID. He knows it won't be one of his men. They'd contact him via radio, through his earpiece.

Orlando doesn't have the caller's full name saved. Instead, it's under SBH.

Senator Bob Hanley.

Orlando answers. "Senator," he says.

"How's San Francisco?" Bob says.

"Bright and beautiful."

"I'm glad to hear it. The package is on the move, coming to you, looking to enjoy its vacation home for the weekend, and I'm pleased to hear that the weather will be accommodating."

"I'm sure they'll have more than enough time to work on their tan."

"Have you? You've been there a while now."

Orlando grins to himself. "You know me. I'm all business."

"Of course, of course."

"Speaking of, we're on top of things here and prepared for the arrival of the package."

"And everything else?"

"Like I said, we're on top of everything."

"Then I'll leave the package in your capable hands. Speak soon."

The senator hangs up. Orlando slips the phone back into his pocket. He drains the last of the coffee, but leaves what remains of the pastry. He gets to his feet and twists side to side, stretching out his body.

That was the signal he has been awaiting. The vacation is over. Things are about to begin. It's time to get serious. It's time to get to work.

5

After circling the block a few times and convinced there was nothing to see and no one lurking, Tom returned to his apartment. He checked it over again to be sure nothing had been taken, and also to see if any bugs had been planted. Stopping short of tearing the apartment apart and removing every socket from the walls, Tom found nothing. Bugs weren't too great of a concern to him – there was nothing to hear. No one has visited him in the apartment. Whenever he's in it, he's alone. There's no conversation to pick up on.

After locking the doors and the windows, Tom retrieved some glass jars from the recycling in the kitchen and tied the tops together with a long piece of string. He dangled them, two jars apiece, from the handles of the front and back door, and the inside of his bedroom. Should anyone try to get in, the jars clinking together would wake him. After that, he went to bed and got a few hours' sleep.

Tom wakes earlier than intended. He lies in the bed, listening to the rest of the apartment. It's still, but he doesn't like it. Doesn't like knowing that someone has been here while he was out, and has gone through his things. Again, he thinks of the van he spotted outside Sam's when he started his shift and still there when he finished, and of how it promptly drove away as he approached.

Around him, the room grows dark. Outside, the sun is gradually lowering. There's still a few hours before Tom's next shift begins. He showers and dresses and heads out into the evening. Despite the darkness in his apartment, it's still light outside. The sun is low and the shadows are long. Tom takes the long way to Harry's Coffee House. He's wary. Makes sure he's not followed. Checks all the vehicles he passes, whether parked or in motion, and keeps a look out for a black Ford van. He doesn't see one.

So far as he can tell, there's no one following. Tom doesn't relax. Stays alert. It's important to always be alert. Not once does the thought cross his mind that he may have forgotten himself last night and closed the bedside drawer all the way. He never has before. That's not who he is. When he has a routine, he sticks to it. He'd never go anywhere without leaving something subtle that would alert him to someone having been where he's staying.

By the time he reaches Harry's Coffee House, there's still no sign of a stalker, or anyone sitting on surveillance. Inside, Nina hasn't arrived yet. Despite being evening, there are plenty of people at the tables drinking coffee. Tom wonders if they work nights, too. On his way in he noticed the opening hours. Harry's Coffee House stays open late. He notices a small stage in the corner, a microphone stand at its front. It doesn't look like anyone is performing tonight, thankfully.

Tom gets a water for himself, and a black coffee for Nina.

If she shows, of course. Still, while he's taking up space in the establishment he feels like he should at least spend some money. He grabs some creamers and sugars and carries everything to a table at the rear of the room, his back to the wall and a clear view of the entrance ahead of him.

After five minutes, Nina walks in. She's in uniform. She looks around. Tom is about to raise his hand to wave to her when she spots him. Her face splits into a smile that she's quick to get under control. She comes to the table.

"I got you a coffee," Tom says. "But I don't know how you like it."

She sits, picking up a creamer and a sugar sachet. She holds the sides of the mug and feels its warmth. "I take it you haven't been here long?" she says, stirring in the creamer and the sugar.

"Just a few minutes."

She looks at his glass of water while she sips her drink. "Is that all you're having?"

"I've never been much of a coffee drinker."

"While working nights?" She whistles low. "That's hardcore, man. How do you get through?"

"I've never needed it. What can I say?"

"Just a high-energy guy. You look like you keep in shape."

"Thanks. So do you."

"Part of the job. I'm not sure the same can be said for a short-order cook."

"You have to commit yourself to something."

Nina smiles. "How was your day?"

Tom doesn't tell her about his belief that someone broke into his apartment. Doesn't tell her about his search for the culprits. "Fine," he says. "I slept."

"I hear that. I'm not actually supposed to be working

tonight. Last night was supposed to be my last night shift on the current rotation, but I found out right at the beginning that *uh-uh*, I'm on tonight, too."

"How come?"

"Someone called in sick. Flu."

"And you had to pick up the slack?"

"I suppose someone had to." She drinks.

Tom looks around the room. "Do you come here a lot?" he says.

"Pretty much every day," Nina says.

"A regular, huh? I should've asked them at the counter what your usual drink is, rather than chancing it with plain coffee."

"I'll take it any way it comes. I'm here for the caffeine." She laughs. "Harry's stays open late – did you notice that? And I don't live far from here, so it's an easy stop-off on my way to the station, whatever shift I'm working."

"I notice they have a stage."

"You thinking about getting up there with your guitar, Rollins? You got a backlog of folk classics you want to work through?"

"I don't have a guitar," Tom says. "And folk? I mean, sure, I'll listen to it, but what makes you think that would be my go-to?"

She laughs. "Don't take it personally. You come in here on a night there's a performance, you're gonna hear a folk song. Bad covers of Dylan, or Simon and Garfunkel, or other stuff I don't know who does it originally."

"And it's painful?"

"You have no idea. When there's someone playing, I don't tend to stay here too long."

"It sounds like a great time. I'll have to come back when

someone's on stage. I see flyers in the window. Doesn't look like I'll have to wait long."

Nina laughs. "Sure, more power to you."

"Oh, I'll drag you along with me. We'll stand front and centre, lighters in the air, shouting for an encore."

Nina spits out some coffee. Tom passes her a napkin so she can wipe her mouth. She shakes her head at him. "You're a bad man."

"Folk isn't to your taste?"

"I don't mind it. It's the pretentious guys who come in and play it that I struggle with. And don't get me started on the poets."

"Poets? How bad does it get? Are we talking bongos, turtlenecks, berets, the whole works?"

"Don't forget the wispy little chin beards."

"I'd never dream of forgetting the wispy little chin beards."

"Are you trying to make me laugh so hard I spit again?"

Tom grins. "I enjoyed the first one so much. But okay, I take your point. It sounds terrible. What *do* you listen to?"

"Soul," she says. "I was raised on it. My parents had this huge record collection, all soul, and they'd spin a few every single night. Aretha Franklin, Al Green, Roberta Flack, Erykah Badu, Nina Simone… I'm named for Ms Simone."

"Yeah?"

Nina nods. "Uh-huh. My folks met at the bar at one of her shows. When they got married, their first dance was to 'Feeling Good'. When I was born, they figured no other choice was good enough."

"That's a nice story."

"Yeah. I think they would've liked it if I was musically inclined, but that was never me. I mean, I like music, of course, but I can't play it, and I can't sing. They tried giving me piano lessons, but they never took. I don't have that kind of dexterity, try as I might. Your parents ever encourage you to learn an instrument?"

Tom hesitates, thinking how best to answer.

"What?" Nina says, picking up on his hesitation.

"Well, not any musical instruments. Me and my brother, we were raised by our father. After our mom died, our dad got wrapped up in his grief. Moved us outside of our town in New Mexico and raised us as survivalists and doomsday preppers. So, instead of pianos or guitars, he taught us how to strip and clean rifles, and how to shoot. How to catch and skin animals, cook them up."

"Wow. That sounds intense."

"It turned out for the best."

"For the intense rigours of a short-order cook?"

Tom smiles. "For a lot of things."

They talk a while longer, neither of them paying attention to the time, until finally Nina glances at her watch. "Shit," she says. "I really need to get going."

Tom checks the time. His shift starts in half an hour. "Same."

"You need a ride?"

"No, I'm good. I have time enough to walk." And, again, Tom wants to check to make sure that no one is following him, and that no one is parked outside the diner again.

"This was fun," Nina says, getting to her feet. "We should do it again sometime. I shouldn't always have to come around to pick up a collar just to see you."

Tom stands, too. "Sure. But I have to confess something."

"Yeah?"

"I know you said it's close to your home, but it feels like a betrayal to know that you come to Harry's Coffee House when Sam's is always open and waiting, and as far as I'm aware you've never stopped in there for a coffee, or food."

"That's fair," Nina says. "I should try to rectify that. Maybe sometime soon. I'd hate for that betrayed feeling to linger. Maybe I'll make it up to you later. We finish around the same time, right? If I'm not held up, could be I'll call by."

"If your timings work out, you know I'll be there."

Nina leaves the coffee house. Tom watches her go until she's in her car and has pulled away. When she's out of view, Tom leaves and makes his way to Sam's.

6

Nina's phone rings as she pulls up to the station. The ID reads Dante Walker. Her ex-boyfriend. She takes a deep breath and exhales hard before she answers. "Dante," she says.

"Hey, girl," Dante says. "It a good time to talk?"

She thinks it's never a good time to talk to him, but she refrains from saying so. "I'm about to start my shift, so it'll have to be quick."

"Yeah, sure, I'll be fast. I was just thinking how I've still got some of my stuff at your place –"

"You've got a box of stuff at my place, and it's been there since I kicked you out six months ago. You're lucky I haven't thrown it out already."

"Don't throw it out –"

"There's nothing important in there, Dante. I've checked. It's just old computer parts and two pairs of underwear."

"Yeah, but I need those parts. Anyway, that's why I'm calling, right? I've got some free time in a couple of days. If you're gonna be in, I can call by and pick them up."

Nina sighs, but keeps her mouth away from the phone when she does so. She doubts he'll actually do as he says. "Sure," she says. "Fine. Let me know in advance when you're planning on calling by and I can make sure I'm there."

"I can hear your doubts, Nina," Dante says. "You've never been any good at hiding your disappointment in me."

"And yet you've always been a superstar at living up to those low expectations." She glances up at the building. She needs to go inside.

"We gonna argue now? I didn't call to fight. We've done enough of that already. I thought you'd be pleased that I was gonna come and get my shit. You've hassled me about it enough times."

"I gave up on hassling you about three months ago."

"Y'know, you wouldn't have to complain if you'd just come and drop it off yourself."

"I made it very clear that I won't come to you, Dante. I've done more than enough for you. You're the one who destroyed our relationship. You want me to keep hold of your stuff, fine, I can put it in a cupboard and out of my mind, but don't ever expect me to do you any favours." She looks up at the station again. It's time to cut the conversation short. "I'm going now, Dante. I have to work." She hangs up before he can say anything else.

She composes herself as she gets out of the car, breathing deeply. In the station, after she clocks in, she passes Liz Farr on her way out.

"I thought your rotation was over?" Liz says, pausing in the corridor. Liz is also Black. She wears her hair long. She and Nina met at the academy and have been friends ever since.

"Supposed to be," Nina says. "Tompkins has the flu."

"Ah, damn. How you feeling?"

"I'm fine. It's fine. What's one more night, huh?"

Liz tilts her head. "Something wrong? Something happened?"

"That obvious? It's nothing serious. I just got off the phone with Dante."

"He still hasn't picked up his stuff?"

"Of course not. Why would I expect him to actually do something so simple within a timely manner?"

"Okay, well, you look mad as hell. Maybe keep hold of that energy for a bit, because Simon Arditti and his people are on their way out, too."

"Mm," Nina says. "Maybe I'll just try and avoid them. I'm already angry enough. You seen David?"

"Break room, last time I saw him."

"Cool. I'll go find him there."

They say their goodbyes and Nina makes her way through the station toward the break room. It's upstairs, toward the rear of the building.

The Bayview Heights Police Station is one of the bigger departments in San Francisco. As its name would suggest, it's located at the top of Bayview, at the top of a hill. The cruisers outside are all parked on a slant. From the lobby, Nina passes by the toilets and the offices and heads for the staircase. The ground floor is for administrative works, and processing perps. The cells are on the ground floor, too. There are interrogation rooms down the hall from the cells. Upstairs they have more interview rooms, though these are usually used for witnesses to crimes and are painted a more comforting hue than the grim gunmetal grey of the interrogation rooms.

Beneath the building, in the basement, are the armoury and the evidence lockers. The gym is there, too. Nina spent a lot of time in that gym not so long ago, while going through her breakup with Dante. She had a lot of frustration that needed somewhere to go, and she took it out on the weights, the treadmills, rowing machines, and the heavy bags.

Upstairs, she passes by Chief Bolton's office on the way to the break room. His office door is closed and locked, the room beyond in darkness. He doesn't work nights. Of course he doesn't – a perk of being the chief.

David Remsburg is in the break room, leaning back on a chair at one of the round tables, a plastic cup of coffee in his hand resting on the table, his other holding his phone close to his face while he flicks through social media. He looks up as Nina enters. He's the only person present. "There she is," he says. "This is late for you, isn't it?"

"I got held up," Nina says. "A phone call."

David winces. "Judging from the look on your face, let me guess – Dante?"

"Got it in one," she says. "And you know, it had been such a pleasant evening up to that point."

David chuckles. He's a handsome man, almost too handsome. Hard to believe he's a cop sometimes. Dante would get jealous of them working together, spending so much time together on patrol. Dante being jealous was stupid for two reasons. First and foremost, Nina is not David's type. He's gay. Secondly, Dante was the one cheating on *her*.

"You see Simon on your way in?" David says.

"No, managed to avoid him and his buddies," Nina says. "Liz gave me a heads-up."

"Has his case got a date yet?"

"I was told it could be another couple of months." Simon Arditti has been under investigation from Internal Affairs. One brutality case too many came to their attention. Nina saw one of them first hand. They were policing a protest at the time. Kids marching in the street in protest at an overseas war. It was a peaceful protest, but Simon Arditti is an antagonistic prick at the best of times. The kid must have run his mouth at him or something. Simon hauled him away, down an alleyway, starting laying into him with his boots. Nina had to drag him off. She remembers the look in his eyes, blazing with such a sudden hatred. She's arrested people with those same eyes, that same baleful expression, like murder is just one quick step away for them.

David whistles at the timeframe.

"Yeah."

"And they're not suspending him until then?"

"Can't afford to spare him. But also they say there's lack of evidence. Until I testify, that is."

"Plenty of witnesses on the street, from what I heard."

"Not all of them came forward, and the few who did didn't exactly have clean records."

"So it falls to you."

"Exactly."

"What are you gonna do until it goes to court? Just avoid him?"

Nina shrugs. "I don't need to avoid him. He needs to avoid *me*. I didn't do anything wrong. It's not my career on the line. If he or his people were to say or try anything with me, that would be the worst thing they could do. It wouldn't reflect well on him, or them."

David nods. He drains his coffee, then stretches as he gets to his feet and slips his cell into his pocket. "Shall we begin?" he says. "Those streets aren't going to keep themselves lawful."

Nina grins. She nods. "Let's go."

7

For a Thursday night, Sam's has been surprisingly busy. The shift started off quiet, as expected. It picked up after midnight. A large group of drunks out for a birthday party wandered in, looking for something quick to eat. Mandy and Amira were out front again, finding themselves rushed off their feet. Tom managed to keep on top of the orders coming through. His organisation of the kitchen made it easier.

He was pleased for the rush. It meant that Mandy and Amira weren't able to keep bugging him, asking him if he'd met up with Nina and how it went, which they did at the start of the night.

"A gentleman never tells," he said, and answered nothing else.

"Whoever accused you of being a gentleman?" Mandy said.

"Well, Tom does walk me home regularly," Amira said. "So I feel like I have to defend him there. *I* would certainly call him a gentleman."

Mandy rolled her eyes. "Whose side are you on here?" she said.

The rush has ended, and the end of their shift is soon to come, too. Tom has a couple of days off coming up. He's not going to rest, as he usually would. He intends to be busy. Finding out who was in his apartment, and why, and what they want.

Whenever there's been a lull, he's checked the road outside the diner. There's been no sign of the black Ford van. It hasn't returned. If it was following him, watching him, it would be stupid of it to return after he'd spotted it. On his break, he took a walk around the block, checking for anything concerning. Once again, he found nothing. He won't ignore his paranoia, however. He always listens to it. It's rarely wrong.

Tom is in the kitchen, cleaning, wiping down the grill and stacking the crockery. He straightens up and stretches out his spine and neck, feeling tendons pop. He rolls his shoulders. Amira comes into the kitchen. She's grinning. "I'm not gonna need you to walk me back this morning," she says.

"Two mornings in a row," Tom says, raising an eyebrow. "Is it something I said?"

Amira's face is beaming. There's a sparkle in her eye. She's keeping something from him. "No, it's fine. I just think we might be going in different directions is all."

Tom tilts his head. He looks toward the pass, through it, into the diner. He sees the reason for Amira suppressing her girlish giggles.

Nina has come by. She's sitting in a booth by the door, sipping a coffee.

"I see that smile," Amira says. "You're trying to hide it, but you can't."

Tom looks at her. She laughs and leaves the kitchen.

Tom is done cleaning. He takes off the apron, puts it in the washer, and heads through into the diner. Mandy and Amira are whispering as he passes. He goes to Nina's booth.

"I think you have a couple of fans," Nina says when he slides in opposite her.

"I think it's more that they're fans of you," Tom says.

Nina holds up her mug. "I couldn't live with embarrassing you, so I came and gave it a try."

"The verdict?"

"It's okay. I can tell you're not a coffee drinker. If you were, you'd know that it can't compare to Harry's Coffee House."

"Now you know for sure, at least."

"I couldn't live with the doubt, either."

"So your shift finished on time."

Nina nods. "It did. Am I right in thinking that yours ends soon, too?"

"Five minutes."

Nina takes a drink. Her eyes lock with his over the top of the cup. "And after that?"

"No plans. You?"

"Same. I have a couple of days off."

"That so? Just so happens I do, too."

"Tom, you can go now," Amira calls across the diner. "We've got this. You go and enjoy your days off." Beside her, Mandy giggles.

Tom looks at Nina. "Sounds like I'm getting an early finish."

"A whole four minutes."

"I'm not complaining."

They stand and leave the diner together. It's light outside. "Would you like to get breakfast?" Nina says. "My treat. Have someone cook for you instead."

"You have somewhere in mind?"

Nina walks toward her car, and motions for Tom to follow. He does. "Would you be surprised if I told you Harry's Coffee House makes a mean breakfast?"

"Should I be disappointed again?" They get into her car.

"You can, but it'll be short-lived. Because once you've had a plate, you'll understand."

"I look forward to finding out."

Nina starts the car. She pulls away from the front of Sam's. As they pass by, Tom checks the other parked vehicles. He watches the mirrors as they go, to make sure no one is following them. No one is.

"Harry's Coffee House is close to your place, isn't that right?" Tom says.

He sees Nina smile at the corner of her mouth. "Not far at all."

8

Orlando sits in the warehouse, holding down the fort. He's not alone. His second-in-command, Stuart Lynch, is napping on the cots at the rear. The other four members of the team are out in the field, following their target.

They're not staying too close to Rollins. They can't. He's already made them once. An observant son of a bitch. Orlando is almost impressed. Instead, the team keep their distance, Corey and Eddie having hacked into local CCTV and keeping an eye on him through the cameras. They follow him at a distance, always keeping out of his way, always a couple of steps either ahead or behind him.

Josh Chlebek has kept in regular contact with Orlando, updating him through the night. "He's suspicious, no doubt," Josh said last time he checked in, contacting Orlando via his earpiece. "He's at work right now, but he must be on a break or something because he just came out and circled the block. He's subtle about it, but he's checking all the parked vehicles."

"And where are you?"

"We're a couple of blocks away. He's already going back into the diner. We're out of his view, and out of his reach."

The team have been careful. Rollins spotted the van, and so they've adapted. It necessitated Corey and Eddie going out into the field, but that's fine. They're soldiers, same as the rest of them, and they can handle themselves. Orlando wouldn't have them on his team if they couldn't. And, in their roles as his tech guys, they can work from anywhere.

Stuart has been sleeping for the last eight hours. It was his turn. When Orlando first got back to the warehouse last night he slept until midnight, then took over the command centre.

Orlando sips coffee. It's not the good stuff he's become accustomed to during his mini-vacation visiting the sights of San Francisco. It's cheap and filtered, and has a burnt taste, but he's not drinking it for the taste. He can easily ignore that. He drinks it for the caffeine. Their operation isn't quite in full swing, but it's getting there. They're in the beginning stages. Often, this is the most important phase of all.

He checks the time. Rollins will have finished his shift by now.

Rollins strikes him as an interesting man. Ex-Army, ex-CIA black ops. He's spent the last few years criss-crossing the country and getting himself in and out of trouble on a regular basis. And yet now he's in San Francisco, cooking burgers and frying eggs. Orlando doesn't understand it. It's clear that the man still craves action. It seems he seeks it out no matter where he goes. And yet, he works as a cook? From Orlando's viewpoint, it would make more sense for him to still serve, or perhaps to work as a mercenary. For well-trained men such as themselves, there's always work to be found – and it can be very well-paid work at that.

But maybe it goes deeper than that. Maybe it's not about the money for him. Could be he's in it for the rush, the adrenaline. Could be he's one of those types who craves their freedom, yet simultaneously misses the order and control of their days in service. Orlando has met both types. He's met *all* types. Those who thrive in the military, they're a specific type of man. Those who thrive *outside* of it, yet with its training, are a separate beast altogether. Orlando is one of the latter. He feels this Rollins could be, too. The kind who was born for this way of life. The kind for whom no other road was available, not really.

Orlando is roused from his thoughts by Josh Chlebek. Orlando hears his voice in his ear. "Orlando, come in."

"What's happening?" Orlando says.

"The target is on the move, and he's not alone," Josh says.

"Oh?"

"The same woman cop that came by last night after his fight with the robber. They left Sam's a little while ago, and now they're having breakfast together."

"This isn't an issue."

"No, but from the looks of it they're getting real close. Could be that they end up spending more time together than we expect them to."

"Oh really? The filthy flirt. Well, if he's going to get some action, good for him. He doesn't realise this will be his last chance."

"What if they stick together?"

"Put on Corey or Eddie."

There's a pause as Josh alerts the techs that Orlando wants to speak with them. Eddie comes on. "Sir?"

"Is the presence of the woman going to be an issue?"

Eddie thinks before he answers. "We don't know for sure that she's going to be hanging around."

"And if she does? Are you adaptable?"

Again, Eddie thinks. Orlando hears him conferring briefly with Corey, their voices muffled. Eddie comes back on. "It shouldn't be a problem, sir," he says. "We're adaptable."

"Even with her being a cop?"

"We can find a way to spin it."

"I'm glad to hear it," Orlando says. "I assume you'll start work on that now?"

"Absolutely. No other choice, sir."

"Good. You have today to get it done."

"We won't let you down."

Orlando hangs up and leans back in his chair. He thinks of Rollins and the cop, on their date from the sound of it. He chuckles to himself. If the woman's lucky, she'll have gone her own way before the time to strike arrives. If she hasn't... Well, if it comes to that, he hopes they're having a good time right now. Neither of them knows it will be their last.

9

Tom spent Friday with Nina. He spent Friday night with her, too.

No one had followed them here. Tom checked the road outside Nina's home before he went to sleep. He didn't want to alarm her by setting traps. Besides, her house has an alarm system. She locked the door and set it before they went upstairs.

Tom slept reasonably well. Every couple of hours he awoke and checked the window, careful not to disturb Nina. She slept soundly. She'd kicked the blankets off herself through the night, and she lay with one bare leg stretching toward his side of the bed. Tom would check the street, find nothing, and then get back into bed, resting one hand upon her thigh.

In the morning, they both wake early. They have breakfast together. Tom makes eggs.

"So this is what it's like at Sam's, huh?" Nina says, forking up eggs. "Maybe I *should* make the detour some mornings."

"Why pay those prices when you've got me free and private?"

"True. But sometimes you'll be working."

"Then I'll expect you on those mornings."

They eat in silence for a while. After spending a day and a night together, and most of that time being intimate, their silence is comfortable.

"Do you have plans for the rest of today?" Nina says.

"No."

"Not even on a Saturday?"

"Do you?"

"I can find something. Do you want to join me?"

"Some spoken word, perhaps?"

Nina laughs. "Play your cards right and I'll take you to an open mic."

"I thought I played my cards right already."

Nina whistles. "You need a shower? Get dressed and we'll head out, find some way to pass the time."

Tom takes her up on the offer of a shower. He heads upstairs. Looks out the windows yet again before he gets under the hot water. It's still early in the morning. Just after eight. It doesn't take Tom long to shower. He dries, dresses, and returns downstairs to Nina. She already has her boots on. She wears black jeans that cling tightly to her legs, and a black blouse. She slips into a leather jacket. "You good?"

Tom puts his own boots on. "I'm good. And I'm looking forward to seeing where you take us."

They leave her house together. Nina locks the door. They head toward her car.

Tom spots a car approaching from the left. As he turns toward it, he spots something coming faster from the right out the corner of his eye.

It's the black Ford van.

As Tom reaches out for Nina, the car approaching from the left speeds up and mounts the sidewalk, skidding to a halt next to them. The rear window is open. An M4 is sticking out, covering them both. The man beyond, holding it, is masked.

From the right, the van halts, the back door thrown open. Another man leaps out, again armed with an M4, again masked. He approaches.

"Not a fucking move," says the man in the back of the car, getting out. "Twitch a fucking muscle and I'll cut you in half."

Tom and Nina exchange glances. They raise their hands.

The man from the van reaches them. Behind him, Tom notices another masked, armed man has gotten out of the van and is covering them. The driver's door is open. In the car behind them, another masked man is behind the steering wheel. Four men in total, presumably all armed.

What happens next comes fast. The first man from the van, the one closest to them, he spins the M4 and strikes Tom across the jaw with its stock. Tom drops to a knee. The stock is driven down again into the bridge of his nose. Tom feels it split, and blood run down the sides of his nostrils and to his mouth.

The attacker lashes out at Nina next, smacking her across the face with a backfist. She spins and hits her car then falls to the ground. Tom sees, through dazed and blurred vision, that her cheek has been split open.

A bag is pulled over Tom's head, and he assumes the same has happened to Nina. He's hauled to his feet and dragged to the van, thrown inside. He feels himself patted down, checked for a weapon.

"He's clean," the person patting him down says. "Her?"

"Service revolver," a voice responds.

Tom's wrists and ankles are pressed tight together and bound with plastic ties. The rear doors of the van slam shut. He hears it locked from the outside. The van starts moving. It pulls away fast. Tom rolls to the side as it takes a corner. Nina rolls too, landing against him. She manages to stay close. "Rollins?" she says. She keeps her voice low, raising it only to above the level of the roaring engine.

"Yeah."

"These people here for you, or me?"

"Right now, I don't think it matters."

10

Masked and bound, the van carries Tom and Nina far. Tom can't gauge the turns. Can't make sense of the direction they're going. It feels like they drive for a long time, like they could be leaving the city.

At one point, Tom tries to push himself up, pulling his knees under his body and pushing himself onto his elbows, testing if there is any kind of gap at the base of the sack over his head. There is a slight line of light. If he can get up, he can see out the windshield, see where they are, potentially get some kind of idea as to where they're going.

"Lie back down," says a voice familiar from when they were first taken. "Don't try anything stupid, either of you."

Tom lowers himself back to the ground. The man riding shotgun is watching. No doubt he has his M4 trained upon their prone forms, or at least close to hand should they try anything.

Eventually, the van stops and Tom and Nina are dragged from the rear. They're hauled to their feet, and then the binds are cut from their ankles so they can walk. Tom feels a hand grab him by the left elbow, and the barrel of the M4 is jabbed into his back, forcing him forward.

Tom sniffs. Through the sack, he can smell water. Sea, or perhaps river. He thinks they've been taken to the outskirts of the city. The sun is rising, and with it the temperature. Then, suddenly, the quality of the air changes. It's cooler. It's darker, even through the hood. He can't smell the sea anymore. They're inside a building, dragged through it to what feels like the rear. Then, they're thrown forward. Nina bumps into Tom. There's a metal clanging as something is slammed shut behind them.

"Take two steps forward and put your wrists through the bars, and then you can take off the hoods." The voice is different to the ones Tom has heard so far. "Rollins first."

The use of his name answers Nina's earlier question – whoever these people are, they're here for him. The same people who broke into his apartment, no doubt. Tom has made plenty of enemies over the years. He wonders if this group is familiar to him already.

Tom takes two steps forward. If they're willing to cut him loose, he's not going to complain. He reaches out and feels the cold steel of the bars, then slips his bound wrists through. A moment later, the plastic tie is cut. Tom takes a step back and pulls off the hood.

The first thing he notices, the men are no longer wearing masks. This isn't a good sign.

The second thing Tom notices is that they appear to be in an old warehouse, the walls and the ceiling corrugated steel. There are patches of rust where they interlock at the ceiling. The building hasn't been maintained in a long time. As he suspected, he and Nina have been taken into a rear room. They've been shoved into a cell. The steel bars are shiny and new and undamaged, and Tom can see where they've been welded together. The cell looks as if it has only recently been constructed, within the last few weeks, or possibly even days. The floor is concrete, and there is no mattress or blankets, only a bucket in the corner for waste.

There's six men standing in front of them. They're dressed alike in an all-black combat uniform that reminds Tom of his years running black ops. They wear tactical vests, carrying extra magazines, a flashlight, a first aid kit, and a radio. They all have a dangling key, too. Tom glances at the cell's lock and sees they're the same style as the key. They all appear to be the same cut, though it's hard to be certain when looking at them from afar.

The man at the front has his thumbs hooked through his vest. He looks Tom over. He smiles. "Now you, Nina," he says without taking his eyes from Tom. He seems to be in charge. "Three steps for you. Of course, if Rollins there is a true gentleman, he could always guide you."

Tom places a hand on Nina's arm and leads her closer to the bars. The big man to the speaker's right, Buck 120 knife already out, steps forward and cuts her free, then returns to his previous position.

With both hands, Nina pulls the hood from her head and looks around, blinking. She sees the men in front of them. "Where are we?" she says, her tone demanding an answer, the cop in her coming through loud and clear in her voice. "Who are you, and what do you want?"

The man at the front, his thumbs hooked through the vest, raises his eyebrows and looks around. "So many questions," he says, his own tone mocking. "Especially from someone in no position to be asking any."

Nina glares at him.

The man at the front has a slim build, like a swimmer, but Tom notices how the others, though bulkier and in some cases taller, all defer to him. How they smile when he smiles, and stare when he stares.

All six of the men are armed. They carry M4s, held across the front of their chests, balanced on their vests. On their left hips they each have a Buck 120, and on their right they have Sig Sauer P320s. Only the man at the front does not have an M4. He does carry the knife and the handgun, however, though his hands are nowhere near them.

His hair is cut short and his face is clean-shaven. His features are narrow and angular, and there is a wicked glint in his eyes, especially when he smiles. There is humour there. He's enjoying himself. He's enjoying this, whatever *this* is. The man to his left is thick with muscle. He's Black, the only Black man in the group, and his hair is also short, and while his cheeks are also smooth, around his mouth he sports a goatee beard. The man to the leader's right, the one who cut Tom and Nina loose, is the biggest of the six men. His biceps and deltoids bulge through his black, long-sleeved shirt. His neck is the same thickness as his head. His traps almost reach his ears. There is an uncomfortable, almost bloated look about his appearance, like he could be on the verge of a heart attack. Tom has no doubts that he is on steroids.

Of the remaining three men, one of them has a mullet. Another, who stands close to Mullet, is bald with a thick, red beard. He looks like a Viking. The remaining member of the team stands slightly apart from the others. He has long hair and a beard. Unlike the others, there are three M67 grenades hanging from the front of his vest. He's obviously not expecting to be shot at with the bombs hanging in such a dangerous location. He strokes one of them. When he spots Tom looking, he opens his mouth in a smile and runs his tongue across his top row of teeth.

Tom turns his attention back to the leader. "You want me, right? Let her go. Whatever your problem is, she doesn't have any part in it."

"We can accommodate for her," the leader says.

"What's that supposed to mean?"

The leader doesn't answer. He just smiles. "The two of you just need to sit tight. I know we haven't provided anything in the way of amenities – save for the bucket there – but try to make yourselves comfortable. This will all be over soon." He lets go of the vest with his right hand long enough to click his fingers. "Before you know it. Just like that."

Tom and Nina glance at each other.

"What are you talking about?" Nina says. "What will be over?"

The leader doesn't answer her. He motions to the big guy, the steroid freak, on his right. "Chlebek, you stay back here with our guests. Keep a close eye on them. Don't let them do anything stupid."

"Wouldn't dream of it," Chlebek says, his voice strained and rough. As well as his apparent steroid addiction, it sounds like he might be a heavy smoker, too.

"The rest of you, with me," the leader says, and then he turns and heads out into the main part of the building, the other four men following him.

Chlebek rests his hands on the M4. He stands ramrod straight, his head raised, looking down his nose at Tom and Nina.

Tom makes a show of looking around. "I love what you've done with this place," he says. "You planning on staying here long?"

Chlebek smirks with the corner of his mouth, but he says nothing.

Tom turns to Nina. "I think this could be a long day," he says, and jerks his thumb toward their guard. "He doesn't seem like much of a talker."

11

Orlando leads his team away from Tom and Nina, through into the main part of the warehouse. The door to the back room is closed, and so Orlando doesn't need to lower his voice.

"Nina," he says, looking toward Corey Crewe and Eddie Mitchell. Corey has a mullet and Eddie is bald. "You said you were adaptable, so tell me how we work her in."

Eddie scratches at his chin through his thick beard. "Well, we've been watching Rollins a while through the security cameras in Sam's."

"We have all the footage on him we need," Corey says.

"But we didn't realise Nina was gonna become a part of this," Eddie resumes. "So we weren't paying her too much attention. But we have enough to make it work. The doctored footage isn't as in-depth as with Rollins, but we can factor her into backgrounds, etc."

"We can make her look like a getaway driver," Corey says. "I've already put the footage together."

"When we're done here, I want to see that," Orlando says.

Corey nods. He looks pleased with himself. "At such short notice, I've made it work. I think you'll find it more than acceptable."

"And now we've got her here under lock and key, we can always get additional footage," Eddie says. "Extra scans. If needed."

Harris Elkin speaks up. "They met up a lot in the diner," he says, moving on. "Rollins and Nina, that is. There's a backstory there. I took a look through the footage and it was clear they were flirting, even without volume. Any fool could see it." Harris isn't a computer guy. He's Orlando's bomb expert. After Corey and Eddie, he's perhaps the most important part of this operation. Orlando has to keep it all together, of course, and Stuart Lynch is his right hand, but both Stuart and Josh Chlebek are here as muscle. They're here to make sure things go smoothly, and to handle Rollins.

Stuart strokes his goatee, nodding along. "Whenever Rollins dealt with a robbery, Nina and her partner were the cops who turned up to cart the bad guys away. Nina always hung around longer than she needed to."

Orlando looks between Stuart and Harris. "And you're certain of this? They weren't just making polite small talk?"

"We're all sure of it," Corey says.

"Not that it would matter anyway," Stuart says. "It's how it *looked* that matters. *We* know something more was going on – hell, they spent the day and night together yesterday, and I doubt they were playing board games."

"The waitresses knew it, too," Harris says. "They'd try and tease Rollins about it."

Orlando listens. "So there's enough evidence of them meeting up, talking, spending time together. Enough witnesses to it, too. We doctor the footage, put it out, people will believe that they were an item. It's not like no one saw them together before."

Stuart grunts, nodding. "Exactly. Nobody knows what they were talking about. Rollins got in her ear. He indoctrinated her. Radicalised her."

"All right," Orlando says. "I like it. It'll work."

"Will it fly with Hanley?" Stuart says.

"He trusts our judgement," Orlando says. "So long as we make it work, he's happy. Our ends justify our means, and all he cares about is the end result."

12

Tom and Nina stand close at the rear of the cell. Chlebek hasn't moved from where he's planted himself. He watches them both. His eyes have never left them. His hands rest upon the M4 strapped across his chest.

Nina speaks in a low voice, turning her back to Chlebek. "Do you know these people?"

Tom shakes his head. He leans against the bars with his arms folded, thinking.

"Any idea what might be going on here? Why they've taken us?"

"I know as much as you do," Tom says.

Nina steps back, looking around the cell as if searching for a weak point. "I don't like that they took their masks off," she says. "That they're not concerned about showing us their faces."

"It's not a good sign, no," Tom says. It means the men don't care if they're seen. If they don't care, it means they don't expect Tom and Nina to be around to identify them later. No matter what they have planned, or why they've kept them alive for now, they have no plans for keeping them alive indefinitely. Showing their faces, mentioning names, was as good as a death sentence.

"They were pretty free about using this one's name, too," she says, tilting her head back toward Chlebek.

Tom's eyes have never left their guard. Unwavering, Chlebek stares right back at him. With his muscles and his steadfast stare, he strikes Tom as the kind of man desperate to challenge himself. He's sizing Tom up. Wondering what he has to offer.

Tom is doing the same to him. Gauging him. Searching out potential weak points. It's hard to find any when the man is standing as still as a statue.

It could be that his weakness isn't physical. It could be psychological. A pathological need to prove that he's stronger than everyone else. To prove that he can't be defeated. To test himself against Tom, and come out on top. It could be enough for Tom to work with.

"Listen," Tom says to Nina. "Whatever's happening here, I think this has more to do with me than it does you. I think you're collateral. You've been dragged in because you happened to be with me."

"Why do you say that?"

"Because I used to be CIA black ops, and these guys strike me as black ops, too," Tom says. "And because a couple of days ago I noticed someone had been in my apartment. They didn't take anything, and they were careful to put everything back where they found it, but it was searched. I noticed a black Ford van had been sat outside Sam's all night, too, and when I approached it it drove away. The same black Ford van we were bundled into the back of and brought here."

"Yeah, well, if it *is* targeted solely at you, we're both in it now." Nina pauses, then adds, "But why do they want you?"

"I don't know," Tom says. "I don't know who these people are or what they have planned. Frankly, I don't know why we're alive right now. When everything else is factored in, it almost seems like it would make more sense for us to be dead."

"Maybe they've been hired to capture you," Nina says.

Tom considers this. "It's a possibility. I'm sure someone out there has a bounty on my head."

"If we get out of here, you're going to have to give me a full rundown of where you've been and what you've done before you came to San Francisco. If anyone else is gunning for you, I want to know about it."

"We'll get out of here," Tom says, his eyes having never left Chlebek. "I'm working on it."

"Oh really? What are you thinking?"

"Just wait here. When it's time to move, you'll know. Be ready. In the meantime, follow my lead."

Tom pushes himself off the bars, unfolding his arms. He steps toward the door of the cell, closer to Chlebek. He leans against these bars, his arms resting on the horizontal support bar, his hands dangling. Chlebek's attention is upon him. Tom nods toward the door where the rest of the team went. "You don't get to play with the others?"

Chlebek doesn't respond.

"They're probably talking strategy, right?" Tom says. "Discussing plans, where to go from here, all that stuff, right? The important stuff. The stuff that takes brains." Tom taps the side of his head. He smiles at Chlebek.

Chlebek grunts. "Whatever you're trying, save your breath. I'm here to watch you and make sure you don't try anything, and that's what I'm going to do."

"Of course," Tom says. "I didn't expect anything else." He glances toward the door to the rest of the warehouse again. It's for show, but it also allows him to check that no one is returning. "I mean, you're the muscle, right? You're not one of the thinkers. Those other guys, they're all smaller than you. They're the thinkers, right? Except for the Black guy – he looked almost as big as you are."

Tom notices how the corner of Chlebek's mouth twitches at this. He disagrees about the size comparison.

"I mean, I didn't see him for very long – maybe he was bigger?" Tom tilts his head like he's thinking. "No, that can't be right. *You're* the guard dog. That means *you're* the muscle, right? If the Black guy was bigger, he'd be here right now instead of you. He'd be on watch. What do you think, Nina?"

"That sounds about right to me," she says.

"Exactly. Plus, the Black guy, he looked natural, right?"

"Looked natural to me," Nina says. "Good genetics."

"Yeah, whereas this guy, he's a juicehead. Clear as day, right?"

"First thing I thought when I saw him," Nina says.

"You and everybody else who lays eyes on him," Tom says. He laughs. "Looks like a tomato about to burst. But yeah, it all makes sense now. No one ever accused a juicehead of being smart, right? That's why they're through there, and you're here. That's why you're not involved."

Chlebek takes a deep breath. "I know what you're trying to do."

Tom raises an eyebrow. "And what's that?"

Chlebek smirks. It quickly fades when Tom next speaks.

"He can't articulate it, Nina," Tom says. "I understand why they left him behind, even if he doesn't. Poor guy. It feels strange that we're the ones behind the bars, because it's like we're at the zoo, and this guy's the big dumb gorilla trying to form a thought."

Chlebek sneers. He's seething. His face is bright red. He breathes deep, shaking his head, calming himself down. "You're talking tough for someone who was taken without a fight."

"Can't fight a bullet," Tom says. "You'll find that out soon enough."

"Yeah?" Chlebek says. He moves now, stepping a little closer, tilting his head. Tom is getting on his nerves. "What's that supposed to mean? You got a gun we don't know about? I patted you down myself. You got one hidden away, stuck up your asshole?"

"How about I bend over and you check?"

"I don't go in for none of that bullshit."

"Then you'll never know. No, see, what I'm gonna do is, I'm gonna shoot you with *your* gun. And those guys out there, I'm gonna shoot them with your gun, too. Ordinarily, I like to know why I kill a person, but since you bundled me and my friend here in the back of a van without so much as a kind word, I'll make an exception. I can always find out the answers after, right?"

Chlebek smirks. "Sure."

"Or, you know, you could make it easier and quicker for all of us. Why *are* we here, Chlebek? You got an answer for us? Hell, do you *know* the answer? Were you allowed in on that one?"

Without realising he's doing it, Chlebek takes another step forward. In his anger he's getting closer, and he doesn't realise it's happening. Tom doesn't move a muscle. He stays right where he is, smirking up at the big man, keeping his eyes locked on his.

"Oh, I know why you're here," Chlebek says. He comes closer. Another step, and he'll be within reach.

"You wanna share with the class?" Tom keeps smirking. Keeps his eyes on the big man's. He can see that the unbroken, unblinking eye contact is driving him crazy. Chlebek is used to being the most intimidating man in the room. He doesn't like it when the person he's looking at doesn't back down. That's why he comes closer. To give a better idea of his size, and of how he dwarves Tom. To give him a closer look at his own eyes. Killer's eyes.

Tom is unfazed. He has killer's eyes, too.

"I ain't gonna share shit with you," Chlebek says. "You're gonna sit nice in your little cage. If you ever come out breathing, it'll be too late for what we got planned."

Chlebek is slipping up. In his anger, his growing roid rage, he's not thinking straight. "Why not just kill us now?" Tom says.

"Insurance," Chlebek says. "A just-in-case. You ran black ops, right? You should know how it is."

"I never ran an operation like this."

"Yeah, well, you ain't as hardcore as us."

"I'm sure. But that doesn't answer why we're still breathing."

"It's all gotta look good," Chlebek says. "The two of you are the scapegoats. It was just supposed to be you, Rollins, but then you had to go and spend the night fucking and this dumb bitch has got caught up in the ride."

"Scapegoats?" Nina says. "Scapegoats for what?"

Chlebek grins. He shows his teeth. "You'll never know.

You play your part just by sitting in that cage. When the time comes, you're dead in the street. How's that sound, tough guy? An ignominious end for an ignominious asshole."

"Wow, you hear that, Nina? He just used a pretty big word. Maybe he's not as dumb as we thought."

"I'm not so sure he used it right the second time," Nina says.

Tom nods along. "Maybe not. Think he got caught up in the moment. Remembered what his word-a-day calendar said this morning and was so desperate to use it, he used it twice."

Chlebek's nostrils flare. "I'm getting real sick of you calling me stupid."

"There's a lot of things I could call you, juicehead. I'm just afraid that if I put them all out there, you're gonna keel over of a heart attack. You already look like your head's gonna burst."

"Like a zit," Nina says.

Chlebek takes another step closer. Tom hasn't moved, so he's not expecting him to try anything. He doesn't realise how close he's just gotten. *Too* close. He shifts the M4, squeezing the grip and the barrel tight, like he wants to turn it upon them. "You know, maybe you're right," he says. "Maybe we don't need to keep you alive."

"It's too late now," Tom says.

Chlebek's eyes narrow. "Too late? Heh, you said yourself you can't fight a bullet." He starts to turn the barrel of the M4 toward them. He wants to spook them. Hell, the way he looks right now, how hard he's breathing, he might just go ahead and pull the trigger.

"I think it's time for you to shut up," Tom says.

Chlebek pauses. "What?"

"I said you need to shut up," Tom says. "It's time for me to work."

Too late, Chlebek realises his mistake. Tom's arms lash out, fast. His left goes to the back of Chlebek's skull, catching him by surprise. His right goes to his vest, grabbing the key. In one movement, catching Chlebek by surprise, he drags him in by the back of his meaty neck and slams his forehead into the bars. At the same time, he pulls the key loose. He tosses it back toward Nina, then laces both hands behind Chlebek's head and pulls him in again. His head splits, blood running down the centre of his face.

"Shame you can't build muscle there, huh?" Tom says.

He shoves Chlebek, spinning him around, and wraps an arm around his throat, putting pressure on his carotid artery. While he does so, Nina hurries to the cell door beside him with the key. Chlebek sputters, spraying blood from his lips. He's dazed from the head blows. He tries to reach for his weapons, but he's fading fast and can't grip them properly.

Nina gets out of the cell. She disarms Chlebek, removing the Sig Sauer and the Buck 120 from his hips. She can't get the M4 from around his neck but she doesn't need to. Chlebek slides down the bars, unconscious.

Tom steps out of the cell and removes the M4. He checks the magazine. It's full. Both armed, Nina tilts her head toward the door. Tom nods.

"They haven't come rushing in," Nina says. "They mustn't have heard."

"Unless they've already left."

"Let's find out," Nina says. "I trust you can handle that? When they see us, I don't think they're going to be in the mood to talk and explain themselves."

"Maybe they'll surprise us," Tom says. "Maybe they're reasonable guys once you get to know them."

"You always joke so much?"

"Depends on how serious the looming gunfight might be."

"I'm expecting it to be pretty damn serious."

Tom grunts. "Me too. Let's go."

13

Tom and Nina don't know what the rest of the warehouse looks like. They were still wearing the hoods when they were dragged through. They'll have to be careful.

They stand either side of the door leading through to the main part of the building. They exchange looks, checking they're each ready. They nod. Tom opens the door, just a crack. He peers through.

Two members of the team – the bald guy and the guy with the mullet – are at computers. The bald guy is typing, but the other is sitting back, playing a video, or a loop of footage, on his laptop. The leader of the group and the Black guy are standing behind him, watching. The long-haired guy sits in a chair nearby, tilting back on its legs while he inspects his fingernails. He looks bored.

Tom looks around the rest of the open space. There is no sign of what the warehouse used to be used for. There are, however, some old, rusted oil barrels scattered around the floor. Three of them are standing erect close to the door.

Around the rest of the room, there are a few tables and chairs. There are some cots in the corner, and he imagines the team has been staying here for a while. Where the four members of the team are gathered around the laptops, Tom notices a cork board on the wall in front of them. It's covered in maps of San Francisco, parts of it circled in red ink. Tom is too far away to work out what it signifies or what it might mean.

All five of the men have put down their M4s. They're resting against the wall close to where the leader stands.

Tom opens the door wide enough to slip through, then goes to the nearby oil drums for cover. Nina softly closes the door behind them and follows, keeping low, Sig Sauer raised. They duck behind the drums. Silently, they confer. Tom counts them off from three, then they stand, guns raised.

"Police!" Nina says. "Drop your weapons and put your hands in the air!"

The long-haired man sitting separate in the chair spots them first. He does not comply. Instead, he throws himself back and crawls toward a table, upending it to provide cover.

The other four spin at the sound of Nina's voice. They don't hesitate. They reach for their handguns. "They were warned," Tom says, then opens fire.

The man with long hair is first to shoot back, bullets from his Sig Sauer ricocheting off the drums.

Tom ducks down and peers through the drums. He spots the four who were gathered around the laptops get to cover. The bald guy and the guy with the mullet gather up their computers. The leader lunges for the standing M4s. Tom blasts in his direction and he lunges back. The leader shouts something that Tom can't make out over the gunfire. The four turn and flee from the warehouse, heading toward the vehicles outside.

The long-haired man slams a fresh magazine into his Sig Sauer, then tears a grenade from his vest. He pulls the pin and throws it toward the drums. Tom and Nina duck down and it explodes before it reaches them, but it serves its purpose – it provides him cover as he runs back, laying down suppressive fire toward the drums, keeping Tom and Nina pinned behind cover. When he gets close to the exit he spins and runs.

Tom jumps out from behind the drums and pursues. As he reaches the exit he sees the long-haired man jump through the open rear door of the black Ford van, already in motion. The door slams shut. Once he's on board, the van speeds away. Tom raises the M4 and aims for the tyres, but his bullets find only road. The van speeds off.

14

Orlando slams his fists against the dash. "What the hell happened back there?"

Stuart doesn't answer. He's driving. He focuses on the road ahead.

"Chlebek must've dropped the ball," Harris says, breathing hard after diving into the back of the van.

Orlando slams the dash again. He's angry. He's *furious*. The team say nothing. None of them dares.

Orlando breathes deep, trying to calm himself. It's hard. He rolls his neck and feels the tendons popping. He clenches his jaw. He turns to Stuart. "Take us to the cache," he says. They have a stash of weapons elsewhere in the city. They didn't expect to need them, but they're professionals and they always prepare for all eventualities.

"Already on the way," Stuart says.

Orlando pats him on the arm. "All right," he says, running his hands back through his hair and turning so he can get into the back of the van. He stands and holds onto the roof to keep his balance. "This isn't ideal, but it's not exactly a disaster – not yet. Harris, tell me you have the detonators."

Harris grins. He pats one of the pockets of his vest.

"Good. Here's what we do – Stuart, can you hear me up there?"

"Loud and clear."

"We need to initiate the operation now. It's ahead of schedule, but we don't have any other choice."

"Hanley will need to know," Corey says.

"Don't worry about Hanley," Orlando says. "I'll deal with him. He's not going to like it, but we can adapt to this. That's why he uses us, and he knows it. Everything happens as planned, but the early phases need to move at an accelerated pace."

"If we move too early, is that going to scare off the target?" Eddie says.

"It shouldn't," Orlando says. "And you still have eyes on his home, right? We're keeping everything removed from him, at a distance, it shouldn't look like it has anything to do with him, but if he looks spooked and tries to leave we intercept. Everyone clear?"

They all answer in the affirmative.

"What about Chlebek?" Harris says. "If he's still alive, he's still back there with them. He could talk. Tell them what we're doing."

"They won't have enough time to make him talk," Orlando says. "We don't *need* Rollins and Nina to be alive for what comes next."

"But, Chlebek?" Corey says.

"Fuck Chlebek," Orlando says. "He was stupid enough to let them get free. Now he's going to have to deal with the consequences of that." He looks at Harris. "Light them up."

Harris doesn't hesitate. Doesn't concern himself with Chlebek's whereabouts. He pulls out a detonator and checks it. "We need to get closer for the signal," he says.

"Stuart, you heard him."

Stuart is already turning the van. "On it."

15

Grabbing Chlebek by the ankles, Tom drags him through into the main part of the building. He sits him up in a chair and binds him to it with plastic ties he finds in his tactical vest.

"What are you going to do?" Nina says.

"I'm going to make him talk," Tom says.

Nina hesitates. "What's that supposed to mean? We should call my department, tell them what's happened, get them down here."

"We might not have time. You see those maps? Those red circles? What does that mean? Where has the team gone now? What have they got planned? We can't wait around for answers."

"So – what? You're going to torture him?"

Tom looks at her. "I'm going to make him talk."

"Tom, I can't let you do that. I can't let you torture this man."

"Nina, you saw them. They're an elite team. They're heavily armed. Just because I managed to piss this gorilla off enough that he made a stupid mistake, can we trust that the rest of them are so dumb? They're up to something and we need to know what. Lives could be in danger."

Nina motions toward the M4s. "All they have is handguns and knives."

"They can still do a lot of damage with those, but do you think they won't have another cache stashed somewhere nearby?"

"Listen, I don't know how you did things when you were black ops, but right now we're going to do things by the book. I can see that he has a phone. I'm going to call my department and then –"

Before she can finish, they notice that Chlebek is beginning to wake. He grunts and snorts, coming around. He raises his head, blinking. His eyes are wet and bleary. He coughs, his throat no doubt raw. Looking around, realising where he is and what's happened, he becomes alarmed. When he tries to move he finds that he's been bound. He looks down at the chair, shifting his weight, the legs bouncing. "What's happened? Where's everyone else?" His voice, already rough, is now barely more than a rasp.

"They ran off," Tom says. "Left you behind. Seems you really are the weak link of the team, huh?"

Chlebek's eyes go wide. "They're gone?"

"Do you see them anywhere around here?"

Chlebek's head snaps side to side. "Shit! Get me out of this chair. We need to get out of here!"

Tom frowns. "*We*?"

"Yes, we! We need to go!"

Nina raises her hands, trying to calm him. "What's wrong? What's happening right now?"

"We need to go! This building is gonna blow! It's laced with Semtex. We need to go right fucking now!"

Tom looks around the building. Chlebek could be trying to trick them, but his terror seems genuine. "Where?" Tom says.

"I don't know. I didn't plant it – that's Harris's job – but he said it's fucking *everywhere*!" Chlebek tries to twist in the chair, looking around. "It'll be on the ceiling, in the corners. The whole building is supposed to come down!"

Tom takes a step back, checking the ceiling.

"Maybe we should take him out just to be safe," Nina says.

Tom spots the Semtex. South-west corner, in the shadows. The plastic explosive is moulded to the corrugated steel, blending in. To its right, Tom spots the detonator. There is a small light on its side to show if it's active. The light is currently off. He motions back toward Nina. "Cut him loose," he says.

Nina approaches Chlebek with the Buck 120 she took from him. "Hurry!" he says.

Tom's eyes never leave the detonator. Nina cuts through the plastic ties. Because of Chlebek's size, Tom used a lot of them. Nina gets through the first one on his right ankle when the light on the detonator comes on.

Tom doesn't say a word. He turns and scoops Nina up, slinging her over his shoulder and running for the door.

"No!" Chlebek cries out behind them. "Stop! Stop, you motherfuckers, *stop*!"

The warehouse explodes.

16

Tom hears the explosion, and he keeps running. He's clear of the building, Nina still over his shoulder. He runs until he feels the blast wave lift him from his feet and knock him down. They both go rolling. When they stop, Tom throws himself on top of Nina, covering her to protect her from falling and burning debris. Some of it lands nearby but luckily none of it hits them.

Tom falls back, sitting up, wiping sweat from his brow. Nina pushes herself up and looks back with him. "Shit," she says, looking at the demolished warehouse. "There's no way he survived that." She coughs. "There's no way *we* would've survived that if you hadn't been so fast."

"You tend to find out how fast you really are when you realise a bomb's about to go off."

Tom looks around, checking the surrounding area for the black van. It would have had to return in order to be within range of the detonator. Tom doesn't see it nearby. He keeps watch, but the van doesn't appear. They must have expected them to die in the blast, and then they turned and left the area again. It's sloppy, Tom thinks. They should have checked. Why would they just turn around and leave without checking? They'd have time before the cops arrive. What's their rush?

He looks at Nina. She doesn't have the Sig Sauer. He doesn't have the M4. Both weapons were lost to the explosion. The other M4s are unlikely to have survived. Nina doesn't have the Buck 120, either. He heard her drop it when he picked her up. They're unarmed again. Tom gets to his feet and offers Nina a hand.

"The cops will be coming," Nina says, accepting the help. She looks around. "There are other warehouses here, and they look like they're still active. They must've called it in by now. It won't take long before someone's here."

Tom looks toward the fallen warehouse. It's flaming still, hot, even at a distance. Tom puts a hand to the back of his neck. The hairs there have been singed. His skin is hot. If he'd been any closer to the blast, he'd have been burned. Nina too. If he'd hesitated for just a second, their skin would be bloody and peeling right now. As it is, they're lucky it's going to feel more like sunburn than a fire burn.

"You okay?" Nina says. "You landed pretty hard, and with me on top of you."

"I'm good," Tom says. "You don't weigh that much."

Nina turns back to the road, her hands on her hips, watching for the cops to arrive. Minutes go by. Five. Ten. There's no sign of the cops.

"How long does it usually take you all to get to an emergency?" Tom says.

Nina looks across the road, toward the other warehouses. "They should have called it in," she says.

"Unless they thought this was a controlled demolition," Tom says. "The warehouse clearly wasn't in use."

"But there was no warning, no demolition crews, no security measures."

"True. But are they really going to care if an old warehouse suddenly falls down?"

"Maybe we should head over there, see if we can use their phone."

Tom hears something in the distance, deeper in the city. A low, brief rumbling. He notices how Nina reacts to it too, her head turning to hear it better.

Tom steps up closer to her. "You hear that too?"

"I hear it all right," she says. "That sounded like a..." She holds off saying it. She doesn't want to. Doesn't want to believe that it could be.

"An explosion," Tom says for her. "It was another explosion. Bigger than this one."

"A lot bigger," Nina says.

A moment later, they can finally hear sirens. The city has come alive with them, howling through the distant buildings. They aren't coming this way. They aren't coming to the blown-up warehouse. They're going the other direction. They're heading deeper into the city, the sound of the sirens growing fainter.

"Could it be...could it be the same guys who did this?" Nina says. "It's Saturday morning, early. Depending on the roads they took it might be quiet enough that they could have gotten that far since they blew this warehouse... That explosion was so *loud*..." She runs a hand down her mouth. "Did you see where was circled on the map?"

Tom shakes his head. "There wasn't enough time," he says. "I didn't expect the place to be laced with Semtex. I thought we'd have time to check once we'd dealt with Chlebek."

Nina stares toward the city, the direction of the explosion and the sirens that race toward it. Tom sees how she frets. Sees the concern and worry on her face.

"We need to go," Tom says. "There's no point hanging around here."

Nina nods. "I have to go help."

17

Orlando and his team remain on the move, heading to their backup hideout. It contains a cache of weapons – extra M4s and ammo. After they blew up the warehouse, they headed into the city, downtown, and set off the next bomb.

Around them, post-explosion, the city has erupted into chaos. It's still early morning, but it's a Saturday and it was already getting busy around the SF Downtown Federal Building. They didn't get too close. Didn't need to. They stayed a couple of blocks away, on the edge of the detonator's signal. The explosion came from a car parked in front of the building. Harris parked the vehicle a night ago, close enough to the building for optimum damage. The car's trunk, hood, and body were packed with Semtex. Corey and Eddie had put the nearby security cameras onto a loop, erasing evidence of who left the car. They're working now to insert their own created footage of Rollins parking the car, then leaving, picked up in a separate vehicle by Nina.

After the explosion, Stuart calmly pulled the van back

into traffic, heading away from the scene. Everyone else on the road is going slowly and Stuart matches their speed. Some cars have pulled over. They look back toward the bombing, hands atop their heads, faces concerned. Some of them head that way on foot. Some people blare their horns at the holdup, but Stuart does not. He's patient. He doesn't rush. He doesn't hassle anyone. Doesn't draw any attention to them.

Cop cars, ambulances, and fire trucks race past them, going the other way, toward the bombed building. In the front of the van, Stuart has pulled on a jacket to conceal his tactical gear. He drives calmly, pulling aside to let the emergency vehicles past. Orlando is in the back of the van with the others. Corey and Eddie have brought up the footage in the area around the federal building. Orlando watches. Smoke billows. People stumble, dazed and bloody. Bodies lie on the ground, missing limbs. The east corner of the SF Downtown Federal Building, where Harris parked the car, has collapsed. The car itself is almost completely gone, a crater in the road where it used to be. Emergency services rush to the scene and try to get control of the situation. He sees cops searching other parked cars, checking them for further explosives.

Orlando turns to Harris. "Nicely done."

Harris nods, once.

"Damage?" Stuart asks, calling back.

"Optimal," Orlando says.

"Have you heard from Hanley?"

"Not yet. But I expect to – as soon as he's able."

Sure enough, after ten minutes, Orlando's phone begins to ring. They're stuck in traffic and still far from their hideout. Orlando answers the phone.

"That was earlier than I expected," Hanley says. Orlando can hear wind whipping around him. He's making this call outside, away from anyone who could overhear or listen in.

"There was a slight complication," Orlando says. "But we've dealt with it."

"That might answer my next question," Hanley says. "I heard there were two explosions. None of this is what I was expecting."

"Don't expect and you won't be disappointed," Orlando says. "We had to adapt, so we did. The warehouse had to be sacrificed, but it's fine. It was always part of the plan for it to go boom." He explains what happened with Rollins and Nina back in the warehouse, and with Chlebek.

"So there'll be a third body there," Hanley says. "One of yours. How is that going to be explained? Can't he be linked back to you?"

"My people are already erasing any tangential connection he might have had to us. He'll just be another acolyte of Rollins, same as Nina."

"And what about the target later tonight?" Hanley says. "If Rollins and Nina are already dead, how are they supposed to take the blame?"

"There's always a story that can be spun. A conspiracy theory that can be bled out. Either the bombs were on a timer, or Rollins has another follower running around out there, following through on what he started after he moronically blew himself up in his own hideout."

"And you're sure they're dead?"

"After everything I've just told you, what do you think?"

Hanley is silent.

"All eventualities are planned for," Orlando says. "Don't worry about it. We can spin everything. It's all about leaking out the right kind of information to the right kind of people who want to hear it."

Hanley takes a deep breath. "Has the footage been planted?"

Orlando looks at Corey and Eddie. Corey gives him a thumbs-up. "It'll be found soon."

"All right. I'm trusting your judgement here, Orlando."

"As you should. Sit back and wait. There was a minor hiccup, but we're back on track. We've adapted, and everything is according to plan again. Not long now, and we're all going to be very rich."

This last statement doesn't cheer Hanley as much as Orlando expected it would. Instead, he just grunts.

"Don't go getting regrets, senator," Orlando says.

"It's not that," Hanley says quickly. "It's not regrets, it's not cold feet, it's nothing like that. It's *concern*. The sooner this is all over and done with, the better. *Then* I can breathe easy."

"I'm breathing just fine," Orlando says. "You should follow my lead. Talk soon." Orlando hangs up.

18

On foot, Tom and Nina head to a nearby bus stop and ride it back to her home. It stops a block away. As they head to her house on foot, they can see black smoke rising from downtown.

"What has *happened*?" Nina says to herself, quietly. Tom sees the concern etched on her face. "Was this *them*?" she says, louder, addressing Tom.

"If it's not, it's a hell of a coincidence," Tom says.

When they reach her house, Tom tells her to wait outside. "I want to check it for explosives," he says. He also wants to check if the team got ahead of them and have left anyone lying in wait, covering a base in case they survived the warehouse explosion.

"I'm a cop, Rollins," Nina says. "I'm capable of checking my own home."

"And if there *is* a bomb," Tom says, "I need to make sure I can get out of there *fast*. If there's two of us, that complicates things, slows us both down."

Nina pauses for a moment, thinking over what he's said. "All right," she says. "You're right."

"Did they take your keys?"

She nods. "There's a spare under the plant pot."

Tom nods. "If you see anyone coming, shout out."

He goes to the front door, taking the spare key from under the plant pot. There's no plant in it, just dirt. Tom unlocks the door and enters the house. He steps lightly, careful for tripwires, eyes scanning the walls and the ceiling. He moves room to room, throughout the house, upstairs and down. There's no one present, and he can't find any explosives, either. He goes back to the open front door and gives Nina the all-clear. He has to whistle to get her attention. She's standing, arms folded, staring toward the smoke.

Nina heads for the stairs, pausing at the bottom. "I'm going to get into uniform and head out there, see what I can do to help," she says. "Maybe you should come with me to the station. It's going to be busy out there, but you can tell them what happened – how we were taken, and how those people are probably responsible for this attack."

Tom nods. "Okay. I'll put the TV on while you change, see if it has any information."

Tom goes into the living room while Nina runs upstairs. He puts on the set and watches it, standing. He glances outside, to the road, regularly checking to make sure no one has pulled up, their friends from earlier back looking for them. It's been long enough now for them to go through the warehouse and see that they weren't caught up in the blast. The warehouse could be swarming with cops, though, and they might have avoided it for that reason. If they think Tom and Nina are dead, that's in Tom and Nina's favour.

On the TV, the news is showing the direct aftermath of

the explosion. It focuses mainly on the crumbling federal building, and the crater where the car that exploded was parked. Its camera doesn't pull back for wide shots. Tom can imagine why. There'll be blood on the road and the sidewalk. There's probably still limbs lying around. There'll be body bags. The presenter says that initial estimates put the death toll at forty-two, and the injured currently at ninety-six, and likely to rise.

Tom clenches his jaw. It's a grim situation. If the people who kidnapped them are responsible, he'll make them pay for all of this death and destruction.

The news presenter comes back onscreen with a breaking update. As it plays out, Tom feels his face begin to fall. He stares for a moment in disbelief, making sure he's understanding completely, then he calls for Nina. "You need to come and see this," he says.

"What is it?"

Tom remembers what Chlebek said. They were going to be the scapegoats. "We're getting the blame," he says.

Nina runs down the stairs. She's not in her uniform yet. She's abandoned that idea after hearing Tom's words. She's pulled her jeans back on, buttoning them as she runs down the stairs. "*What*?"

Tom motions toward the television. "There's footage," he says. It's grainy, but it's clear enough. It replays over and over. They watch as Tom parks the car filled with explosives, and then Nina pulls up alongside him and drives him away. Both of their faces are clear as day through the windshield, caught under the illumination of a nearby streetlamp.

"It's fake," Nina says.

"Of course it is," Tom says. "But by the time anyone figures it out it's going to be too late."

"They won't have played this footage as soon as they got it," Nina says. "They won't have been allowed. They'll have sat on it for a while."

"To give the cops time to come looking for us," Tom says.

"There's only two places they can look," Nina says. "Your place –"

"And here," Tom says. "We need to go."

Then, they hear the sirens.

19

As the cruisers – three of them – screech to a halt in front of Nina's home, she and Tom race through her house to the back door. They burst through into the back yard, scaling the fence at the end and dropping down into the alley below.

A fourth cruiser is rolling down the alleyway, flanking them for this escape attempt. Its siren is off. When it spots them, it speeds up. Tom and Nina run across the alley to the fence opposite, scaling it into the yard beyond.

One of the cops hops out of the passenger side, raising his standard issue Sig Sauer P226. "Freeze!"

Tom and Nina drop down into the yard as he fires. It flies over the top of the fence. Nina lands flat and looks back. "He shot at us," she says.

Tom drags her back to her feet. The cop can see them through the gaps in the fence and he's re-aiming. They run as his bullets blast through the wood.

They pass down the side of the house, Tom leading the

way. He shoulders through the wooden gate there, Nina following close behind.

While he runs, Tom's mind races with what has happened. They're getting the blame for the bombing. He can't think about it right now. Can't think about how they're going to clear their name and bring down the people truly responsible. What he has to do is keep running. They need to get clear. Unless they stay free, they have no hope.

From the front of the house they cross the road, running at full speed. Tom hears the screeching of tyres behind them. He doesn't look back. Looking back puts him at risk of tripping. There's no siren, but he's sure it'll be one of the cruisers that pulled up in front of Nina's house. It roars down the road behind them. Tom can only hear the one vehicle. The others are likely coming from different directions, trying to cut them off.

Tom and Nina run down the sidewalk, heading downhill. Tom keeps his breathing under control. He's not breathing hard yet. He's not struggling. He keeps in shape for moments like this. Beside him, he can hear that Nina is the same. She's breathing through her nose, same as him, slow and controlled breaths.

The cruiser mounts the sidewalk. Tom hears it gaining. On their left are houses. Lawns. Tom dives to the left, toward Nina, wrapping her in his arms and rolling across the lawn with her. The cruiser speeds on, screeching to a halt.

Tom and Nina roll through. They head down the side of the house whose lawn they're on, leaping over the short metal gate there. In the back yard, they find the occupants of the house sitting outside. Despite the early hour, they're drinking beers. Tom can smell weed smoke in the air. The two people – one male, one female – double-take as Tom and Nina race through.

"Hey, what –" the woman says.

Tom and Nina reach the fence and climb it, jumping down and continuing to run.

"Follow me," Nina says. "I've got an idea."

Tom falls slightly back, following her lead. She knows the area better. Hopefully she knows somewhere they can hide out where the cops won't find them.

They cross the road and clear the divider, hopping the metal railing there. Cars on the road swerve to avoid them, blaring their horns in frustration. Tom and Nina push on, Nina leading. As they round a corner, Tom chances a look back. They've managed to give the cruisers the slip, however brief it may be. They're still close. They'll still be looking. They're no doubt on their way to this location.

They keep running downhill, their boots slapping hard on the sidewalk. Nina takes left and right turns and Tom follows. She takes a zig-zag route. Tom doesn't think it's a shortcut. She's putting distance between themselves and the other cops, as well as houses and streets to make them harder to spot.

"This way," she says, reaching the end of a street. "Nearly there." She looks back, makes sure no one can see them. They cross a patch of dried-out grass. There's a sheer drop beyond it with a concrete border. Nina doesn't slow. She jumps down the drop, and then doubles back toward it. The drop is only a six-foot fall into a descending concrete ramp. It's dry, but Tom can see patches of wet around its edges, shallow standing water. There's a faint, foul smell in the air.

Tom soon sees why. Nina is leading them into a sewer outlet.

"Do you have a flashlight?" Tom says.

"Funnily enough, I didn't have time to grab one," Nina says. She's breathing harder now, catching her breath. She breathes through her mouth and covers her nose with a hand and Tom does the same, each trying their best to minimise the smell. They ignore it as best they can. "I had to chase a perp down here once. I've got a vague idea of where to go. It shouldn't take long for our eyes to adjust."

They keep walking, sticking close to each other. Nina holds onto Tom's hand, guiding him through. They stick to the edges of the sewer system, out of the water.

"They didn't give us much of a chance to explain what's going on," Tom says.

"Maybe we shouldn't have run," Nina says.

"It wouldn't have made a difference. You saw the footage. We know it's fake, but to anyone else it was pretty damn convincing." Tom pauses a moment. "I'm sorry I got you caught up in this."

Nina stops abruptly. She turns back to him, their faces close so she can see his eyes and he can see hers. "No," she says. "Don't say that. I'm not sorry at all. Would you rather you were going through this alone? Hell, if we hadn't spent the night together and I'd seen that footage without context, I'd be running you down just as hard as them, because I'd be *real* pissed off that I was attracted to you and then it turned out you were a terrorist."

Tom nods. "I appreciate that," he says. "But would you have shot me in the street without giving me a chance to explain, like they were trying to do to us?"

"No comment," she says, then kisses him. She turns and starts walking again, still holding onto his hand. "That shocked me, though," she says without turning. "That they would fire on us like that. They were shooting to kill."

"Emotions are running high," Tom says. "A lot of people have died today. A lot of injuries, too. A lot of lives changed forever. Those cops coming after us, they might have had people of their own affected."

"I get that, but I'm a colleague. They could have at least granted me some kind of professional courtesy and *tried* to take me in alive. Give me a chance to talk."

"I'm not saying it makes it right. I'm just offering an idea. It seems like they've made up their minds, and they want us dead for what happened." Tom's eyes have adjusted to the darkness. He assumes Nina's have, too. They step easier now, and walk faster. "That footage is going to circulate, and fast. Our faces are going to be known to the whole city – the whole country. It's not just going to be the cops out for our blood."

"Then we need to keep our heads low," Nina says. "Right now, down here in the sewers might be the best place for us."

20

Simon Arditti hasn't been anywhere near the explosion. He's been on traffic duty, keeping vehicles moving, diverting them away from downtown, making sure the bombing doesn't cause unending gridlock and bring this part of the city to more of a standstill that it already is. Barricades have been erected and things are under better control, and Simon is no longer downtown. He's back at Bayview Heights Police Station. He's in the locker room. He's not alone. He placed some calls.

With him is Christie Llewellyn, Bill Kuzniar, and Jorge Da Costa. The three other cops in the department he trusts the most. The three he knows he can talk freely with.

"So that goddamn bitch is a bomber, huh?" he says, the others huddled around him. The station is mostly quiet. There is a lot of activity upstairs after what has happened, but most of the uniforms are out on the streets, doing what they can, attempting to hunt down the two responsible. Because of that, Simon figured this might be the safest, most private place for them to talk. "Ain't that a pisser, huh? She spills her guts about me to Internal Affairs, and all along she's a fucking terrorist in waiting."

The other three nod along with him.

"You hear that Harwood and Jackson took shots at them?" Bill says.

"Nearly got them, from what I heard," Christie says. "Came real close. Jackson says he must've missed the guy by just an inch."

"Tompkins nearly ran them down, too," Jorge says. "They managed to give him and the rest the slip, though. Said it was like they just disappeared. There's a team still out there looking for them, but it doesn't look like they're gonna find them."

"You think Nina really did it, though?" Bill says. "She's always been such a straight arrow."

"You saw the footage, didn't you?" Jorge says.

"Listen, that's what I called you all here for," Simon says. "You have doubts, it doesn't matter. I saw the footage, same as everyone else, and it looked pretty damning to me. But frankly I don't care if she did it or not. She could be a *suspect* and I wouldn't give a shit. This is an opportunity I *need*. She wanted to testify against me, and then gets herself caught up in something so stupid? Well, now she's got a target on her head, and ain't no one gonna ask any questions if *we're* the ones to gun her down. Shit, we'll be heroes."

"I like the sound of that," Christie says. "I'll do it more for the satisfaction than the medal."

"You and me both," Simon says.

"All of us," Bill says.

"And the guy?" Jorge says.

"They're a package deal, I guess," Simon says, shrugging.

"I reckon they're gonna be sticking together. We want her, we're probably gonna have to deal with him, too."

"But how are we gonna find them?" Bill says. "It's a big city and they could be anywhere. Chances are slim."

Simon has already thought about this. "Here's what we do – we run a pool on who takes them out first. Spread the word, but only to people we trust. But make it clear *we* want the privilege of putting them in the ground. They find them and get the info to us and we tag and bag them, *they* win the pool. We all got that?"

"And if *they* bag them?" Christie says.

"They get a *cut* of the pool," Simon says. "We wanna incentivise them to do things right."

The three smile. They nod.

"Then let's get to it," Simon says. "Like you said, it's a big city."

21

Tom and Nina pause beneath a manhole cover. "This will bring us out around the back of an old factory," Nina says. "There shouldn't be anyone around to see us – whole area's a bit of a dead zone."

"You chased a perp all the way through here?" Tom says.

Nina nods. "He was a junkie with a long line of breaking and entering felonies. This one night, he'd tried to rob an old lady in her home. She fought him off, but he gave her a hell of a shiner. Me and my partner David – you've met him – we chased him down. On the surface David went one way and I went another. I saw the guy slip into the same sewage outlet we came in through. Nearly missed him. If I didn't see him come this way he'd have been lost for good. Turned out he'd been using the sewers to get around, break into houses, and then disappear underground. The factory where we'll come out, that's where he was holing up."

"Just him?"

"Just him. I caught him inside, trying to hide in an old

locker. He'd turned one of the back offices into his crash pad. The floor was covered in all these tatty old pillows he must've taken out of dumpsters or something. He was using newspapers for blankets. If it wasn't for all the break-ins, the robberies, and the occasional assault, I would've felt bad for him."

"And the factory is still empty now? Has anyone else settled into it?"

"Not the last time I checked," Nina says. "It got added to my beat. I come by regularly."

Tom nods. "When we come up out of the sewer, let's head into the factory to lie low, figure out our next move."

Nina makes her way up, opening the manhole cover an inch and looking around to make sure it's clear. She tells Tom it is and then climbs all the way out. He follows, then replaces the cover and follows her into the factory through a door with a busted lock. It was chained closed at one time, but the chain has been cut in half.

They stay on the ground floor. The windows at the front of the building have been boarded over. No one can see in. Beyond them, Tom can hear traffic passing.

Nina sniffs her clothes. "It's not too bad," she says. "But it's not great, either. It's gonna be hard to keep a low profile when we smell like this."

"A change of clothes should be our first priority," Tom says. "The cops back at your home saw what we're wearing. If we can get hats, too, baseball caps to cover our faces from security cameras. And then we need to figure out what the hell's going on here, and why we're being used to blame for this bombing."

"And why did they choose *you* to blame?" Nina says.

"I've been wondering that," Tom says. "I figure it must be my background. They've presumably spent some time looking for a viable candidate to play their fall guy, and they found one in me."

"And there must be something more going on," Nina says. "They struck me as a professional team, not a bunch of whackos looking to prove a point. Not necessarily the best of the best, but they had elite gear. Chlebek could've been the weak link, but the rest of them might not be so careless. How'd it read to you?"

"Same," Tom says. "But sometimes it can be hard to tell. Maybe all they wanted to do was blow up a government building and have someone else to blame it on, then they'll move on and do the same thing somewhere else. Or it could be there's more going on, and the bombing was some kind of false flag, a diversion, but for what?" He pauses a moment, thinking. "If it's the former, they're likely already gone by now. If it's the latter, they're probably still in the city. We need to find them, find out what they're doing, what their end goal is – if they have one. Without them, it's going to be hard for us to clear our names."

"We're unarmed," Nina says. "And they had heavy weaponry. With the bombs, too, who knows what else they might be packing? We can't go up against them with just fists and good intentions."

"That's another problem we need to resolve."

"It's not like anyone's going to sell them to *us*. Our faces are known. People are more likely to put a bullet *in* us than let us purchase them."

"We'll have to think on it. First things first, we need different clothes. And we need to keep moving. I don't want to stay in any one place for too long. We're alone out here. It's just the two of us, and we don't want to risk that anyone sees us, and if they do we can't hang around long enough for them to bring anyone else to us."

Nina looks to the side, thinking. Tom notices. Her brow furrows, like she's trying to figure something out.

"What is it?"

She pauses. "We might...we might *not* be completely alone," she says. "I have a friend, on the force. Liz Farr. I think she'll believe us. I think she'll help us."

"You *think*?"

"I can't know for sure, but I've known Liz a long time. I trust her."

"How much do you trust her? Because it's a big risk to take."

"*Completely*," Nina says. "I'd trust her with my life. She wouldn't believe that I'd do this. And if I tell her you didn't either, she'll believe *that*, too."

"How can you be sure?"

"Because if our roles were reversed, and it was *her* on that footage, I wouldn't believe she was responsible."

Tom takes a deep breath. "Well, let's hope you're right, because trusting her with our lives is exactly what we'll be doing."

"Do you know anyone who could help us out?"

It doesn't take Tom long to answer. "Cindy Vaughan. She's a hacker. She'll have seen right through that footage. If we can get hold of a phone, or a computer, I could contact her. She'd find some way to prove the footage is fake."

"Where is she?"

"Texas."

Nina whistles. "That's pretty far."

"She doesn't need to be here. She can do it all remotely."

"Then we know what we need to do," Nina says, beginning to count off on her fingers. "Clothes, phone, Liz, Cindy."

Tom nods. Wordlessly, they head back out of the factory, senses on high alert, knowing that no matter where they go, they're in danger. The whole city is against them.

22

Stuart Lynch paces the floor. He's agitated. Concerned.

Orlando, on the other hand, is not so worried.

They've found out that Rollins and Nina are still alive. Hence Stuart's agitation. Eddie picked up on the news. His radio is tuned in to police radio traffic, and he turned it up so they could all listen as the cops tried to run down Rollins and Nina from her home.

The team lie low in their hideout, a loft office space, currently unused. They stored their spare cache of weapons here, and the Semtex before it was put to use. For now, they wait. For some of them, the waiting is easier than for others.

Corey and Eddie are hard at work on their laptops. As well as keeping tabs on their upcoming target, they also search for Rollins and Nina's whereabouts. They remain tuned in to cop traffic, and they've set up alerts for facial recognition throughout the city.

Harris lies flat on the floor, staring at the ceiling. He

appears to have sunk into a meditative state. Orlando would think he was sleeping if it weren't for his open eyes.

Stuart pauses his pacing long enough to ask the techs, "Anything?"

Corey shakes his head. "Nothing. Not yet."

"Goddamnit." He takes a step back, lacing his hands atop his head. He turns to Orlando. Orlando sits in a swivel chair, twisting softly side to side. "This isn't eating you up?"

Orlando shrugs. "Why should it?"

"Why? Because they're out there running wild, that's why!"

Again, Orlando shrugs. "What can they do? The footage is out. They're the bombers. There's nowhere they can go, no one they can turn to. This isn't as great a concern as you're making it out to be, Stuart." He tilts his head back toward Harris. "Take a note out of his book. Just lie down and breathe through it. Feel all of your concerns melt away."

Stuart's eyes narrow, glaring at Orlando and his blasé attitude. "I don't like it," he says.

"None of us *like* it, but it is what it is. This situation will resolve itself. They can't hide forever."

"And what if someone catches them? What if they speak?"

"Rollins was in the Army. He was in the CIA. He was raised by a nutty father who trained him in survivalism and prepping. Do you really think they're going to get caught?"

"It's always a possibility. It's a risk."

"The cops are shooting on sight. It doesn't sound to me like they *want* to question them. They want revenge for what has happened to their city. Everyone here does. They're out for blood. They're not interested in talk. Besides, on the slim chance they're taken alive, other than our faces Rollins doesn't know who we are. He doesn't know why we're here. He has no idea who or what our true target is."

Stuart remains doubtful. He resumes pacing.

"When have I ever led you wrong?" Orlando says. "Stuart – *Stuart* – take a seat. You know what *is* driving me crazy right now? *This*. This pacing you're doing. Sit down."

Reluctantly, Stuart does as he's told.

"There. Doesn't that feel better?"

Stuart's leg bounces.

"Corey and Eddie will find them," Orlando says. "And when they do, *we'll* deal with them. Rollins and Nina might be able to give her fellow cops the slip, but they can't stay out of *our* grasp. Once we know where they are, they're ours."

Stuart forces himself to sit back, folding his arms. "Fine," he says. "But the sooner the better. I don't like this. It feels sloppy."

"Mistakes will happen," Orlando says. "Harris, back when you were a Marine, what was that slogan they used to have?"

Harris doesn't move, doesn't react to his name being called, but he responds without raising his head. "They still have it," he says. "Improvise, adapt, overcome."

Orlando looks at Stuart. "Improvise, adapt, overcome," he says. "See? We're currently doing the first two. It won't be long before we overcome. You'll see. By the end of today, we'll have left this city behind. We'll be riding out of here to our meet-up point with Tony and Chet, and I'll remind you of this moment, and when I do we're all going to laugh in your face."

Orlando glances around the room. Corey and Eddie

don't look up. Harris remains staring at the ceiling, slowly breathing in and out. Stuart is angry and miserable. Right now, it doesn't look like any of them are prepared to laugh, but they'll see. By tonight, Orlando's point will be proven. He's right. He's always right. That's why he's the team leader.

23

Simon and Christie have hung around the station. David Remsburg was called in to help with the explosion. He was at the bombsite. He's returned to the station now and he looks like hell. He's tired and dirty. He goes to the lockers, hits the shower. Simon and Christie wait for him to get out. The station is still quiet, most other people rushing around still. They're the only three in the locker room, and David doesn't realise they're here.

When he gets out of the shower, wrapped in a towel, he gives a start.

"Surprised to see you back here so fast, David," Simon says.

"Sergeant said I looked dead on my feet," David says. "The situation is under control down there. He told me to get cleaned up and head home."

"We haven't been to the site," Christie says. "What's it like?"

"It's like a warzone," David says, his features pinched. "You're better off not going. You don't wanna see it."

Simon folds his arms and leans against the nearest locker.

David looks the two of them over. He frowns. "The two of you want something, or...?"

"Hell of a thing about your partner," Simon says. "She being the one to *cause* that warzone."

David grimaces. He steps past them, heading for his locker. Simon and Christie follow.

David pauses, looking back at them. "What do you want? You think I had something to do with it?"

"You're not in the footage, David," Simon says.

"Unless there's something you want to admit to us?" Christie says.

David clenches his jaw. "I'm not gonna answer that," he says. "I'm not gonna dignify it."

"We're not implying anything, David," Simon says. "We don't think you're responsible for anything that's happened. Of course not. We just wanna talk about your erstwhile partner."

"You wanna talk about Nina?" David says. "You think I haven't already been asked? I've got nothing more to say about Nina."

"It doesn't piss you off?" Christie says. "Knowing what she's done? Knowing who you were on beat with, knowing who you were sat next to all that time, all those long nights, and it turns out she was a murderous bitch that you never really knew at all?"

David turns back to them. "I know Nina pretty damn well," he says. He's fierce now. "And I saw the footage, and I don't care how it looked. I don't believe it."

"You don't believe it?" Simon says. "You don't believe your own eyes?"

"That kind of thing can be faked."

Christie snorts. "It's a pretty convincing fake."

"Nina wouldn't do that." David doesn't want to believe it. Simon can see that. To admit that she helped plant the bombs feels like a betrayal of his partner, despite her blatant betrayal of him.

"Then why's she running?" Simon says.

"Probably because she was shot at before she was given a chance to explain anything," David says.

"Nothing much to explain," Christie says.

"What about the man?" Simon says. "This Rollins character. You know much about him?"

"I know he can fight," David says. "Listen, that's enough. I don't wanna talk about this. I wanna change and go home." He starts to turn back to his locker.

Simon exchanges a glance with Christie. She nods. She spins David and presses him up against the row of lockers. His towel drops. She grabs him by the testicles and she squeezes.

"Jesus Christ!" David says, his voice choked off with the pressure and the shooting pain.

"You can go home when we're done talking to you," Simon says, leaning in close, his chin almost resting on David's shoulder. "You're holding out on us, David. I can tell. You've still got too much trust in Nina. It's misplaced. You're gonna get yourself into trouble, David, holding out like this."

Christie squeezes harder. David grunts and coughs.

"Tell us about Rollins."

David's voice is choked. "I barely know anything about the guy," he says. "We'd go by the diner to deal with the attempted robbers he'd beat up. He and Nina would flirt. That's as much as I know."

"She ever talk about him away from the diner?"

David shakes his head. "No."

"All right, whatever. That's not what's important. You know what's important, right?"

David says nothing.

"What's important is finding out where she's gone."

"This is personal for you," David says. "It's because she was going to testify. This doesn't have anything to do with what's happened."

Simon shrugs. He doesn't deny it. "We're just trying to do the right thing, Davey." He makes sure David can see his smirk. "So where could she be? You know her pretty damn well. Give us some clues."

"I don't know where she is."

Christie starts to twist his testicles.

David falls to his knees. He cries out. Christie follows him down. Tears stream down his face.

Simon gets down to a knee. "You're gonna have to give us *something*, David. It's the only way to get Christie here off you."

"What do you expect me to fucking say?"

Christie gives him another twist. David falls onto his front. He retches.

"Come on, man," Simon says. "There must be some kind of idea in that big handsome head of yours. Just tell us where she could've gone. Somewhere she might try to hide out, or someone she might turn to for help."

After a moment David raises his head. He's not looking so handsome right now. His face is bright red. His eyes are streaming. Mucus drips from his nose and spit hangs from his lips. The veins in his neck and at his temples pop. His mouth is twisted. “I don’t know,” he says, the words coming out slowly. “Try asking Liz.”

Christie prepares to twist again, but Simon holds up his hand. “Wait a minute,” he says. “Liz Farr, that right?”

David manages to nod.

“Two of them have always been tight,” Christie says.

“Where is she right now?” Simon says, asking anyone who might know the answer.

“Probably like everyone else,” Christie says. “Probably out in the city somewhere, trying to help.”

Simon nods. He turns back to David. “You know her address?”

David hesitates, but Christie’s hand is still wrapped tight around his testicles. “Yeah, I know it.”

Simon pulls out his notepad. “Keep hold of him until I’ve written this down, Christie, then you can let him go.”

“You’re a son of a bitch,” David says, gasping. “You’re a goddamn asshole.”

“Sure,” Simon says. “But I’m the asshole who’s gonna have his Internal Affairs investigation thrown out. I’m the asshole who’s gonna be the hero that gunned down the San Francisco bombers.” He pauses a moment, then grins and adds, “I’m also gonna be the asshole who takes home the pool.”

“Depends on who gets them first,” Christie says, smirking.

“I’m up for the challenge,” Simon says. He taps David’s forehead with the end of his pen. “Now give me that address.”

24

Tom and Nina travel on foot, keeping their faces down, features obscured by the peaks of their newfound baseball caps.

They went to a thrift store Nina knew, cases of clothes outside the front of the building, under the shade of a canopy. There weren't many people around. Things are quieter than they would ordinarily be since the explosion, especially closer to downtown. Further out, there are still plenty of vehicles and pedestrians.

Tom and Nina picked out clothes, trying to keep their faces turned away from the window so the proprietor inside wouldn't see them and potentially recognise them. They grabbed what they needed and they ran, disappearing around a block. They heard the store owner cursing them out as they fled, but they're too desperate to feel any guilt. "I shop there a lot," Nina says. "When this is all over, if we're still alive, I'll go back and pay them for what we took."

Tom grabbed a pair of black jeans and a white T-shirt, along with a grey huntsman jacket. Nina grabbed a pair of blue jeans, a size too small but she's able to squeeze into them. A red blouse with buttons down the front, tucked into the jeans. A long, green jacket that hangs down to her knees, and a hood that she wears up over her cap as extra disguise. Tom was able to grab a couple of black Giants baseball caps from a sporting store that they passed after they'd been to the thrift store. He walked inside, concealed them under his new jacket, and then walked straight back out without anyone noticing.

Now, they need a phone. "We get a phone, we call Liz," Nina says. "I know her number. Got it memorised. What about Cindy? You know it off the top of your head?"

Tom nods. "I know it."

Nina leads the way through the city. She sticks to quiet streets, places where she knows there's the least amount of security cameras, as well as areas where security cameras have been smashed. They pass drug dealers on corners, seemingly unperturbed by the news of the downtown explosion. No one gives them a second glance. Their business is unaffected.

"There's a store down here, they sell unlocked phones," Nina says. "They're used as burners by the dealers."

"How are we gonna get hold of one? We don't have any money."

"They're on display. They're in plastic cases, but not all of them are secured to the wall. You distract the guy behind the counter, I'll grab one of the boxes. We'll have to break it open, but I'm sure we'll find a way."

When they reach the store, on a corner at the end of the block, Tom goes in first. He keeps his hands in his pockets and pretends to be looking around, struggling to find what he's looking for. The store sells mostly candy, some tinned goods, as well as alcohol and cigarettes. The man behind the counter is also behind a sheet of bulletproof glass. Tom goes up to him. On his way, he spots the cell phones on display to his right. The phones are old. Look like they're all second hand. The plastic cases hold four phones each. Tom can't see which of them aren't connected to the walls.

"Help you?" the man behind the counter says, glancing up from his own cell phone.

Tom acts twitchy, like he might be one of the junkies he spotted outside. He keeps turning his head left to right, his baseball cap pulled low to further obscure his face, doing everything he can to make his features harder to make out. "Yeah, man," Tom says. "I was just wondering, you got any, uh, Rolling Rock?"

The man behind the counter looks at him, unimpressed. "What, you didn't use your eyes? You walked right past it, man – *twice*. It's right over there. Second shelf from the bottom."

Tom turns, makes like he's struggling to see it.

"Keep your head still for two seconds and you might find it," the man says.

Tom turns. The door opens. It's Nina. She's already running. She races past Tom from behind, grabs one of the cases containing the cell phones, and then bolts for the door again.

"Hey!" the man shouts. He grabs something from under the counter and then unlocks the door to the side, stepping out. In his hand he has a sawn-off shotgun. He's raising it as he heads for the door. Tom steps up beside him and pushes the shotgun up. It goes off and plaster rains down around them. Tom keeps raising the gun, slamming the hot barrel hard into the centre of the man's face. He stumbles back, tripping over his own feet and falling flat onto his back. Tom sprints out of the store after Nina.

They keep running until they've put a few blocks between themselves and the store. Nina slips down an alley and Tom follows. They find themselves at the back of an abandoned house. It's rundown, its windows either smashed or boarded up. The grass here is overgrown, and vines are crawling up the walls.

Nina turns the plastic case around in her hands, figuring out how best to break it open. "I heard a shotgun go off," she says.

"Storekeeper was coming after you," Tom says. "I persuaded him it wasn't a good idea."

"He hurt?"

"Bust nose. Maybe a chipped tooth. Nothing serious. Certainly nothing as serious as what was coming out the end of that shotgun." Tom looks around the overgrown area, searching for a rock. He looks at the house, and sees that some of the bricks on the corner are loose. He goes to them and kicks at them until a few of them fall to the ground. Nina brings the plastic case over and Tom balances it against the foot of the building, then uses the corner of one of the bricks to crack it open. He opens it wide and takes out two phones. He hands one to Nina. They switch them on. They're both fully charged.

Tom thinks for a moment, remembering Cindy's number, and then dials it. He presses the phone to his ear. Nina waits. She watches.

The call rings, and rings. It goes to voice message. Tom frowns, hangs up, then tries again. Again, she doesn't answer.

"Nothing," he says, slipping the phone into his pocket.

"She won't recognise the number," Nina says.

"Doesn't make a difference. She'd still answer. I know Cindy."

"You think she's ignoring the calls, thinking it could be you?"

"Cindy wouldn't do that. Whenever I've called in the past, no matter the time of day or night, she's always answered. She knows it's the same if she calls me."

"You always answer straight away? Even if you're busy?"

"I suppose not. If I'm busy, I call her back when I'm not."

"She's not going to know this is you."

Tom takes the phone back out and sends her a message. It's brief and to the point.

This is Tom. Call me when you get this.

He nods. "Hopefully she'll be in touch soon. We can't wait around for her to get back to me."

Nina calls Liz. While she does, Tom goes to the corner of the alleyway and looks out. The street beyond is clear. He can hear Nina talking on the phone. Liz has answered. Tom leaves her and goes down the alleyway to the end, checking up and down the road. It's quiet. There's no one around. No one has followed them. The shopkeeper has not given chase. After the blast in the face with the hot barrel of the shotgun, he probably didn't even leave the store.

Tom returns to Nina. She's off the phone.

"I got through," she says. "She was at the bombsite, and she doesn't believe for a second that I had anything to do with it." She seems relieved at this, pleased to know that her trust in her friend was justified.

"I hope she feels the same way about me."

"You're with me, so if I say you didn't have anything to do with it, she'll believe you. I didn't have time to explain everything to her on the call. I kept it brief. We can tell her everything when we see her."

"And where will we see her?"

"We go to her place. She says because of the traffic it'll probably take her a couple of hours to get there."

"How long will it take us?"

"From here, and on foot, about ninety minutes."

"Then let's go," Tom says. "I want to get there early. Make sure there's no one waiting for us."

"Liz wouldn't betray us like that."

"I'm not saying she would. But people in your station know that you're friends, right? Then they're probably going to be watching everywhere you might go, just to be sure you don't turn up there."

Nina looks like she feels sick. They start walking. "Pass me your phone," she says. "We need to exchange numbers in case anything happens and we get split up."

Tom pulls out his phone and hands it over. Nina punches her number into his phone while they walk, then does the same with her own. When she's done, they pick up the pace.

25

When Tom and Nina reach Liz's home they get in via the back door. Tom has to break the glass to get it open, carefully slipping his arm through and undoing the latch.

"When this is through, I'm going to owe a lot of people a lot of money," Nina says.

They stay low as they get into the house. Tom crawls through into the living room at the front, then peers out the window there, checking the road. He spots an unmarked car parked on the other side of the street, two people in the front, watching. He ducks back down.

"Someone's outside," he says.

They stay in the kitchen, staying low and drinking water. Tom sits with his back against the drawers, watching the front of the house. Nina sits opposite, watching out the back door. It takes another half-hour before Liz arrives. Tom moves out of sight so he's not the first person she sees in her home. Nina slides into view, pressing a finger to her lips. Liz already understands. She moves at a casual pace toward the kitchen.

"Did you spot the guys outside?" she says as she enters the kitchen, getting into a position where the car outside won't be able to see her through the window. She spots Tom. He's standing now. Tom nods. Liz eyes him warily.

"We saw them," Nina says.

Liz notices the smashed window on her back door. She raises an eyebrow. "You gonna pay me for that?"

"You know I'm good for it," Nina says. "So long as we survive."

"You must be Rollins," Liz says to Tom. "Wish I could say I was pleased to meet you."

"Wish I could say the same." Now that she's seen him and hasn't been caught by surprise, Tom moves back into a better position so he can see through the living room and to the window. To the car parked outside and the people within. They're still there. They haven't gotten out since Liz returned.

Nina explains to Liz everything that has happened. The true version of events.

Liz nods along. "I never believed it for a second," she says. "That ain't you. It's not who you are. I tried telling people, but no one would listen. Of course, everything going on, it's not like there was much time to talk. We had work to be doing. Obviously, I wasn't so sure about this one." She nods her head toward Tom. "But if you say he's not the bomber, then he's not the bomber. But listen, the two of you need to hear this – there's a rumour going around that there's a pool on who can kill you and Rollins first. This is very much a shoot first, ask questions later situation – if any questions are asked at all."

"Jesus..." Nina says. "Did you hear we've been shot at already?"

"By Simon?"

Nina tilts her head. "Simon wasn't there. It wasn't any of his group of hangers-on, either. What's it got to do with him?"

"He's the one running the pool."

"Shit... I mean, I guess I shouldn't be surprised."

"People want your blood for what's happened. Both of you. No one's listening to anything I have to say, and Simon and his buddies are taking this as an opportunity to get you out of their lives. Pre-emptive revenge for preparing to testify against him."

"Who's Simon?" Tom says.

Nina gives him a quick rundown of their past history, and why he holds a vendetta against her.

"A bad cop," Tom says when she's done. "I've had run-ins with my fair share of them."

Nina turns to Liz. "If they're firing on us on sight, what do they believe?"

"Well, the media are painting your friend here as a disgruntled ex-Army vet striking back at a country he believes has failed him – hence the bombing of a *federal* building. They're colouring it all very Timothy McVeigh coded. And you play into it as his brainwashed sidekick."

Nina bites her lip and shakes her head.

"The team who kidnapped us," Tom says, "they're the ones most likely responsible for this. We're working off the assumption that the federal building wasn't their final target, and that they have another objective out there. It's our only hope of tracking them down and clearing our names. If they *do* have another target, we need to find out who or what it is and stop them before they can strike again."

"And how are you going to find them?" Liz says.

"I know the van they're driving. I've memorised the license plates. If we can get into security footage we might be able to track the van down, and find where they've gone, too."

"What about the men themselves?" Liz says. "Did you catch any names? You said they weren't hiding who they were."

"Only one," Nina says. "Chlebek, but he's dead. By the time forensics pull an ID on him from the warehouse, it's going to be no good to us."

"If these guys are as under the radar as we suspect," Tom says, "it could just be twisted so Chlebek is made out to be another of my followers, especially if he's ex-military, too."

"We need to know who you're up against," Liz says. "Right now, you're flailing blind."

Tom nods. "If we track down the van via security footage, we might catch a glimpse of their faces, too. We get their faces, we can search them online, find out who they are. Maybe find out if they're answering to anyone else, and who *they* are."

Nina clicks her fingers. "The warehouse where we were held, there were other warehouses nearby and they were functional. They must've had security cameras outside. It would be an oversight if they don't. If we're lucky, they might have even been pointing toward the road. They could have picked up on these guys going to and from their HQ."

"You any good with computers?" Tom says. "This is usually the kind of stuff Cindy helps me out with, but she's still not calling back."

"Cindy?" Liz says.

"A friend," Tom says.

"I'm good enough with computers," Nina says. "I can get us what we need. So long as they have them, the security footage from the warehouses will be kept onsite. If we get inside the one with the best camera angles, we can retrieve the images from there."

"Last I heard, there's still a lot of cops down there," Liz says.

"So they finally showed up, huh?" Nina says. "We waited a long time after it blew, and no one came."

"What happened downtown drew everyone away," Liz says. "It needed everyone. More important than an old warehouse. Except, now that it's looking like it was your apparent base of operations, it's getting more attention."

"Then we'll have to be careful," Tom says. He tilts his head through the living room, toward the window he's been keeping an eye on. "Another car has just pulled up," he says. "This one's marked. Two people are coming this way. They're in uniform."

"Stay out of sight," Liz says, then peers out of the kitchen to see. "*Shit*," she says, then glances back at Nina. "Simon and Christie."

Nina's face is grim. She turns to Tom. "Simon has a tight crew. They're all as rough and ready as each other. As well as Christie Llewellyn, he has Bill Kuzniar and Jorge Da Costa running around after him like loyal pups, too. Wouldn't surprise me if they were the two already outside."

There's a knock on the front door. It's hard and insistent, demanding a prompt response.

"You two go out the back," Liz says. "I'll keep them busy at the front."

26

Tom and Nina slide out of the back door while Liz heads to the front to keep Simon and Christie preoccupied.

"Back to the warehouse?" Nina says.

"Back to the warehouse," Tom says.

Before they can set off, they find they're in a trap. The two cops who were already outside the house when they arrived, waiting in the car, have come around the back. Two men. Tom assumes them to be Bill Kuzniar and Jorge Da Costa. Judging by their ethnicities, Tom can guess which is which.

Their guns are already out, raised and ready. When they spot Tom and Nina, Jorge gives a start, almost surprised, but Bill does not hesitate. He opens fire.

Tom, however, has reacted faster. He grabs the lid from Liz's trash can and hurls it at them like a discus. It hits Bill in the chest and knocks his aim off, his right arm knocked to the side with the spinning impact, his gunshot taking a chunk out of Liz's home. He stumbles back into Jorge, and

Jorge fires wild into the air as he tumbles back onto his ass.

"Nina!" Liz shouts from inside the house. "Rollins! *Run*!"

They're already moving, fleeing across Liz's backyard. Tom hears gunshots behind. Flowerpots explode. Tom reaches the fence first. He doesn't scale it. He throws himself against it, knocking it flat. Nina grabs him by the back of the jacket as she passes, helping haul him back to his feet.

They run. Simon and his people follow.

Tom follows Nina's lead. She knows the area. She knows alleyways to slip down, and where to hop fences and cross yards. Unfortunately, Simon and his people seem to know the same shortcuts, and they can't give them the slip.

They get away from the residential area. Closer to businesses. They run across the road and Tom slides across the hood of a screeching car skidding to a halt. The car horn blares as he races to catch up to Nina. The driver curses him out of the open window. Tom and Nina make their way down another alleyway. This one is between taller buildings, as opposed to the houses they've been passing by and through. Tom pauses, slipping down a cut and pressing his back against the wall. Nina is still running. She hasn't noticed he's stopped.

Tom waits. It doesn't take long before he hears footsteps pounding down the alleyway in pursuit. Only one set, but it still means that when Tom's finished here it's going to be one set less coming after them.

When the racing footsteps are almost upon him, Tom sidesteps out from behind the corner, raising his arm and slamming the back of his elbow into the centre of Bill's jaw. He goes down hard and fast, landing with a thud on the ground. Tom looks back down the alleyway. No one is there.

They either haven't caught up, or they've taken an alternate route.

Bill is pained, but he's not out. He pushes himself up onto his hands, then sees Tom. He grabs for his handgun. Tom kicks him across the face, knocking him flat. He reaches for the gun, but then hears another pair of footsteps reaching the end of the alleyway. It's a man Tom hasn't seen. He assumes this must be Simon Arditti. Simon spots Tom and stops running, raising his gun in both hands. Tom starts moving before he can fire. His bullets ricochet off the brick-work around him, raining down concrete dust and shards of brick.

Tom reaches the end of the alley and jumps to the left, out of view of Simon. Nina turned to the left when she reached the end, too. He spots her running down the hill. She pauses at the sound of the gunshots, though, realising that Tom is no longer beside or directly behind her. She stops, waiting for him to catch up. Tom runs after, waving for her to continue on.

A cable car is descending nearby. Nina is still looking his way and Tom motions to it. She nods, understanding. As it passes, Tom leaps onto its rear, then hangs off it as it passes close to Nina, his right hand wrapped around one of its railings. He grabs Nina and pulls her onboard.

There are gunshots. They hit the deck together. The back window of the cable car shatters. From the direction of the fire, Tom thinks it must have come from Simon. Glancing that direction, Tom sees the cops chasing on foot, gaining on them.

The cable car is half-full. The people inside scream and throw themselves to the ground. Tom hauls Nina into the body of the car, where everyone else is. It continues moving.

Tom isn't sure how the cable cars work, but he feels like it's sped up since the gunshot. They're going downhill – he could have just imagined the speed change. Wishful thinking.

Two more bodies leap onto the rear of the cable car. Jorge Da Costa and Christie Llewellyn. They spot Tom and Nina on the ground, just inside the body of the car. The cops reach for their handguns. Jorge is closest to Tom. Tom waits until he brings out the Sig Sauer. Tom kicks it from his hand. It skitters toward the edge of the cable car. Tom jumps to his feet as Jorge scrambles for the gun. Tom slams into his side, driving him out of the body of the car and throwing him against the railing. Jorge goes down and reaches for the gun. Tom kicks it off the cable car. Undeterred, Jorge lunges for Tom's legs, knocking him off balance.

Nina charges at Christie, wrestling her own gun away from her. They battle at the rear railing of the car. Christie is bigger than Nina, heavier, and she takes control. She wraps her hands around Nina's throat and presses her against the railing, arching her back over it.

Tom is on the ground. Jorge scrambles toward him. He punches at his face. Tom moves his head to the right. Jorge's fist hits the ground. He cries out, grabbing at his wrist. Tom kicks him in the ribs, twisting him up. Tom sits up and grabs him by the side of the head, slamming him into the metal lining of the nearest chair.

The occupants of the car are gathered together inside, at the front, away from the fighting. The car remains in motion. It takes a right turn. Everyone tilts.

At the railing, Nina breaks Christie's grip on her neck, slamming her fists down on her elbows. She jabs Christie on either side of her ribs, then brings up a knee into her midsection. She pushes Christie back and kicks her off the car.

Tom has Jorge. Holding him by the back of the neck, he throws him over the rear railing. He checks Nina over, making sure she's okay.

The car is still moving. The passengers are talking. It takes a moment before Tom makes out what they're saying. The passengers have realised who he and Nina are.

"They're the bombers," Tom hears someone say.

"Get them!"

The biggest guy in the group is pushed forward. He drags his smaller friend with him. He's not going to tackle Tom and Nina on his own. Behind them, the rest of the group swells forward, forcing them on, the mass of bodies encroaching.

The cable car is nearly at the bottom of the hill. "We need to go," Nina says. "This is going to get nasty."

Nina prepares to leap off the car, but the friend of the biggest guy is close to her and he grabs for her arm. Nina grabs his thumb and twists it, forcing him off. She shoves him back.

The bigger guy is eyeing Tom. "I'm gonna tear you apart, you goddamn butcher," the big guy says. He lunges. Tom leans back against the rear railing and raises his legs, slamming both boots into the chest of the biggest guy, pushing him back with all of his strength. The big guy falls, arms spread wide, catches all those immediately behind him on his downfall and causing a ripple effect. Everyone goes down. The cable car is at the bottom of the hill. Tom and Nina leap from it and start running.

27

In the hideout, everyone on the team is standing. They're gathered around Corey and Eddie's laptops, watching. Eddie got a hit first – Nina, emerging from a gap between two buildings, Rollins following shortly after. Both of them in too much of a rush to be careful. And then they saw why – a cop, firing at them both, before they jumped onto the back of a cable car.

"Stuart, Harris," Orlando says, "tool up and get out there. We have them now. We'll keep them in sight and direct you from here."

"Dead or alive?" Stuart says. Harris is already equipping himself, checking the magazine of his M4 and then slamming it into place.

"Living is best," Corey says. "A lot has already gone wrong today. If we need more footage of them, it's best we have them alive for the scans."

"Use your head," Orlando says, breathing deep. "Judge the situation. I trust you. What I *want* is for them brought back, kneecapped, but I understand that might not be doable."

Stuart nods. He and Harris leave.

"Don't lose them," Orlando says to Corey and Eddie. "This is the best hit we've had. We need to keep eyes on them."

"Doing my best," Corey says. "They're goddamn careful. They're already trying to get away from cameras. They know what they're doing."

"They've changed their clothes," Orlando points out. "We know what they're wearing now. That'll help, right?"

"Doing everything I can," Corey says, fingers hammering at the keys, eyes flickering between the half-dozen screens he has open on his laptop.

Orlando glances at Eddie's screen. He's not continuing the hunt. He's going back through footage. Retracing the chase as far back as he's able.

"What are you doing?" Orlando says.

"Those cops," Eddie says, and then trails off momentarily while he watches something. He turns to Orlando. "They looked particularly bloodthirsty, right? All that gunfire, leaping onto the cable car like that. And this bit – watch." He scrolls through the footage to where they first got the facial hit on Nina emerging from the alleyway. Shortly after Rollins appears, and the cop behind him, firing, Eddie pauses it on his face. "Look at that expression," he says, pointing to the screen. "There's something in his face..."

"It looks personal," Orlando says. He folds his arms, a finger tapping his shoulder while he thinks. "It *should* be personal – as far as they know, these two are bombers, right? They've killed all those people today. But there's more there. We're not just imagining that."

Eddie nods in agreement. "Saw it as soon as he appeared. Saw it with all of them, to be honest. They way they jumped on the cable car, there was desperation there. I mean, they could've called it in – cut off the cable car, get someone to go where it is, or to intercept it on the way. But not one of them reached for their radio."

Beside Eddie, they hear Corey linking up with Stuart and Harris, directing them. "I'm catching glimpses," he says. "They're being *very* careful, okay? I'll tell you where to go, but you're gonna have to rely on your own eyes as much as mine. You saw what they were wearing now though, right?"

"It looked personal, that's for sure," Eddie says, his screen still fixed on the image of the shooting cop emerging from the alley. "I mean, all the cops we've seen before, they've been bloodthirsty, right? But none of them have had that face. They're angry, like, it *is* personal for them, but it's still their job. They look angry more than anything else. Disappointed, even. This guy looks like a jilted ex or something. I'm not just imagining that, right?"

"No," Orlando says. "You're not. I see it."

"The other cops we saw shooting, they looked like they were shooting to wound. Hell, I'll be honest, it looked like they were shooting wide on purpose. They feel betrayed by Nina, but they can't bring themselves to put her down. Rollins, it's not the same, but it's different for her. There's a part in them that still sees a sister cop. These guys, though, they were on target. Shooting to kill."

"You've got their faces," Orlando says. "Look into them. Find out what you can. Find out if it *is* personal."

"Then what?"

"Then I'm going to talk to them," Orlando says. "If the cops gun Rollins and Nina down in the street, publicly, it's not the worst thing in the world, but maybe I can rein this overzealous group in. Put them to work for us. Won't hurt to have some extra bodies on side, just in case they get away from Stuart and Harris. They've been a slippery pair so far. It's best we prepare for all outcomes."

28

Tom and Nina return to the warehouse district they escaped from only a few hours ago. They stay low while they're in the area, avoiding being seen. They keep their caps pulled low.

It's already been a long day for them. They're both tired, but neither of them lets it show. They push on. They push through. All those hours spent in the gym are in preparation for moments exactly like this.

There are still cops at the bombed-out warehouse, but only a couple of them. They stand by their cruiser and watch the forensic team as they sift through the wreckage, bagging anything that looks of interest. Tom and Nina give the area a wide berth. They don't need to be close to it. They go to the other warehouses. The ones still in business.

They're not so active right now. Tom and Nina walk past them, keeping their heads down but glancing inside. "They look like they've shut down for the day," Tom says.

"Could be because of the explosion," Nina says. "They've

maybe been told to close. Could be there's a worry about more bombs in the area."

"It's also Saturday," Tom says. "They might work half-days on Saturdays."

"Plenty of factories out there that go for twenty-four hours, no matter the day of the week. I reckon it's more likely because of the bomb. Maybe coupled with the bombing in the city, too. It's been a big damn day for San Francisco."

Tom looks back toward the warehouse where they were earlier held captive. "I'm surprised at the lack of media presence."

"I'm sure they're coming," Nina says. "They've probably already been, but there's not as much excitement here. They've got their hands full with what happened downtown. There's more story there. A *lot* more."

They check the cameras on the functioning warehouses. None of them point toward where they need. Tom isn't surprised. "They would've checked in advance," he says. "We saw the footage they faked – they know cameras."

"Maybe one of them covers the road," Nina says, looking around. "It could have caught them coming in or going out or whatever."

Tom tilts his chin, spotting one with promise. He goes toward a camera high up on the side of one of the warehouse buildings. It's pointing toward the entrance to the district. He stands beneath it and looks in the direction it's aiming. He follows the road to the warehouse. It's the main road. The team must have used it. He turns back to Nina. "I think we've got a winner."

They go to the back of the warehouse and find the rear door. It's made of the same corrugated steel as the rest of the building. Tom tests the handle, but it's locked.

"Worth a shot," he says.

"Any further ideas?"

"Force," Tom says, taking a step back. He kicks at it. It's firm in the frame, but the metal dents a little around the lock. The sound reverberates through the building. They both freeze and make sure no one comes to investigate. No one does.

"Kick it with me," Tom says.

They stand together and count off. On three, they kick the door together. It flies inward, the door bending around the lock and the catch slipping out of home.

Tom steps in first. The warehouse is in darkness. He blinks, giving his eyes a moment to adjust. Nina follows. They look around and spot the back office. There's a glow coming from it, where the security cameras are still running.

"You go make a start. I'll make sure there's no security or anyone coming," Tom says.

Nina heads to the back office. Tom takes a walk around the warehouse. It's a big space. It's filled with car parts. Most of them look new, packaged up and ready to be transported out. Some of them are old, used. Damaged. To be repurposed, perhaps. There's the smell of motor oil hanging in the air. He checks down every aisle to make sure there's no on-duty security guard, lying low, ready to call them in. There's no one. Next, he goes to the front of the building. He's able to unlock the door from the inside. He pushes it open just a crack and peers out. The area beyond remains as quiet and desolate as it was when he and Nina first arrived and took a look around. He relocks the door and then heads to the back office.

Nina is already in the system and searching through footage. "I'm looking for the black van," she says. There are three screens, each of them covering different parts of the warehouse. The one on top shows the road – the camera they came in here to investigate. The screen to the left of it shows the front of the building. The one Nina is looking through, when it's not being used to go through footage, presumably shows the inside of the warehouse.

Tom watches over her shoulder. "How far back have you gone?"

"This is yesterday," she says. The footage plays in reverse. Her eyes never leave the screen. "I spotted the van on this morning's footage, but it was while it was driving away and all I got was its rear. We already know its licence plate. No faces, so no good to us."

"What about when they first arrived with us?"

"Only the driver was visible, and he was wearing a mask at that time."

Nina goes back further. Another day. Tom wonders if the team were using any of the other vehicles that they've seen. He remembers the car that pulled up on him and Nina early this morning. He doesn't think he's seen it on the footage.

"Ah!" Nina says suddenly, freezing the screen.

Two days ago. The black Ford van, coming this way. The two men in front, one white, one Black, neither of them masked. They recognise both of them. The Black man is driving. The white man riding in the passenger seat was the leader of the group.

"That should be enough," Nina says. "I can search them with this. This is a clear shot of their faces." She points to the white man. "And we know he's in charge, so I'll search him first."

"Can you do that here?" Tom says.

Nina nods toward the closed laptop on the nearby desk. "Fire it up," she says.

As Tom moves, something on the live footage above catches his attention.

It's the black Ford van.

"We have company," he says.

Nina looks up. "Shit," she says. "Do you think they're coming here?"

"I doubt they're going to the old warehouse."

Nina curses again. "Okay, it's fine. I can just email this image to myself and we can look it up somewhere else."

"Don't email it," Tom says. He searches the desk around the closed laptop, opening draws and rummaging inside them. "The team has tech guys, right? They could be in your emails. We don't want them to see this, to know what we've found." He pulls out a USB stick and hands it over.

Nina nods and downloads the image onto the stick. Tom goes to the office door and looks out, waiting for the men to turn up from the black van. Is it just the two of them who were riding up front, or are there more in the back? He thinks they're going to find out soon enough.

Nina appears beside him with the stick. She holds it up. "Got it," she says.

They leave the office, hurrying toward the rear door where they entered.

They approach it from the side. The door opens. The end of an M4 pokes through.

29

Tom spots the open door and the end of the rifle and grabs Nina's arm, pulling her away and hiding down an aisle of stacked mechanical parts. They duck down onto their haunches and Tom peers through a gap in the boxes to see the Black man entering the warehouse from the broken rear door. He's alone. He steps lightly, moving the M4 from left to right, sweeping the area. He heads deeper into the building.

Tom and Nina stay low and move as quickly and quietly as they can, slipping into another aisle.

At the front of the warehouse, Tom spots a brief flash of light as the front door is opened. It's promptly closed again, and the dimness returns. However the other team member got the door open, he was quiet about it. Picked the lock, perhaps. Tom wonders if he re-locked it from the inside. Wonders if he noticed it can be unlocked from the inside, as Tom did earlier.

He turns to Nina. "We head for the front," he whispers. "Stay close. We're going wide."

Nina nods. Tom turns and, rising to a stoop, he starts moving, looking ahead and behind for the two members of the team. He doesn't hear or see any sign of anyone else being here, unless the other team members are still outside, guarding the front of the building. If they are, that's a risk Tom and Nina are going to have to take. They need to get outside. They need to get away. They can't stand up against the M4s.

They need weaponry of their own. Tom is sick of being caught short.

Plus, if they can get outside, he's not sure the two men will take a risk on shooting at them, not with cops parked so close. Everything about their operation has been careful. They won't want noise here. They won't want to draw attention to themselves.

Tom stops. The Black member of the team is close. Tom spots his movement through the stacked crates. He's careful, and he's quiet, but he moves *fast*.

The other man catches up to him. The long-hair with the grenades on the front of his vest.

"They've been here," the Black man says, his voice low. The two men don't look at each other. Instead, their heads are on a swivel, on lookout. They keep their M4s raised while they scan the warehouse. "Back door was kicked in."

"Any sign?"

"Nothing yet."

"They could have left."

"I don't think so. Not yet. They haven't been here long enough."

"Why would they even come here?"

The Black man considers this. "I don't know," he says. "But they're still here somewhere. I'm sure of it."

"Maybe we should try and spook them out," the other man says. "They're probably hiding among all these damn aisles. Want me to toss a grenade?"

"Are you nuts? We don't want the noise. Just find them."

Tom waits until they're moving again, each man going in separate directions, M4s poised. He reaches back for Nina, taps her on the side to be alert, then starts moving again. She follows close.

At the end of the aisle, the Black man appears. He's not looking their way. Tom cuts right with Nina. They go straight, looking back to make sure the other man isn't near. He's disappeared from view. They get to the end of the aisle. In front of them is a clearing. The front of the warehouse is twenty yards away. Twenty yards with nothing between them and the front door.

Tom looks left. The Black man is gone, has disappeared down the aisle where they gave him the slip. Tom waits another moment for him to get deeper, to get further away from where they are. He brings Nina up beside him.

"We need to make a break for it," he says. "Straight for the door. You ready?"

"Always."

"On my mark." Tom looks around. "*Go.*"

They run.

As they near the door, Tom hears a startled noise behind them. He hears the Black man's voice, calling out. "They're on the move!"

They're close to the door. Tom sees that it's been locked. There's gunfire. He throws himself forward, rolling through, the bullets rattling off the steel walls. He gets to the door and unlocks it, throwing it open. Behind, he hears footsteps pounding across the concrete ground, giving chase.

Tom pulls Nina out of the warehouse with him and then slams the door closed. He looks around, deciding where to go. He can't take long. He looks toward the old warehouse. The cops aren't active. They didn't hear the gunfire, or if they did they've dismissed it. But, if they run that way and the cops realise who they are, they're going to gun them down. Tom looks right, down the road, toward the end of the warehouse area. There's a chain-link fence, and on the other side of it is scrubland. And then, the water.

A boat is coming. It's close.

"This way!" He starts running and Nina follows without question.

The two men from the warehouse burst out, search where they've gone, and give pursuit. Tom glances back. He sees the white man raise his rifle but the other pushes it aside, gesturing back toward where the cops are.

The top of the chain-link fence has barbed wire. They're closing in on it. Tom is in the lead. He slips out of his jacket and throws it to the top of the fence, covering the barbs. He turns, pressing his back to the chain link, and stoops down, lacing his fingers together to boost Nina over. She understands and runs right at him, placing her right boot in his hands. He pushes up and she vaults over, placing her hands onto the jacket. As she's descending, Tom turns and jumps up, hands on the jacket, hauling himself over. He pulls the jacket down with him, not wanting to make it easier for their pursuers.

"The boat!" Tom says, catching up to Nina.

It's passing by now. It's below the edge of the scrubland. It's a cruising boat, slowing as it nears the port. They can only see the top of it.

Together, hand in hand, Tom and Nina jump. They land

on the back of the boat, shaking it violently. The two people already aboard, a younger couple in swimming shorts and open shirts, give a start and turn.

"Keep going!" Tom waves. "Don't stop the boat!"

The pilot turns and does as he's told. Tom looks back toward the scrubland. Their pursuers reach the edge. They run alongside it, trying to catch up to the boat, but it gets away from them.

"Tom," Nina says, breathless, getting his attention.

Tom turns. Nina tilts her head toward the young couple whose boat they've landed upon. The woman is pointing a revolver at them. "I know who you are!" she says. "I saw you both, on my phone! I know what you did! Don't move!"

Nina has already raised her hands. Tom does the same. "I'm sorry we dropped in like this," Tom says. "Why don't we just get off your boat?"

"No!" the woman says. "Stay right where you are! We're taking you in!" She leans her head closer to her boyfriend/husband/whomever he is. "Do you think there's a reward?" she says.

"I don't know," the man says. "Maybe? I mean, it stands to reason that there *should* be, right?"

While they're talking to each other, distracted, Tom seizes the opportunity. They're clear of the warehouse area now. The two men chasing them have been left behind. They're not far from shore, either. Tom is a strong swimmer. He doesn't know about Nina. If she's not, he can drag her along beside him. He catches her eye and tilts his head back. She understands. She nods.

They dive off the side of the boat and start swimming.

"Hey!" the woman on the boat cries.

"Shit! Shoot them!" the man says.

The woman starts shooting. She's not a good aim. The bullets splash into the water, wide. Tom holds his breath and goes under, getting deep and then continuing in a straight line, so if a bullet happens to come near him the density of the water will slow its impact until it's harmless. He looks back. Nina has done the same. The water stings his eyes but he keeps them open, sweeping his arms and kicking his legs to keep him moving toward the shore. He looks for the bottom of the boat. He spots it. It's still moving. It's getting further away.

Tom and Nina return to the surface and fill their lungs. They float into the shore. It's made up of rocks and isn't comfortable when Tom lies flat upon it. It's clear, though. There's no one else around. They take the opportunity to catch their breath.

Nina coughs and spits out water. "This is *not* how I expected my day to go," she says, wiping water from her face and splashing it onto the stones.

Tom sits up. "You mean you *didn't* expect an entire city to be gunning for you?"

"Funnily enough..." Nina says.

"I doubt the USB survived that," Tom says.

Nina pulls it out, expecting the worst. She examines it and her face lightens. "Oh," she says. She holds it out for him to see. "Someone splashed out when they bought this – pun intended. It's water resistant."

Tom laughs. "Some good news."

"Fleeting as it may be," Nina says, slipping the USB back into her pocket. "We need a computer. Somewhere we can look into these men now that we've got a couple of their faces on camera."

"We need weapons, too," Tom says.

"Outnumbered and outgunned," Nina says, staring across the water. Ripples still play across the surface from the boat they jumped onto, and then promptly off. The boat itself is almost gone from view now, pulling into the harbour.

"We need to get moving," Tom says, dragging himself to his feet. He holds out a hand for Nina.

She takes it, but pauses. She's thinking. Hesitating. "We need guns," she says. "And we need information." She hesitates again. Tom doesn't hurry her. "Bayview Heights Police Station has both of those things." She gets to her feet using his hand.

"We break into your station?" Tom says.

"I was thinking more we *sneak* in," Nina says.

"Won't the guns be under lock and key?"

"I'll deal with that," Nina says. "I'll find a way in. Hell, with everything else we're wanted for, what difference is a little theft gonna make?"

"Sounds like a pretty big theft to me."

"So long as we stay alive, I can smooth it over after."

30

Orlando is in the field. He had Eddie keep an eye on Simon Arditti, the apparent ringleader of the group of cops fervently pursuing Rollins and Nina. It was wise to do so – soon after, Stuart and Harris called in. Once again, Rollins and Nina got away. They jumped onto a boat, apparently. By the time Stuart and Harris got to the harbour and found the boat they'd escaped on, they'd already jumped off into the water, according to the boat's occupants.

Like Orlando said to Eddie, it's best to prepare for all outcomes.

Orlando remains dressed in all-black, though he's concealed the tactical vest and his weaponry in the trunk of the car he drove here. Simon Arditti is nearby. He's getting coffee. He's alone. Corey and Eddie have kept eyes on the rest of his group, ever since they lost visuals on Rollins and Nina. The rest of them – Christie Llewellyn, Bill Kuzniar, and Jorge Da Costa – are doing the same thing they are: they're searching.

Orlando waits in the shadows of the alleyway next to the coffee house. When Simon emerges, his brow is furrowed, his lips pursed. He's lost in thought. Whatever it is he's thinking about, it's not making him happy.

It didn't take long for Eddie to work out the cause of Simon's drive. Nina was prepared to testify against him in an Internal Affairs investigation. Seems Simon is a little too eager to get his hands dirty. Orlando likes that. He can use it.

"Officer Arditti," Orlando says, calling to him from the alleyway before he can get into his car.

Simon pauses, turning back, frowning. "Yeah?"

"Mind if I talk to you briefly?" Orlando says, stepping out enough for Simon to see him.

"I'm busy," Simon says, opening his door. His tone drips with sarcasm. "Big case. You might've heard about it. Can't hang around. You got a problem, call 911."

"I think you'll want to talk to me, Simon," Orlando says, causing the policeman to pause. "It's about Nina Perry and Tom Rollins."

This gets Simon's attention. He closes his door but doesn't come any closer. He looks into Orlando's face, trying to work out if he knows him.

Orlando beckons him to come closer, stepping back into the alley, giving the impression of this being a clandestine meeting.

Simon puts his coffee on the top of his cruiser and cautiously steps forward, one hand resting on the handle of his pistol.

"No need for that," Orlando says.

"How'd you know my name?" Simon says.

"We've been watching you today, your reaction to the bombing, and we're impressed."

"We? Who's we?"

"Do you really expect me to say?"

Simon frowns so hard his right eye is almost completely closed. "Who are you?"

"My name is Higgs," Orlando says. He puts on his most serious voice, and makes his expression grave. "And my team and I have been tasked with capturing Rollins and Perry for their actions today. We've been monitoring them for a while now, and we regret that we weren't able to intervene early enough to stop them from following through on what they've done. We're going to have to live with that for the rest of our days."

Simon's eyes widen at this. "Are you with the government?"

Orlando nods. It's not a complete lie.

"Do you – do you have ID?"

Orlando glares at him. "I'm working black ops, Arditti. This is all hush-hush. Do you *think* I'm carrying ID? Is knowing your name, and where to find you, not enough?"

Simon considers this. He swallows. He decides it is. "So what do you want with me?"

"Assistance," Orlando says. "As you may have guessed, we're struggling to find them, and my own people are stretched thin already. We're doing all we can, but we need more bodies, more eyes. That's where you come in. Like I said, we've been impressed by what we've seen so far. You have promise, Simon. And you know this city. You know Nina Perry."

Simon nods enthusiastically. He's become caught up in the moment, in its conspiratorial nature. "You can count on us," he says. "Me and my people, we're gonna deal with them. We've even put a little incentive out there, if you get what I'm saying."

Orlando cocks his head. "An incentive?"

"I've organised a pool," Simon says, looking and sounding pleased with himself. "Whoever takes them out gets the pot. Like I said, an incentive."

Simon is beaming broadly. Orlando considers what he has said. "How many people are participating in this pool?"

Simon hesitates. Orlando imagines that not everyone on the force has been made aware of its existence. Only a select few – the type of cops who would jump in with Simon while he was kicking an already downed protester. "People I could rely on," he says tactfully. "People I trust."

"All cops?"

"Yeah, of course."

"Okay. You need to amend the rules of your pool, Simon."

"What do you mean?"

"We need them alive."

"Alive?"

Orlando nods.

"I don't understand. After what they've done, why would you want them alive?"

"Do you really think that they're working alone here, Simon?" Orlando says, leaning closer, making his eyes fierce. "Rollins may be part of something much bigger, something that reaches much higher. Do you think he's the only person we've been watching? Like I said, my forces are spread thin. This is the closest we've come to capturing someone who belongs to the cell he's working with. We need answers. The information he can give us is no good if he's dead."

"What about – what about Nina?"

"We need her alive, too. Rollins may have passed information on to her. From what we understand, she hasn't been a part of this as long as he has. She might break easier than he will. But there's more, Simon, a more pressing matter."

"What's that?"

"There could be more bombs. Here, in San Francisco."

Even in the shadows, Orlando sees how Simon's face blanches. He hadn't considered this.

"If there are, we need to know *where* they are. We find out where they are, we can stop them from going off. We can stop more death."

Simon nods along. "Of course, yeah, of course. I'll – I'll make some calls."

"I'm going to give you a number, Simon. If you find them, don't call it in. Contact *me*. Don't try to apprehend them unless you have no other option. My team and I will take them off your hands. That clear?"

Simon nods. He pulls out his cell phone and hands it over. Orlando puts a number in. "What if you need to contact me?" Simon says.

"I already know how to contact you," Orlando says.

Simon nods, wide-eyed.

"Tell no one of this meeting, Simon," Orlando says. "This stays strictly between us, and those closest to you. Christie, Bill, and Jorge."

Simon seems overwhelmed by his knowledge. He nods.

"But no one beyond your inner circle. If you bring Rollins and Perry to us, your government will be forever grateful to you. Naturally a monetary reward will be on the table, for your invaluable assistance in dealing with this disgusting terrorist threat."

Simon is clearly impressed. His eyes light up at the

mention of money. "I'm on it," he says. "You can count on me." He turns and hurries out of the alley, back to his cruiser. He forgets his coffee. He speeds off, the takeaway cup somersaulting through the air and landing with a splash in the gutter.

Orlando contacts Eddie and Corey, speaking into the microphone in his sleeve at his wrist. "Did you hear all that?"

"We got it," Corey says, his voice coming through Orlando's earpiece.

"It appears we've gotten this situation under control at least," Orlando says.

"Do you expect them to actually find the targets?" Eddie says.

"Not particularly, no," Orlando says. "But there's no harm in having some extra eyes on our side. Plus, I feel these idiots were likely to cause us more problems if we'd let them continue to run unfettered. Best we keep things as neat as we can."

31

It's late afternoon. The sun is still shining, and has mostly dried Tom and Nina's clothes.

They've lain on the roof of the building next to Bayview Heights Police Station for the last hour, watching. The scene of the bombing downtown has likely calmed, is under control, and there is more activity around the station as the cops who were called in either return to their regular duties, or prepare to go home.

They're uphill. They're atop a small apartment building with a flat roof. It has three floors, presumably one apartment for each floor. They climbed up the fire escape at the side, out of view of the station.

Bayview Heights Police Station is on a downhill slope. On either side are houses and apartments, and at the bottom of the hill, on the corner, there is a café. Cruisers are lined up outside the station, parked on the other side of the road. Directly opposite the station, beyond the cruisers, is a green space. Bushes and trees. Further down, elevated and flattened, there is a basketball court. Four small children, of different races, pass a ball around and attempt trick shots at the hoop. Tom doesn't watch them for long. He looks around briefly every so often, checking the area, seeing how it is. He keeps himself alert to everything, not just the station.

On the way over, Nina tried calling Liz. She didn't have high hopes that she would answer, but it was worth a try. If they were able to get in touch, Liz could get them inside. She'd be able to look up the information they need, too. "Nothing," she said when the call rang out.

"Would they have taken her in?" Tom said. "For talking to us, having us hide out in her house?"

Nina's face was grim. "Probably. At the very least they'd take her in, see what else she knows. And plus, this was Simon and his people. Any excuse to hassle someone close to me."

They continue to watch the building, Nina pointing out to Tom the various rooms on this side of the station. "Ideally, I'd like to wait longer, so we could get in when it's quieter," she says. "But I don't think we've got that kind of time."

"We need a diversion," Tom says. "I'll make it. Draw as many of the cops out as I can. I do that, you get inside. You know the way around. It'll be faster for you by yourself."

"What are you going to do?" Nina says.

"I don't know yet. There's gonna be a chase involved, I know that much. When you get out and get clear, you can call me and we'll arrange where we meet."

"The guns?"

"Stash them. When things calm down we can come back for them."

Nina looks across to the cruisers. "I have an idea for you," she says. "You see that car there?" She points to one of the cruisers, parked third from the end. "That's Garcia's car. He leaves his keys in. No matter how many times he's warned about it, he keeps doing it. Puts them behind the sun visor."

"Got it," Tom says. He starts to move away from the edge of the roof.

"You're going now?" Nina says.

Tom keeps crawling back toward the edge. He stays flat. Doesn't want to risk being seen by straightening up. "No time like the present."

32

Simon calls his people into the station. They meet with him in the break room. He keeps it clear for their arrival. When they arrive, they huddle by the door, stay standing. Simon doesn't want anyone to walk in on them. He doesn't want anyone hovering outside, either, and overhearing them.

"All right, I'm glad you all got here fast," Simon says. He looks around each of them, taking them in, locking eyes, impressing upon them how important what he's about to say is. They're bruised and beat up from their run-in with Rollins and Nina at the cable car. So far, Simon is unscathed in comparison. "We need to talk. This is serious. Someone came to see me."

Christie looks confused. "Someone came to see you? What do you mean by that?"

"Someone from the government." He glances out the crack of the break room door. It's clear outside. "He recruited me. Recruited *us*."

The others lean in. They're intrigued.

Simon tells them how Higgs approached him. Tells them what he told them.

"What kind of monetary reward?" Bill says when he's finished.

"Is that the first thing you think of?" Simon says. "This is a government agent. He picked out *me* – *us*. He's recruited us. I mean, it's obviously gonna be a hefty reward. I don't think we've gotta worry about that. But look at the bigger picture here, man."

"Okay, sure," Bill says. "What part of the government was he from?"

Simon blinks. He forgot to ask. "It was – it was secretive, y'know? He couldn't say. Black ops. This is the kind of shit you don't just talk about. For them to reach out to us, it's a big deal."

Bill avoids the severe look that Christie gives him.

"But they want them alive, right?" Jorge says.

"That's what he said," Simon says. "I mean, I don't think it matters if we hurt them, but yeah, we've gotta keep them breathing."

"And you're okay with that? You wanted Nina dead."

"Look, she can't testify against me anymore, can she? No way. We hand her over, you know what the government is gonna do with her, right? She's never gonna see the light of day again. It's gonna be like Guantanamo Bay-type shit for what she's helped do. Her life's gonna be a living Hell. Knowing she's suffering like that, I'm gonna go to sleep with a smile on my face every night."

"Shit, for what they've done, the governor might even consider lifting the moratorium on the death penalty," Christie says. "They'd deserve it."

Simon nods. "Yeah, exactly. So yeah, I'm okay with it. I'm

satisfied with it. If the government wants to either prolong the bitch's suffering, or cut it short in the electric chair, I don't care. I'm all on board."

"We better make some calls," Bill says. "Adjust the rules of the pool."

"Do that now," Simon says. "We don't want anyone to fuck this up for us."

33

Tom crosses the road to Garcia's car. He strides like he has nothing to hide, the collar of his jacket pulled up to conceal the sides of his face. In front of the Bayview Heights Police Station, though, he's hiding in plain sight. The cops wouldn't expect to see him here, and so the few of them who are hanging around outside aren't looking for him.

Tom makes his way to the cruiser parked three from the end. It's unlocked. He gets inside. He pulls down the sun visor and the keys fall out. Just like Nina said. He catches them. Before he puts them into the ignition he glances into the rear-view mirror. The three cops outside are still talking among themselves. They haven't seen him get into the car. Tom wasn't trying to be subtle. He wanted to be seen. It's time to get noticed.

He starts the engine and reverses it out of the space. The cops still don't look up. They're probably accustomed to cruisers regularly pulling in and out, coming and going. They don't register it anymore.

Tom rolls down the hill until he stops directly in front of them. He puts the window down. "Excuse me, gentlemen," he says. "Which way to the Golden Gate Bridge?"

They turn to him, frowning. At first, they see a civilian behind the steering wheel of a cop car. Then, they realise exactly who they're looking at. Tom sees the recognition dawn on their faces.

Tom winks at them, and then he speeds down the hill.

Watching the mirror, he sees two of the men race to their cruisers. The third runs back into the station to sound the alarm, on his radio as he goes.

At the bottom of the hill, Tom takes a right. A cruiser is coming from this direction. When it spots him, it puts on its lights. The word is already getting out, it seems. Tom swerves past it. The cruiser skids sideways, turning around to pursue.

Further back, Tom sees two cruisers descend the hill from the station. They're coming fast. More will be on their way. Tom takes the next left and continues downhill.

34

Nina descended the side of the building soon after Tom, waiting until she saw him start to cross the road. She hid at the corner, concealing herself, and watched as Tom got into Garcia's cruiser and made himself known to the station.

She waits and watches as more cops spill outside, hurrying to their cruisers to give chase. In the flurry of movement, while they're all distracted, Nina leaves the corner and goes to the rear of the station. She enters through the fire door. It's never locked, but it is alarmed. She does this on purpose. It adds to the chaos and the confusion.

Sure enough, as she enters the station, the alarm bells are ringing. She ducks into a supply closet as a couple of cops run by, peering out until they've passed. When they're gone, she hurries down the hall and heads down to the basement. To the armoury.

The armourer's name is Kyle. He's a pale, dour guy, his days all spent underground, away from the sun, and with little social interaction. He's nice, though. Nina has never had any problems with him. He rarely smiles, but he often cracks jokes. Nina likes him. Because of that, she feels bad when she has to sneak up on him from behind and choke him out as he's leaving the armoury.

He goes down without much struggle, caught completely by surprise. His legs land inside the armoury door and keep it wedged open. When he's unconscious, Nina gently lowers his head to the floor. She makes a mental note for yet another apology she's going to have to make. Kyle doesn't know it's her who's put him down, but Nina wouldn't be able to live with the knowledge.

Of course, as she keeps reminding herself, she might not be living at all come tomorrow, or an hour from now, or even the next few minutes.

She enters the armoury. The alarm is still ringing shrilly in her ears. It'll take them a couple more minutes to turn it off, once they're sure there isn't any fire. She needs to be fast. In and out of here, and then on to the database.

She grabs a carry bag and fills it with weapons and ammo. She puts in a couple of Sig Sauer P226s and two AR15s. She fills the space remaining in the bag with magazines for both. Done, she steps lightly over Kyle's prone body, then runs back upstairs. Checking the hall is clear, she heads to a back door further down, away from the fire door. She unlocks it from the inside via the catch, then heads to the nearest dumpster. She throws open the lid and then dumps the bag of guns inside, pulling a box over the top to keep it covered. She goes back into the station and lets the door close behind her. She doesn't relock it.

The alarm is still ringing. Nina heads upstairs. She glances in the rooms she passes. Most of them are clear. Inside an interrogation room, however, she sees Liz. Nina halts, and opens the door. Liz looks up with a start. "Nina," she says, though Nina can barely hear her over the alarm. A klaxon is nearby, and it's deafening.

Nina notices that Liz is not cuffed to the table. "Come on, let's go," she says, waving for her to follow.

Liz jumps up and they head further down the hall. Away from the klaxon they can hear each other better. "They arrested you?" Nina says.

"Not exactly," Liz says. "They can't prove that I've been harbouring you, and there were clearly signs that you'd broken into my house. There was nothing to say that I've been helping you. But I've been brought in and questioned, and they won't let me leave. Keep asking me where you might be, where you'd go. I think they plan on holding me here until they catch you and Rollins. So, they haven't put me in a cell, but they haven't let me out of the interrogation room, either. They don't trust me not to try and help you."

"Who's questioning you? Simon?"

"He's popped in, but no. Hyder and Graham. Where are we going? Why are you here? I doubt you came just to get me."

Nina stops outside an office, grabbing Liz's arm to keep her close. The office is empty. They slip inside. Nina takes a seat and pulls out the USB. "I need to use the database," she says. "And then, if that doesn't have any answers, I need to get online. Watch the door."

Liz does as she says. "Where's Rollins?"

"He's causing a distraction."

"The fire alarm?"

"No, that was me. He took Garcia's car."

Liz shakes her head. "You think he'll learn after this?"

"I think he'll be severely reprimanded after this," Nina says. "I'll add him to the list of people I need to say sorry to."

"There's a list?"

"You're at the top."

Liz chuckles. "It's clear out here."

Nina slams at the keys, working as fast as she can. She runs the two faces through the database. She doesn't get a hit on the leader. She does, however, get a hit on the driver of the van. Stuart Lynch. Assault with a deadly weapon, three years ago in Arizona.

"I have a name," she mutters to herself as she leaves the database and continues her search online. "I can work with a name."

She searches Stuart Lynch. She searches his name, his face, and the face of the group's leader. She searches the name Chlebek, too, in conjunction with the others.

"How long you gonna be?" Liz says.

"Going as fast as I can," Nina says, eyes never leaving the screen, fingers never leaving the keys. "What's it like out there?"

"Still clear for now, but it won't be forever. And you still need to get out of here, don't forget that."

"*We* need to get out," Nina says. "I'm not leaving you here."

Liz doesn't answer.

Nina gets a hit. She has to go deep, chasing links she doesn't have time to double-check for viruses and malware. That's a worry for another day.

The leader of the group is called Orlando Higgs. There's details on his team. Names to the faces. It's not a lot, but it's enough for Nina to work with. They're all ex-military. They all left the forces years ago, different branches and at different times. They were all in trouble for various indiscretions before they either went AWOL or were given the boot. Now that they're out, they've been living off the radar since. There are rumours about them. Stories. Nothing can be corroborated. Nina memorises what information there is.

The alarm falls silent.

It's so abrupt, the ringing continues in Nina's ears for a few seconds longer. "That's not good," Liz says. "Means things are getting under control. We need to go. You got what you came for?"

Nina shuts down the site and gets to her feet. "Let's go."

As they leave the office, a door opens down the hall from them. The door into the break room. Simon emerges. Closely behind him follow Christie, Bill, and Jorge. The two groups lock eyes. Simon blinks, unable to believe what he's seeing.

"Holy shit," Jorge says.

"Get them!" Christie says.

They surprise Nina by not automatically reaching for their guns. Instead, they charge, giving chase. Nina and Liz turn and race down the hall, heading for the stairs. A door opens as they pass but Nina throws her shoulder into it and forces it to close in the face of the person emerging. She hears them cry out. She's probably given them a bloody nose.

Simon and his people are gaining. Nina feels them reaching out, grasping, their hands only inches out of reach.

Suddenly, Liz stops. She spins on her heel and throws herself back at Simon and his group, knocking them down like a bowling ball through pins. Nina stops, feet slipping on the linoleum floor, but Liz waves at her.

"Go!" she says. "*Go!*"

Every fibre of Nina's body tells her to stop and help, but she knows that Liz is right. She needs to get out. Needs to tell Tom what she has found. She sees Liz drive an elbow down into Bill's sternum, sees her clawing at Christie's face, and then she turns and she runs.

She reaches the stairs and leaps down them two at a time. Someone is coming up. They raise their face and see her. Nina recognises him. Atkinson. His eyes go wide. "Nina," he says. He places a hand on his gun. "Stay where you are," he says. "Don't make this difficult." He starts to pull the gun from its holster.

Nina braces herself with her left hand against the wall and her right on the handrail. She lifts herself and kicks Atkinson in the chest, sending him tumbling back down the stairs. She doesn't add him to her list. He was going for his gun.

Nina reaches the bottom and steps over him, and then freezes. A familiar figure stands in front of her. He's out of uniform. David. Her partner.

They lock eyes. There's no one else around, save for Atkinson on the ground.

"Y'know," David says, "I'm supposed to be at home right now. Sleeping. But people are looking for you, and they keep asking me if I know where you are. They keep calling me. Apparently, there's a lot of money at stake. *Money*." He shakes his head, disgusted. "Frankly, I'm getting sick of it."

Nina says nothing. She can't move.

"Simon and Christie nearly pulled my dick off," David says. "I think they've torqued something. I came back to put in a complaint. Looks like I'll be taking your place on the stand." He snorts.

"I didn't do it, David," Nina says. She hears motion

behind her, up the stairs. Simon and his crew getting free of Liz, half of them subduing her, half of them continuing the chase. "I swear to you, we've been set up. But we know who *did* do it, and we can stop them. We're the only ones who can. You have to trust me. You know me – you know I would never –"

"I know," David says. "Deep down, I always knew. It was a shock, but I've processed it now. Of course you didn't." He takes a deep breath. He steps aside. "Go."

Nina runs. She gives him a grateful look, but she can't stop for long. She bursts out the back door she left unlocked, and then she hears David lock it again behind her. She hesitates, looking around. The area is clear. She goes to the dumpster and pulls out the bag of guns. The plan was to come back for them when things have quietened down, but Nina sees the opportunity to get clear. She shoulders the bag and she runs.

35

Tom keeps the cops behind him busy. He ignores red lights and swerves around bend after bend, going uphill and then down. He starts to circle back toward the station, though stays distant from it. He checks the time, wondering if he's given Nina enough.

He hits a long stretch and puts his foot down all the way to the floor, creating distance. Slamming the brakes, he yanks up the handbrake and skids into an abrupt left, heading downhill. Cruisers fly by behind him, struggling to stop. Some of them crash into each other. Tom hears the screech of their brakes and the crumpling of their connecting bodies. He pulls the cruiser into an alleyway and gets out, starts running in the opposite direction. He looks back up the road. None of the cruisers have followed him down yet. He gets a couple of blocks away and then slows to a walk, pulling up the collar of his jacket again. He pulls out his phone and calls Nina.

She answers almost straight away. She's breathless, like she's running. "Are you out?" Tom says.

"I'm clear," Nina says. "Where are you?"

They arrange a meet-up point and Tom heads there at a brisk walk, keeping his hands in his pockets and his face down. He lost the cap after the warehouse, when they had to jump onto the boat and then into the water. The popped collar is the best he can do.

Distantly, opposite to the direction he's going, he can hear the sirens still running from the cruisers that were chasing him. They'll have caught up to the cruiser he dumped by now. They'll be broadening the search. Trawling the area for him. Closing roads and setting up checkpoints. Tom slips down alleyways, avoids main roads as best as he can.

Ten minutes later, he reaches the meet-up point Nina gave him, an underground parking lot. Nina said there aren't any cameras there. He finds her sitting in a dark corner, concealed in the shadows. There aren't many cars parked here. Tom spots a camera. He sees that there's *supposed* to be CCTV here. The camera has been smashed. Probably why there aren't many vehicles present.

"You get away okay?" Nina says when he reaches her.

Tom nods. "You?" He notices the carry bag at her feet.

"It got close, but I got out." She tells him about the help from Liz and David. "Simon and the rest, they didn't go for their guns this time."

Tom considers this. "They were indoors, in the station. Maybe they didn't want to run the risk on shooting their co-workers," he says.

"Maybe, but I ran into someone on the stairs and he didn't hesitate to go for his gun. It's probably nothing, but it feels like a stark contrast to just a few hours ago."

"We've got enough people shooting at us," Tom says. "If a

few people don't take a shot, we've just got to take it as a win."

"It didn't feel right, though. Of all people, I wouldn't expect Simon to hesitate."

"Maybe he's been listening to Liz. Maybe he's starting to come around."

Nina snorts.

"What did you find?"

"Oh, I got names," she says. She runs through them, along with descriptions so Tom can put names to the faces. Orlando Higgs, leader of the team. Stuart Lynch, the only Black member, and Orlando's second-in-command. Corey Crewe and Eddie Mitchell, both of whom, as well as being well-trained soldiers, are computer experts. The tech support for the team. Josh Chlebek they're already familiar with, and is no longer a concern. And finally, Harris Elkin – bomb expert.

"Shit," Tom says. He remembers the grenades Harris wore on the front of his tactical vest, and how he absently stroked them, like they soothed him.

"He's our bomber," Nina says.

Tom nods. "Though I'm sure it's a group effort."

Nina continues telling him about the team. "I couldn't find out too much on them. I didn't have the time. Names and faces is the most I was able to get, but I figured that was enough for now. But it seems like they stick together. They're a team. A motley bunch who would likely be convicts if they'd hung around their various branches long enough to be punished, but a team nonetheless."

"It's enough for now," Tom says. "We have their names, and that's something. Now we need to find if they have another target." He touches the carry bag with the tip of his boot. "I take it we don't need to go back for the guns."

"I saw an opportunity and I took it."

Tom smiles. He crouches down and opens the bag, looking over its contents. He takes out a Sig Sauer, then a magazine. He checks it's fully loaded and then slips the magazine inside. He tucks the gun down the back of his waistband and hides it with the tail of his jacket. "It feels like we've been caught short too many times," he says, straightening. "Now we're on an even playing field."

36

Orlando feels his phone ringing. It doesn't surprise him.

He doesn't answer it straight away. He's in their temporary HQ. The whole team are. They know what's happened in the police station. They know about the chase Rollins led the cops on. Clearly a diversion, but to what end? What did they get from the station? Why did Nina go into it anyway?

But then, why did they go back to the warehouse district? Why were they in the warehouse where Stuart and Harris found them?

"Do they know who we are?" Orlando says to himself, stroking his chin. "Have they learned our names?" He sucks his teeth. If he'd known there was ever any risk of them escaping their cage this morning, he would never have removed his mask, and he wouldn't have let the rest of the team, either. He turns to Stuart. "You have a record, don't you?"

"We all do."

"A police record, I mean," Orlando says. "Something that could be found in a database."

Stuart doesn't answer. He can hear Orlando's phone buzzing. "Are you going to answer that?"

"I already know who it is," Orlando says. "I'm not in a rush to talk to him right now. Answer my question."

"You know I do," Stuart says. "Those racist assholes in Arizona. You were there. It was the man calling you who had to clear that up. Left me with a record though, and a promise I wouldn't go back to that shithole town."

"Mm," Orlando says, nodding. "You nearly killed those men."

"You heard what they called me. I'd do it all over again."

"But it *did* leave you with a record. And this cop bitch has access to a database that will bring up your face and name. And your name could lead them to *me*. To *all* of us."

"She wasn't in there long enough to search every damn face in the database. And another thing – your new recruits didn't exactly excel themselves there, did they?"

Orlando ignores the remark. "What were they doing in the warehouse?"

"How should I know? There was nothing in the warehouse."

"We searched it after we lost them," Harris says. "Unless they were looking for car parts, there was nothing useful in there for them."

Orlando thinks. His phone has stopped buzzing.

Corey speaks up, turning around in his chair. They were watching the footage from inside the station on his laptop. They were watching the chase with Rollins and the cops on Eddie's. "What about the security cameras?" he says.

"What do you mean?" Stuart says, but he sounds annoyed already.

"Did you check in the office? Did you check their on-site footage?"

"No, we didn't," Stuart says. "Because *you*," he jabs a finger at Corey, "and *you*," he points at Eddie, "told us that you'd checked the area, and it was secure. None of the cameras were pointing our way. We were in a blind spot. We were invisible. *You* told us that."

"Yeah, the warehouse we were using was clear, but what about where else their cameras were pointing?" Corey starts to rise. "Some of them were pointing at the road. Did you check what footage they got from the road? Rollins and Nina could have got something from there."

"Again, that was your job to deal with."

"Uh-huh. And we were gonna go and wipe that footage once we were done here. None of this was supposed to happen. If Chlebek didn't fuck up back at the warehouse in the first place, none of this would be a goddamn issue right now."

Stuart and Corey are getting close to each other. Tempers are flaring. They're blaming each other. Orlando doesn't like it. His phone starts buzzing again. "The two of you need to calm down," he says.

"You need to answer that damn phone," Stuart says.

Orlando stares at him. His face is cold. He likes Stuart, but right now he's thinking about pulling his Sig Sauer and putting a bullet between his eyes in order to regain control, and remind them all who's in charge here.

It doesn't come to that. Stuart sees the look on his face. He knows what it means. It doesn't take a mind reader. He realises his mistake and raises his hands in apology. He backs down. Corey does the same.

Orlando clears his throat. "Maybe they know who we are," he says. "But that won't tell them what we have planned. Now I need to deal with this, so try to behave yourselves while I'm on the call." He pulls out his phone and walks away from them while he answers.

It's Hanley. Of course it is. "What the hell is going on over there?" he says.

"I guess that depends on what you've heard," Orlando says.

"I've heard they broke into a fucking police station."

"That's about the top and bottom of it."

"You sound way too laid back for me, Higgs. I don't like it."

"I'm doing my job. Would you prefer if I were cursing and shouting? That would hardly instil confidence now, would it?"

Hanley takes a breath. "I have people breathing down my neck here. You know that. This Rollins, he was the wrong guy to scapegoat."

At this point, Orlando is inclined to agree, but he can't admit that. "Listen, everything is in hand. Everything is set up. There's only a few hours before our plans come to fruition. Rollins and Nina aren't going to be able to find out what's coming in that time, let alone prevent it."

"They need caught."

"I'm well aware. We're working on it."

"This is messy, Orlando. I've never seen things this messy before. I rely on you because you keep things clean. You run a tight ship – *usually*."

"By the end of today this will all be resolved, and by then

it won't matter how messy things have gotten. Things will move forward as planned, we'll all be very rich, and this will be just a hiccup along the way."

Hanley breathes deep. "I hope so."

"I *know* so. Where are you right now?"

"I've come home. It's easier for me to monitor the situation from here without drawing any attention."

"Good."

Hanley pauses, then says, "What will happen to Chlebek's cut? Does he have family?"

"No family," Orlando says. "Just us."

"Every cloud, I suppose."

Orlando grunts. "I need to go." He hangs up and turns to his team. He takes a deep breath before he speaks. "Hanley is right," he says, assuming they were all able to overhear. "This has gotten out of hand. We're losing control."

"We're doing all we can," Eddie says. "We're working nonstop."

Corey nods. "My eyes are burning."

Stuart agrees with Orlando. "You're right," he says. "We need to get this situation in hand. We need Rollins and Nina dead and on ice, and then the cops can take credit when it's over."

Harris is leaning against the wall, arms folded. He shrugs one shoulder. "So what do we do? What more can we do than we already have? Corey and Eddie are making themselves blind trying to find them, and you've already brought some cops into it. It's not like we can go out and pound the pavement. This is a big city. It's not going to do us any good. And like you said, it's just a few hours until we make our move. We're going to need to get into position soon."

Orlando closes his eyes. He takes another deep breath.

They're all right. He knows they're right. They're doing all they can. If Rollins and Nina had more connections in the city, they could go to them, find out what they know or else use them as bait, but Nina's family live too far south, and Rollins's family are even further away. And as for friends, they watched Rollins for a few weeks, and he wasn't taking visitors. He went to work, came home, and that was that. Corey and Eddie have looked into Nina, searched her social media, but most of her friends have either moved away, or they're on the force. No current boyfriend or known hook-ups for either of them – save for each other, of course.

"Short of them messing up and giving themselves away," Stuart says, "there's nothing else we can do."

Orlando opens his eyes. "I'm going to lie down. Come get me if anything shakes loose."

37

Tom and Nina stay on the move. The underground parking lot was secluded, but they couldn't stay there forever.

They stick to quiet streets, Tom following Nina's lead. She knows her way around better than he does. He carries the bag of guns on his back. He has the Sig Sauer on his person, and Nina has one, too. They keep the automatic rifles and the ammo in the bag.

"We have names but we need more information," Tom says. "We need another computer. We need to go deep – dark web deep, maybe."

"Has your friend called back?"

Tom checks the cell just to be sure, but there's nothing. Cindy must be incredibly busy to leave him hanging like this. Of course, she could be out of town. On vacation. She could have left her usual life behind to be undisturbed. "No," he says.

Nina doesn't say anything. She keeps walking. She's thinking. Tom can see it on her face. "What?" he says.

She exhales through her nostrils. She starts to speak but hesitates and stops herself.

"We don't have time for doubts, Nina."

"Yeah, but I've got some pretty big ones about what I'm going to say."

"So just say it, and we'll take it from there."

"My ex," she says. "He works in surveillance. He also knows a lot about computers. As in, he spends most of his free time dismantling and rebuilding them, and when he's not doing that he's going down rabbit holes. He could probably help us find what we need to know."

"How come you didn't mention him earlier?"

Nina hesitates again.

"You don't trust him?"

She shakes her head. "No," she says. "I don't. He cheated on me, so that might give you the kind of idea of how our relationship ended. The fact that I thought it would be a better idea to break into a fully manned police station rather than turning to him is another clue as to our levels of trust. And it's not like with Liz where I knew we could go to her and she would believe me – I doubt Dante will. He'll accept what they're saying on the news and think nothing more about it. For all I know, he could be helping them try to find us." She pauses, biting her lip. "But we're running out of options. I mean, I think we've *already* run out of options. I wouldn't mention him at all if I thought we had anywhere else we could go."

Tom considers this. "Does he live far?"

"About an hour across the city."

"Is he working today?"

"He doesn't work Saturdays, but they might have pulled him in."

"We'll go to his place," Tom says. "If he's home, we won't try to explain ourselves. We'll put him to work and keep a close eye on him. If he's not, we get into his place anyway and use his computers. And you never know, he might surprise you. He might be on your side."

Nina blows air out of her pursed lips. "We'll see."

38

They make the hour trek across the city on foot, staying off main streets and avoiding security cameras. It's early evening by the time they reach Dante's building. This part of the city, closer to downtown, is quiet. Since the explosion this morning and the initial chaos, things have calmed. A hush has descended upon the area. A mourning calm. Further out, away from the scene of the blast, San Francisco remains lively and busy, but here, close to the eye of the storm, it's different. Life is not continuing as normal. This is no ordinary Saturday. The city is in mourning.

Tom and Nina hide down the block, staying out of view of the bar on the corner. The bar is open, but it's so quiet it might as well be shut. There are two men sitting separately at the counter, staring into their drinks. The news plays, but only the bartender is absently watching it.

Nina points to the building. "Third up, right on the corner," she says. "That's Dante's." The light is on. They've seen him move around inside. Dante is home.

Tom looks to the entrance. There's a buzzer. "How do we get in?" he says.

"Next to the buzzer there's a lockbox," Nina says. "There's a spare key inside in case anyone gets locked out and they've forgotten their own key. The etiquette is that once you're inside you're supposed to put the key back."

"You know the code?"

Nina nods. "So long as they haven't changed it in the last six months."

They make their way to the front of the building. Tom keeps watch while Nina punches the code into the lockbox.

"It's the same," she says, bringing out the key and using it to unlock the door. She holds the door open and then puts the key back into the box and closes it. Tom follows her in.

They make their way up to the third floor, then down the hall to Dante's apartment. The building is quiet. They don't see anyone else on the way. They knock on Dante's door and then step to either side, out of view of the spyhole. Tom lowers the bag of guns to the ground.

Tom puts his ear close to the door, listening. Footsteps approach. They're cautious. They pause a few feet from the door, waiting and listening to see if they heard right.

Tom slams the side of his fist against the door again, rattling it in its frame. He imagines the man on the other side giving a start at the sudden noise. The footsteps come closer. He'll be looking through the spyhole, wondering if it's kids playing a prank.

"Hello?" Dante's voice calls through.

Tom and Nina look at each other, bracing. Nina is on the side of the door closest to the handle.

Tom hears footsteps retreating back down the hall. He slams the side of his fist against the door again, summoning

Dante back. He looks around, makes sure no one else comes to investigate. The hallway remains clear. The other apartment doors remain closed.

Dante comes fast to the door, hoping to catch whoever it is in the act. He unlocks the door. As the handle goes down, Tom throws himself into the door, shoulder first, driving Dante back. He quickly grabs him and slams him against the wall, covering his mouth with a hand, then pulling out the Sig Sauer and making sure he can see it. “You need to stay real quiet for me, buddy,” Tom says.

Dante manages to nod, eyes wide.

Nina follows them into the apartment with the bag of guns, closing the door behind them. Dante sees her, his eyes cutting to his right. Nina holds up her empty hands to him. “Dante, we need your help,” she says.

His eyes narrow. They look between her and Tom.

“Whatever you think,” Nina says, “whatever you’ve heard or seen, you need to know that it’s not true. We didn’t plant that bomb. The footage is fake. You can help us to track down the people who really did, Dante. For all we know they could be up to something else. They could have more bombs planted. We need to stop them.”

Tom keeps Dante against the wall, mouth covered. He doesn’t point the gun at him, but he makes sure that Dante keeps it in sight.

“If you promise to be quiet Tom will let you go,” Nina says. “And we can all talk properly, okay? Do you promise?”

Dante looks at Tom again and then he nods. Tom looks at Nina.

“I mean, if he’s lying, you can always just hit him,” Nina says.

"That's a very good point," Tom says, looking at Dante. He takes his hand from his mouth and releases him.

Dante catches his breath. He continues to look between the two of them. There's a wariness about him. Tom doesn't like it, but so long as he doesn't try anything or shout for help there shouldn't be any problems.

"We need your help," Nina says. "I have some names to give you. I need you to look into them. Not surface-level stuff. You need to go *deep*. We need to know where they've been, what they've done, and who, if anyone, they've worked for."

"What are you – what are you talking about?" Dante says. They stay close to his front door. Tom sees how his eyes flicker toward it, trying to gauge if he can make a break for it.

Tom leans over and puts the lock on.

Dante avoids his eyes, like a child who knows he's been caught. "Let's go through to the living room," he says. "My computer..." He edges past Tom, making his way through. Tom puts the Sig Sauer away and looks around the rest of the apartment while Nina and Dante go to his setup in the corner of the living room. Tom checks out the windows, makes sure the streets below are clear. They were careful coming here, but they need to *always* be careful.

Dante clears his throat. "All right," he says. "Give me the names."

Nina reels them off. She stays close to Dante, watching him, monitoring him and what he does. Tom continues to pace the apartment, making sure there's nothing that could be observing them – cameras or microphones. Nina said Dante worked in surveillance. He doesn't see anything concerning. Dante didn't know they were coming. It wouldn't make sense for him to have anything set up, but

Tom has no way of knowing what Dante spends his time doing. Looking around the apartment, he sees computer parts lying on every available surface, and boxes of them stacked up around the floor.

Tom stays close to the windows. Checks outside intermittently. The streets remain clear.

"Tom," Nina says. "We've got stuff on them. You're going to want to see this."

Tom looks at them. They're both wide-eyed. Concerned at whatever it is they've seen.

"This is on the dark web," Nina says. "Only place we could find real stories about them. Coded messages about them, trying to hire them."

"What've they been doing?" Tom says.

"They've been running black ops missions ever since they left the military," Nina says. "Mostly across the United States, but also down in Central and Southern America, and there's stories about them going further afield – the Middle East. It's mostly rumour and conjecture. Snatches of evidence placing them at the scene of assassinations, and false flags."

"False flags," Tom repeats. "Today they bombed a federal building. They planned on placing the blame on us. That screams false flag to me. Like we suspected, they must have something else planned. The question is if it's here in San Francisco, or if it's somewhere else." Tom thinks. He sees the looks on Dante's and Nina's faces. Something has got them spooked. "What is it? Is there something else?"

"There's rumours about who they work for," Nina says. "They're available for hire, but only if they're not working for this person. Some people state who it is as outright fact."

"Who?"

"Senator Bob Hanley."

"I don't know who that is," Tom says.

"I've heard his name, but more to the point, he's a *senator*. What's a senator doing with a private black ops team at his beck and call?" She turns back to the computer and starts clicking through things. "Articles have been written about them – about the team and Senator Hanley – but they've been quashed. Injunctions have been levelled against the writers and their publishers. That's why there's more information here, on the dark web. They're trying to get the story out any way they can."

Dante sits back and holds up his hands. "Look, this is already too heavy for me. This is as deep as I wanna go. You need to use my setup, fine, go ahead, but I don't wanna see any more." He stands.

Tom blocks his way. "Where do you think you're going?"

"I'm not gonna hang around and watch this," Dante says. "I don't wanna see this, man. I don't wanna *know*. I don't even wanna be here right now. I don't want either of *you* here, either. This could get me in trouble, man. This is, like, collusion, conspiracy, whatever. It's probably a lot of bad things that could get me locked up, and I don't want that."

"Well, you're a part of it now."

"I didn't ask for it."

"And neither did we."

Dante looks like he has his doubts about that. Despite everything he's seen and read, he still doesn't trust that Tom and Nina are not responsible for what has happened today.

"You can use my computer, whatever," Dante says. "Just let me be someplace else. I'll stay in the apartment."

"You're not leaving this room."

"This is my home."

"And we've commandeered it. Temporarily."

"Dante, just calm down," Nina says. "Don't you see that this justifies what we've been saying – that we *aren't* the bombers?"

Dante doesn't look at it. He looks at Tom. "All right," he says. "I'll hang around here. But right now, I gotta go piss. Is that all right with you?"

Tom steps aside. He watches Dante as he goes. He doesn't trust him. He can see the bulge of his cell phone in his back pocket. Dante heads down the hall and steps into the bathroom.

Nina starts to say something, but Tom holds up a hand. He follows Dante down the hall and pauses outside the bathroom door, listening. He doesn't hear him using the toilet. Tom doesn't wait around to hear what he *does* do. He kicks the door open. Dante jumps, startled. His cell phone is in his hand. Tom takes it from him, cancels his call to 911, and drops the cell down the toilet.

Tom pulls out the Sig Sauer. He doesn't point it. He doesn't need to. "I think I'm going to have to rescind your bathroom privileges."

39

Dante is bound to a chair, away from the window. Masking tape has been wrapped around his ankles and forearms and chest, binding him tight. He sits and stares while Tom and Nina continue reading up on Orlando Higgs and his team, searching for a potential clue as to where they could be going next. They look into Senator Bob Hanley, too. Search if he could have a potential target for what has happened in San Francisco.

Nina sits back, running her hands down her face. "No known addresses for any of them, other than the senator. What are we going to do, go all the way to DC to talk to him?"

"He might not be in DC," Tom says. "It says he also has property in Nevada, where he represents."

"Nevada is a lot closer."

"But it's still a long way out of our way," Tom says. "We know at least Stuart Lynch and Harris Elkin are still here in the city. The fact they were able to track us at all suggests that Corey Crewe or Eddie Mitchell could still be here too, if not both of them. Is that just to hunt us, or do they have more business here? More bombs, perhaps. If we go to Nevada we're as good as running away. We're the only people in this city that know about them. If they have more planned, we're the only ones who can stop them. We need to be here."

Nina stares at the screen. On a separate laptop she searches more surface-level news reports about Senator Bob Hanley.

"When are you going to let me go?" Dante says.

Tom turns to him. "When you've proved you can behave yourself."

"You didn't tape my mouth and I haven't screamed," Dante says. "That counts for something, right?"

"Sure does."

"Then how much longer I gotta be tied up like this?"

Tom shrugs. "I'll know when I know. You should have really trusted us, Dante. You were reading all the same stuff Nina was. That wasn't enough for you?"

Dante doesn't respond.

"I'm curious as to your line of thinking there, Dante," Tom says.

"It just sounded to me like you were looking for someone you could blame," Dante says.

"Ah. Like how they did to us?"

"All I know is that the two of you are wanted for the bombing, and your faces are all over the news, and I saw the footage."

"I thought Nina said you worked in surveillance. You couldn't tell that was fake?"

Dante says nothing.

"This is interesting," Nina says without turning.

Tom spins back in the chair and looks over her shoulder. She's reading a recent article, a month old, about Hanley's clashes in Congress with Senator Jack Fielder. The two seem to be at constant loggerheads, though no reason why has been given. There's a clear animosity between them that goes beyond the senate floor.

"Senator Fielder represents California," Nina says. "Hanley's state neighbour."

"Okay," Tom says. "Interesting. Are there any rumours as to why they dislike each other?"

"Nothing that I can find. But get this – Jack Fielder has a vacation home here in San Francisco."

"That's very interesting indeed," Tom says, sitting forward.

"I should be able to find the address," Nina says, typing. "There's no way of knowing whether he's there or not – like, they're not going to announce his whereabouts, but it's probably worth us going there, right? It says here that he comes out here every weekend he can with his family. If we can talk to him, he might be willing to listen, given his adversarial history with Hanley. And if he's the next target – the *real* target..."

"If we knew what they were arguing about, that could give us a better idea," Tom says.

"All right, I've got the address," Nina says. "It's in the Sea Cliff neighbourhood."

"Is that far from here?"

"Not as far as it could be," Nina says. She looks beyond Tom, to Dante. "Because we're going to borrow your car. That okay with you?"

Dante holds out his bound hands. "I don't suppose I really have a say in the matter?"

"You might have, if you hadn't tried to dial us in," Nina says. She gets up and goes to the kitchen to find the keys. She walks with purpose and Tom assumes she knows where Dante keeps them.

"Let me come with you," Dante says to Tom. "I could – I could help."

Tom picks up the masking tape he used to bind Dante. "I doubt it." He tears off a strip of tape.

Dante's eyes manically look around the room. "Uh, I need to piss."

"I've heard that one before," Tom says. He slaps a piece of tape onto Dante's mouth, pressing it firmly into place. Dante's protests are muffled.

Nina returns with the car key. "Got it," she says. She looks at Dante. "When this is over, you're going to feel real foolish that you didn't trust us. You can apologise when we come back to free you."

She and Tom leave the apartment, and Dante wriggling in the chair behind them.

40

Dante's car is a Prius. Nina drives. Tom rides shotgun, watching the mirrors while they go. It's getting late, and the shadows are longer, but they keep the sun visors down to hide their faces. Their bag of stolen guns rests on the seat behind them.

"How long does it usually take to get to Sea Cliff?" Tom says.

"Depends on traffic," Nina says. "Everything in this city depends on traffic. But right now, at this time of day, with the *kind* of day it's been, we're probably looking at close to an hour."

Tom watches the mirrors. There are plenty of vehicles on the road, coming and going in both directions, but no one alarms him. No one appears to be following them. The further they get away from downtown, the less it seems like there has been a bombing. At the furthest outreaches of the city, it's a regular day. Business as usual. Of course, by now they are many hours removed from the explosion. Tom looks at the people on the sidewalk, and is sure they're all shaken up about it in their own way. He's sure they're all walking on eggshells, filled with dread that it could happen again, anytime, anywhere.

"Are we thinking that Jack Fielder could be the next target?" Nina says.

"It's an extreme reaction over whatever they've fallen out about," Tom says, "but people have killed for less."

"I know that for a fact."

"Looking at it objectively, the signs all point toward him. Senator Hanley has a private black ops team who run illicit missions for him, doing what they do for who knows what reasons. He has a long-running feud with Senator Fielder and all of a sudden Hanley's black ops turn up in Fielder's back yard, blowing up a federal building and positioning us as scapegoats."

"But why blow up the building?" Nina says. "What purpose does that serve?"

"I don't know," Tom says. "Maybe they have someone else they plan on pinning the blame on. When they deal with us, maybe they'll say we're part of a bigger organisation, and *that's* the group they're really looking to blame. Or, if they're going after Senator Fielder, it could be they're going to use the same modus operandi. They blew up a federal building and blamed me, claiming I'm an unsteady US Army vet with a grudge against the government. They needed proof of that – of my grudge. They blew up the warehouse, too. Obviously that was supposed to happen later, either to look like I was covering my tracks, or else I was careless and blew myself up. Whatever. It doesn't matter. They had to blow it early but it's fine. They can twist that. Just further add to how unhinged I'm supposed to be. A mad bomber, running wild in the city. But they've created a timeline, a story, of what I'm capable of.

If I blow up Fielder on the same day I've already set off two bombs, it's going to make sense, right? People will accept that information, say *of course this is how it ended*. It's all escalating to a point. But we got free, and that threw a wrench in the works."

"It's a lot to take in," Nina says.

"This is all supposition," Tom says. "But we read that Orlando and his team have run false-flag missions before. It adds up."

"What if Fielder *isn't* the target?"

"If he's not, then we'll likely never know who or what is, but that's only if we can reach him and persuade him that we're not responsible for the bombings. If we can talk Fielder around, he'll put the word out and that should spook them."

"And they'll leave the city?"

"Potentially. Unless they hold a grudge and continue to come after us. But that's fine, because I hold a grudge and I plan on tracking them down."

"I'll happily join you on that. See how *they* like being hunted."

"They won't know what's hit them."

Nina pauses a moment. "We're putting a lot of faith in Fielder."

"From what we read, I think that when he hears Hanley's name he's going to be inclined to hear us out. But also, he's kind of our only hope right now. If he won't listen, we're on our own again."

"And then what?"

"We don't give up," Tom says. He checks the mirrors again. There's no black Ford van. There's no one following them. "I'll think of something," he says.

41

Orlando and his team have left their backup HQ behind. They're out in the field, all of them. They're in the van. It's almost time to strike. They're entering the final phase of what today has been all about.

They're in the Sea Cliff neighbourhood. It's an affluent part of San Francisco. One of *the* most affluent. The van is parked down the road from Senator Jack Fielder's vacation home, and away from any of the neighbouring properties, too. They don't want anyone to call the cops on them, describing a van they haven't seen before and suggesting a drive-by to make sure nothing untoward is happening. They're parked next to a patch of grass with a couple of trees. They're not in front of anyone's house. No one should hassle them here, and they're already as close as they need to be.

On their previous reconnaissance, Corey and Eddie have planted cameras outside of Senator Fielder's property. They watch it now on the live feed through their laptops. The house is not in darkness. It's not empty, either, though

Fielder and his family are not present. It's his security. There's two of them inside the house. They can see one of them through the living room window, watching television. The other is a little more active. He looks out the windows. He moves from room to room.

There's more of them outside, too. A car parked on the opposite side of the street, two men inside. Another reason for Orlando's team to park down the road, out of view.

The team are familiar with Fielder's weekend routine. The family are out to dinner right now, probably an Italian place down in the Richmond neighbourhood. They eat early so they can get back by eight to put little Joel Fielder to bed. Joel is six. He's going to die tonight. The whole family is going to die. The security guards, too. There's going to be a lot of dead people in and around the Fielder vacation home.

Orlando doesn't think about it. He doesn't need to. There's nothing about that fact for him to dwell upon. Killing women, killing children, it doesn't make a difference to him. It's all the same. He's never had any issue with it. That's what makes him a good soldier. That's what makes him the leader. He's prepared to do what needs to be done, no matter whom it affects.

Besides, it's not like he's going to get the blame. No one in this van will. No one will know the truth. Tom Rollins and Nina Perry will get the blame.

When the team are done here, they'll be stuck in San Francisco until they can finally deal with the Rollins problem once and for all. He and Nina need to be silenced. It's unlikely that anyone will believe them, but they don't want to run that risk. Plus, something that started out as just business has become personal. They've pissed him off. If they'd just lain down and died, if they'd just stayed in the cage like they were supposed to, this day wouldn't have become anywhere near as long, or as complicated, as it's been.

"What time is it?" Harris says.

"Where's your wristwatch?" Orlando says.

"Battery died."

Orlando shoots him a look and then glances at his own watch. "It's seven."

Harris grunts. "Not long now."

Orlando nods. He turns back to the live feed playing on the laptops.

Not long at all.

42

Tom and Nina reach Senator Jack Fielder's vacation home, but they don't go straight to it. They need to be careful. They approach from the north and they stay distant, watching. They both spot the car parked outside, on the other side of the road, the two men inside watching the house and the road.

"Haven't seen either of those before," Nina says. "They're not on Orlando's team. Security?"

"Senators don't usually have bodyguards," Tom says.

"Not unless they're concerned about something."

Tom looks around. The houses here are Mediterranean style, light colours and tiled roofs, white marble railings. This part of the neighbourhood, the houses are large, bigger than elsewhere in Sea Cliff. They're spaced out, too, so that each property gets its own privacy. "We need to get closer," he says. "We'll go around the back."

The Fielder house is close to the cliffs, with a sea view. There's a green space between them and their neighbour. Tom and Nina head down the side, sticking close to the

Fielder family fence. They get around to the back. Tom peers over the fence. The rear of the house is in darkness. It's still light outside, mid-evening, but the inside of the house is dark enough it should need to be lit.

"Boost me over," Nina says. "I'll go take a closer look."

Tom laces his fingers and helps Nina over. He watches as she makes her way up to the house. Tom watches the windows. No one appears. Nina reaches the house. She stays low, sneaking window to window, peering inside. When she reaches the end she turns and waves for Tom to come and join her. He checks the upstairs windows while Nina keeps watch through the downstairs, then hauls himself over and runs to her.

"What do you see?" Tom says, pressing himself against the wall beside her.

"There's two men inside, but they're at the front of the house."

"Recognise them?"

"No. They're wearing trousers and shirts. No tactical gear. Probably with the two men in the car."

"Any sign of the Fielders?"

"No. But if these people are here, watching the house, then they must be near, right?"

"Let's hope so." Tom peers in through the window. He's looking into the kitchen, but the door is open and he can see through to the living room. Can see one man sitting in a chair and watching the television, and the other standing by the window, looking out. The television is playing the news. Tom can see his own face on the screen, side by side with Nina's. It's talking about the explosion. "Well," Tom says, lowering himself back down. "The security knows who we are."

"Do we wait out here until Fielder gets back?"

Tom looks around. "We shouldn't. When they get back, presumably they'll have more security with them. If they have them at their house, it stands to reason that they wouldn't head out without them. When they return, the security should do a perimeter sweep. They should look back here."

"Then where do we go? Where do we wait?"

Tom spots a window low to the ground, letting light into the basement. He goes to it, lying flat to look through. It's a large space, lavish light fixtures hanging from the ceiling. There's a pool table, and a bar in the corner. It looks like it's been converted into a lounge for entertaining, and has none of the standard use of a regular basement. Tom presses on the frame. It's not locked.

"Looks like they missed it," Nina says, crouching close by.

Tom slips the gun bag off his back and then climbs through first, landing and pausing, listening to make sure that no one has heard and is approaching. When no one does, he turns and reaches up for the bag of guns. After Nina passes it through and he's put it gently on the ground, he holds his hands up for her. She shuffles through and Tom places his hands on her hips to lower her.

Nina keeps her voice low when she speaks, whispering to him. "Now we find a comfortable corner, wait for them to get back, then spring our innocence upon them?"

"Pretty much," Tom says. He steps lightly around the basement, careful not to get too close to anything he could accidentally knock and cause to make a sound, alerting the men upstairs.

"How do we know when they get back?" Nina says.

"That's what I'm trying to figure out," Tom says. There's a

vent in the corner. He goes to it, stands under it. Faintly, he can hear the sound of the television. If the men are to talk, Tom should be able to hear them, too. He's about to step away, point it out to Nina, tell her they'll be able to hear their return through the vent, but then something catches his eye. He pauses, stares up into the darkness. He pulls the cell phone from his pocket and uses the glow of its home screen to shine up into the vent.

Tom freezes.

Semtex.

He steps away from under the vent and looks around the rest of the basement, shining light into its dark spaces.

"What do you see?" Nina says.

Tom doesn't answer straight away. He continues his search. He doesn't find any more Semtex in the basement. Not out in the open, at least. He spots another vent on the opposite side of the room. Standing under it, light shining up, he spots more within.

Tom turns to Nina. "The house is compromised," he says. "They're going to blow it. We were right – Fielder is the target. They weren't done yet."

They're close to the foot of the stairs. Nina pauses, tilting her head, listening. Through the vent, Tom can hear what she hears. The front door opening. The Fielder family returning.

"Shit," Nina says. "What do we do?"

"We need to warn them," Tom says. He can hear voices through the vent. He's not listening close enough to make out what is being said.

"How do we do that?" Nina says. "The second we pop out their security is likely to pop *us*."

Tom stares at the Semtex. If Orlando and his team are

nearby, if they've seen Fielder return, they could activate at any second. "We might not have any choice," he says. "Just... follow me. Keep your hands up. We need to clear this house." Tom starts making his way up the stairs. As he nears the top, he raises his hands to show they're empty. Nina grits her teeth and follows, doing the same.

Tom pauses at the door. He takes a deep breath. Close to the door, he can hear their voices. "Don't shoot," he calls through, and the voices fall silent. "We're unarmed, and we're coming out with our hands up."

Tom presses down on the door handle, but a voice halts him. "Stay where you are! Identify yourself!"

"I'm not sure you'd believe me if I told you," Tom says. Against orders, he opens the door. He does so slowly, and he makes sure they can see his empty, raised hands. As he steps out, he finds six Glocks pointing at him.

"Holy shit," one of the men says. "The bomber..."

"We need to talk about that," Tom says. He spots Senator Jack Fielder, along with his wife and son, behind the wall of men and Glocks. The boy stands close to his mother, holding tight to her hand, pressing close to her leg. Nina steps out beside Tom, hands up.

"Both of them..." one of the men mutters.

"Stay where you are!" says another man, and Tom recognises his voice as the person who told Tom not to open the door.

"I'd really like to comply, but you need to hear what I have to say," Tom says. "Senator Fielder, we need to talk to you. We have information you're going to want to hear."

"Don't talk to him," the head guard says. "You, Rollins, keep your mouth shut. Put your hands on your head, both of you, and get down on your knees."

Tom doesn't. "We don't have time for this," he says. "You need to listen to me. No, I'm not going to shut up. If you shoot me, then everyone in this house is going to die."

"Just let him talk," Jack Fielder says.

The guards fall silent. They keep the guns pointing at Tom and Nina, but they stop barking commands.

"The bombs that went off today, we had nothing to do with them. The men who did are coming for *you*, senator. We need to get out of here right now, all of us, and we can explain what's been happening. It's not safe for us here." If Tom mentions the Semtex straight away, he's not sure how they'll react. It's clear the guards already doubt what he's saying.

"We promise you, it's true," Nina says. "Why would we come here? Why would we expose ourselves like this? Just leave this house with us and we can all talk. What are we going to do? Where are we going to go? You have guns on us right now, it's not like we can try anything."

The head guard glances toward Fielder, checking to see what he wants to do.

It's all taking too long. The Semtex could be active. It could be counting down, the detonator soon to blow. Tom didn't see how much of it was planted in the vents, but judging by the destruction caused at the federal building, there's probably a lot.

Tom grits his teeth. He has no other choice than to tell them. "This house is going to blow," he says, and this gets everyone's attention. "There's Semtex in the basement."

The head guard shakes his head. "Bullshit," he says. "We perform daily sweeps. If there's Semtex down there it's because *you've* just planted it."

"It's hidden in the vents," Nina says. "Did you check in *there*?"

The head guard hesitates.

"Do you want to run the risk on hanging around here?" Tom says. "If the senator and his family are the target, now they're home and it could go off any second."

"We should probably leave," Fielder's wife says. Tom knows her name. He read it earlier. Lauren Fielder. The boy is Joel. He's six. He looks scared.

The head guard shakes his head. "All day we've heard that these two are terrorists," he says. "And now we're just going to take them at face value? We're not going anywhere, not yet." He motions to two of his men. "Go down into the basement and check. Look in the vents. We'll keep them covered up here."

The two men hurry down into the basement. Tom and Nina remain with four Glocks pointed at them, and the Fielder family watching them closely. Tom waits for the Semtex to be found. It shouldn't take long – they've been told where to look – and then they can leave. Get clear. Explain to the senator who is coming after him.

"You need to call this in," Nina says. "We don't know how much explosive is down there. The whole neighbourhood needs to be cleared."

The head guard says nothing.

From down in the basement, one of the men calls up. "I don't see anything," he says.

"He's gonna need a flashlight," Tom says. "We don't have time for this."

The head guard starts to shout down to them. "Use a flashlight," he says. "Use the flashlight on your cell phone."

Before he's finished, the man calls up again. "Wait a minute – there's a light –"

"*Run*," Tom says. He moves before anyone else can react, forgetting about the Glocks pointing his way. He scoops up Joel and grabs the arm of Lauren Fielder, carrying and dragging them out of the house. Nina reacts with him. She throws herself against Jack Fielder, forcing him out after them. They get outside and they keep running. Tom doesn't look back, but he hears Nina and Jack directly behind, and he hears the guards shouting and calling, getting loud, following.

Tom reaches the other side of the road with mother and son. He sees the two guards in the car sitting up, not understanding what's happening. Tom goes to the car. Nina follows, holding onto Jack. They duck down behind the car, throwing themselves flat.

Then, behind them, the house explodes.

43

Orlando leans forward. He's not watching on the laptops. He's looking straight through the windshield. He can see the vacation home. He wanted to see it explode in real time. He sees it happen, but he also sees Rollins and Nina, fleeing with the Fielder family.

The house explodes. They're sheltering behind the car carrying two of the security team. The explosion demolishes the house. It becomes a fireball. Wood, slate, and brickwork scatters through the air up and down the neighbourhood. Some of it falls short of the van.

Orlando leans closer to the glass, hands on the back of the van's front seats, squeezing hard. He waits for the smoke to clear. The family got clear. Rollins and Nina got clear. The Semtex was enough to kill the people *inside* the house, but they weren't inside the fucking house. The flames could have cooked them, though. Falling debris could have crushed them. He needs to see. He needs to *know*.

Stuart comes up next to him. "Is it clear?"

"Not yet," Orlando says.

“The cameras were taken out in the explosion,” Corey calls. “We can’t see shit.”

Orlando’s nostrils flare while he stares, while he waits. It’s so close to being over, but he can’t be sure. He can’t see a damn thing.

Finally, the dust begins to settle and the smoke begins to clear. When it does, he sees some of the security guards stumbling, dazed. Two of them lie dead on the ground, flat on their fronts and unmoving. They weren’t able to get clear enough in time. At the car, the driver’s side window has been smashed, debris has flown through. Orlando can see the driver slumped, blood leaking from the broken window. On the passenger side, the other guard has gotten out, covered in the blood of his partner. That makes three of the security guards still alive, but barely.

And then Orlando spots Rollins, Nina, and the Fielder family, rising from where they covered down the side of the car.

“Are you fucking *kidding* me?” Orlando tears himself away from the windshield. “Tool up. We’re moving out. This ends right fucking *now*. I’m tired of this shit.”

Orlando grabs his M4 and slides open the side door of the van. The rest of his team scramble to follow. Orlando runs toward the explosion zone. Rollins sees him coming up the hill. He alerts Nina and the Fielder family. They bundle Jack, Lauren, and Joel into the back of the car they’ve sheltered behind. Nina gets in the front passenger seat. Rollins drags the corpse from the driver’s seat, and they drive. Orlando opens fire on them. The rear window shatters.

The surviving guards spin at the sound, but they’re dazed and slow. Two of them raise handguns. One of them looks around, searching for his own weapon, having lost it while he fled from the explosion. Orlando notices the back of his head is burnt, his hair scorched away and the exposed flesh there red, raw, and bloody. His shirt has torn up the back, the ripped edges of it blackened. He's unsteady on his feet, swaying, his movements sluggish as he looks for the dropped gun.

Orlando kills him last. He poses the least threat. He mows down the other two guards first with his M4. Neither of them even manages to loose a shot. He turns on the burn victim next. He still hasn't found his gun. He looks back at Orlando with dazed, unfocused eyes. Orlando sees resignation on his face in the split second before he fires a tight burst of bullets into his chest.

The car with Rollins and the rest is gone. Orlando turns and runs back to the van. Corey and Eddie turn at his approach, heading back to it. They never caught up. Harris is already at the van, hanging out of the side door. Stuart is behind the steering wheel. He fires up the engine. Orlando jumps into the front beside him.

Orlando doesn't need to say a word. He doesn't need to. Stuart drives, giving chase to the car.

44

Tom speeds away from Sea Cliff, knowing that Orlando and his men will soon be in pursuit.

Tom drives fast. He glances at the mirrors but his main focus needs to be on what's ahead of them. The inside of the windshield is smeared where Tom has wiped away the dead driver's blood. The blood is all over the front of the car. Tom is sitting in it.

He mounts the sidewalk when they reach a red light, blaring the horn in warning as he drives down it and then swings back out onto the road, turning left, an oncoming car having to swerve to avoid collision.

The Fielder family duck down in the back, covered in the broken glass from the shattered rear screen. As soon as they got in the car, Nina had told them to stay low. She'd spotted Orlando coming for them too, M4 primed and ready, and a furious expression upon his face.

"Are they following?" Jack says, raising his head just a little.

"Not right now," Nina says. She's watching the mirrors. "But they'll be coming."

"Who are they?" Jack says.

"They work for Senator Bob Hanley," Nina says.

Tom glances at the mirror to see Jack Fielder's expression. At first, it's shocked, and then it's angry. Finally, it's focussed. "That son of a bitch," he says.

"Whatever his problem is, it looks like he's sent this team to target you," Nina says. "And he's using us to take the blame."

"I think I can guess what this is about," Jack says. He starts fumbling in his pocket. "There's no time to explain right now. If you keep my family alive, if you get them to safety, I'll make sure people know the truth of today. I'll make sure everyone knows you're not responsible." He pulls out a cell phone. "I need to make a call."

Tom wonders whom he's calling, but there's no time to ask. He keeps driving, making tight turns, hoping to put as much distance between themselves and Orlando and his team as possible. They'll be coming, in that black Ford van of theirs. There's no time to avoid security cameras right now, though he has no doubt that Corey Crewe and Eddie Mitchell will be trying to track them this way. All they have on their side now is time and speed.

Tom doesn't listen to what Jack says on the phone, but he's not talking for long. "I've just spoken to my security detail," he says. "I've appraised them on the situation. They say they can meet us in Marin County."

"They armed?" Nina says.

"They can handle these bastards," Jack says.

Marin County is on the other side of the Golden Gate

Bridge. The bridge isn't far from here. It could be busy. Tom doesn't like it, but there's no other choice. It's the fastest route from where they are. It's the only route.

45

Senator Bob Hanley keeps calling. Over and over again. He must have heard the news.

Orlando ignores his calls. He turns into the back of the van, holding onto the overhead railing to keep from being thrown around while Stuart slams the accelerator pedal flat, pursuing Rollins and Nina and the escaping Fielder family.

"Have you got them?" Orlando says.

"I need eyes!" Stuart says.

"Got them!" Eddie says, not looking up. "Next left, then second right!"

The van screeches and almost tilts as Stuart takes the left.

"They're taking a lot of turns," Corey says while Eddie continues to bark directions. "Obviously trying to lose us."

Harris stands in the back of the van, one hand holding onto a railing, the other stroking one of the grenades on the front of his vest. His eyes are narrowed, looking at nothing in particular. He's thinking. Probably about the explosion.

"A little more Semtex and we might have got them," Orlando says.

Harris raises his eyes. He voices the question they've all been wondering. "How did they know to come here?"

Orlando works his jaw. "I don't know," he says. It's a frustration he can't give in to right now. "But however they figured it out, they did, and now we need to deal with it."

"Uh-huh. And how did they get into the house?" Harris says. "We didn't spot them. The guards didn't spot them. If they hadn't got in the house, they'd all be dead. Mission accomplished."

"Yeah, well, that's not what happened," Orlando says. At this point, he's getting sick of having to adapt. This mission was never supposed to be this difficult. "Which direction are they going?" Orlando says, turning back to Corey.

"Hard to tell right now, all the zig-zagging they're doing," Corey says. "But it looks like they're heading north."

Orlando pulls out his phone. He calls Simon Arditti.

"Hello?" Simon says. "Who is this?"

"Listen to me, and don't say a word," Orlando says. "This is Higgs. You've probably heard about the latest explosion. Their target was Senator Jack Fielder and his family in their Sea Cliff vacation home. The bomb went off early, as the Fielders were arriving home. Rollins and Perry have kidnapped them."

"Jesus," Simon says.

"No interruptions," Orlando says. "They have the family and they're currently heading north. Get your people and head that way right now. If we get a better bead on them I'll send directions. Shoot to kill. No prisoners." Orlando hangs up.

"How do we make this work?" Stuart says, teeth gritted as

he squeezes the steering wheel tightly. "Things have blown wide open here."

"We can still twist this to fit our narrative," Orlando says. "We can still eliminate Fielder and place the blame on Rollins."

"What if the cops you've called get to them first?"

"If they manage to kill Rollins and Nina, then we kill the fucking cops," Orlando says. "Place the blame on Rollins and Nina again."

Eddie shouts directions.

Hanley is still calling. Orlando continues to ignore him. He can imagine he's sweating bullets right now.

Orlando isn't sweating yet, but it won't be long. He's never been on an operation that has turned into such a messy shitshow. He blames Rollins. They should never have used him.

"We can fix this," Orlando says, as much to himself as anyone else. "We just need to catch them. Catch and kill."

"Okay, there's only one place they could be heading right now," Corey says.

Orlando turns to him. "Where?"

"The Golden Gate Bridge. They're trying to leave the city."

"What's the traffic like there?"

Corey checks. "Heavy," he says. "It's busy. It's gonna slow them down."

Orlando grins. He shoots a pleased look at Stuart. Harris steps forward, still stroking his grenade, seeing an opportunity to finish what his explosions could not.

"That's where we'll get them," Orlando says. "Stop driving like a pussy and put your goddamn foot down."

Stuart does not respond to this.

Orlando pulls out his cell. He kills another incoming call from Hanley, then messages Simon Arditti to tell him where they're going. Then, he places another call. "We're going to need a chopper," he says. "ASAP. Extraction from the Golden Gate Bridge. Yes, I know it's not ideal. I don't give a shit. Scramble *right fucking now* and get your asses over there." He hangs up. Hanley calls again. This time, Orlando answers. "I'm fucking busy," he says. "Stop calling. You'll hear from *me*." He puts the phone away and slaps Stuart's thigh. "Let's get these assholes."

46

Tom can see the Golden Gate Bridge. There's no toll heading north, out of the city. Heading into the city, it's busy. It's backed up. This is something in their favour, but it's the only thing. Further ahead, Tom can see the traffic. It's *moving,* but it's moving slowly.

Tom weaves across the three lanes, under- and over-taking the slower vehicles. Ahead, he sees more and more, filling the road. He grits his teeth and pushes on. People blare their horns but he ignores them. He passes under the first arch, unable to get above forty.

Nina tries to look ahead, to see what's causing them to go so slow. "There must have been an accident," she says. "At least we're not gridlocked."

"Not yet," Tom says. "Closer we get to the end, we might be."

Nina checks the mirrors. She carries the bag of guns on her lap. She holds onto it tight.

"We've probably lost them by now, right?" Jack says,

sitting up a little more, keeping his arms over his wife and child.

"Hard to say," Tom says. "They have a couple of tech experts with them. They could have been tracking us, hacking into security cameras and following us that way." Tom points out a couple of cameras on the bridge as they pass by them. "They could know exactly where we are right now."

Jack's face pales.

Tom squeezes through a tight gap between two cars. The vehicle in the middle lane slams its horn and accelerates as if it's going to tailgate, but when it sees the shattered rear window, as well as the cracked windshield and the smashed driver's window with dripping blood, it backs off.

As they pass under the second arch, Nina curses quietly. "Shit," she says. "A very familiar looking van is gaining on us."

Tom looks in the mirror. It's the black Ford. Tom is sick of seeing it now.

"Senator, get down," he says. "And brace yourselves."

The van is coming up fast. Tom is stuck behind three cars spread across the three lanes. The van bears down. It hits them from behind. The car lurches forward, hitting the back of the vehicle in front. The van hits them again. The car in front speeds up, finally gets out of the way. Tom speeds through the gap, but the van stays on them.

Nina pulls out her Sig Sauer. "I'm gonna take a shot," she says.

"They're close enough," Tom says. "This is your best chance."

Nina leans out of her open window and fires back toward

the van. Tom hears Jack's wife cry out. His boy is crying. The family stay as low as they can.

Tom looks at the mirror. The van backs off. An arm appears through its passenger window and starts shooting. Tom reaches over and pulls Nina back inside. Bullets ping off the roof. One smashes the side mirror. A moment later, the van's side door slides open. Harris clips himself onto a railing above and leans out, M4 held.

Tom starts weaving in anticipation. Harris opens fire. Tom sees how the cars near the van hit their brakes, pulling back. The vehicles ahead and between Harris and his target aren't so lucky. His bullets eat through them. Cars swerve and crash into each other and into the barrier between the north and south lanes. One of them flips over. It causes chaos on the already slow-moving southbound side.

A bullet flies through the car from the rear window, cracking the windshield worse than it already is. As it does, Tom sees what has been holding them up on the bridge. A long-haul truck has broken down at the side of the road. The cars are passing through the remaining two lanes. Tom gets through. There's a brief pause as Harris gets back inside the van as they pass by the truck. He's probably reloading, too. It doesn't take long before he's firing upon them again.

Tom keeps the car moving. Keeps it zigzagging, cutting across lanes. Harris's bullets tear into the road. They fire wildly. They take out vehicles heading both north and south. The bridge is in a panic. One car ahead of Tom swerves and crashes into two others. Two of them flip, blocking off the road. Traffic grinds to a halt. The van pulls back, avoiding the crash.

"Get out the guns," Tom says. He hits the brake pedal

and pulls on the handbrake, skidding the car to a halt before it can become part of the wreck.

Nina is already unzipping the bag. Tom turns to the Fielders while she pulls out the two AR15s.

"All of you, look at me," he says. The family look at him, eyes wide, Jack's arms around them. "We need to run. Nina and I will lay down covering fire. Stay between us. Nina will lead the way first and I'll bring up the rear. When she stops, unless she says otherwise, you get ahead of her and then you drop down to a knee and you *stop*. You wait for me, and then you follow me. We keep doing that. You understand?"

Jack and Lauren are nodding. "I'll carry Joel," Jack says.

Tom takes the AR15 from Nina and two extra magazines. He tucks them down the back of his waistband next to the Sig Sauer. "Let's go." Tom gets out of the car, rifle raised. The van spots him. He sees Stuart and Orlando in the front scrambling to get into the back. Tom opens fire, straight through the windshield. He maintains a steady stream until Nina and the Fielders are out of the car and running. Tom watches the van. He doesn't see movement. He takes a tentative step forward, to investigate, but the side door of the van remains open and Orlando steps out, opening fire. Harris promptly joins him.

Tom fires back, sending them scattering, then turns and follows Nina and the Fielders. She stops. The family drops to a knee. Nina lays down covering fire for Tom. Ducking, he gets past. Jack is watching, ready. He gets up and follows Tom.

The bridge is anarchy. People flee from their vehicles. Some of them are caught by Orlando's team's bullets, gunned down by strays while they try to run away. Tom heads for the pile-up of crashed cars. It's cover. More objects to put between themselves and the gunfire, and more places to duck and hide. He stops and turns. The Fielders get past him and take a knee. Nina runs past and takes point while Tom fires.

He sees that Orlando and his team move in a similar fashion. Orlando and Stuart open fire while Harris and Corey run ahead, loosing the occasional shot while they head for cover. Once they're secured, then lay down fire while Orlando and Stuart follow. There are only four of them, now. Tom wonders if his bullets caught one of them in the van. He sees Orlando, Stuart, Harris, and Corey. No sign of Eddie. Tom quickly scans the bridge to make sure Eddie is not attempting a flanking manoeuvre. Tom can't see him anywhere.

In all of the confusion, it's hard for either side to get a clear shot on the other. Tom is more careful with his shooting, not wanting to hit bystanders. Orlando and his men don't have the same compunction. They don't care whom they hit in their pursuit.

Then, Harris throws a grenade.

"Run, *run*!" Tom says as the grenade sails past him.

They break formation and manage to get behind a Toyota as the grenade explodes behind them. Tom feels debris from it fly by close to him, chunks of the road torn up in the blast, and whatever else might be nearby. He feels something cut the top of his left arm and graze his upper back. He keeps running, feeling blood running from the two points. He gets behind the car with Nina and the others.

"There's a truck there," she says, pointing. Tom sees it. "It'll have a thicker body. They open up on this and they're gonna cut us down."

Tom nods. He changes magazine on the AR15 and then

says, "Go," while he stands and opens fire. Orlando and his team are getting close. Most of them take cover behind a nearby van. Corey dives over the partition between lanes and lies flat. Tom's bullets ping off the metalwork. He continues to fire as he runs backward, joining the others at the truck.

He sees a cop car approaching. It's driving fast, coming up the wrong side of the bridge in the southbound lanes. Tom thinks the lanes heading northbound must be backed all the way up if the cruiser has had to use the other side of the bridge. Its siren is not blaring, and its lights are not flashing.

"We've got company," Tom says, ducking behind the truck.

"Who?" Nina says.

"Cops. No sirens. Only one car."

She looks at him. "Simon?"

"Could be. They're not out yet."

"More cops will be coming."

"Does that really help us?" Tom says.

"That's good, right?" Jack says. He's been listening in. "If the cops come, they can help us."

"Not these ones," Tom says. "If they're who we think they are. The fact they've turned up without their sirens going, that concerns me."

"Besides," Nina says, "we're not exactly the city's favourite people right now. They see us, they're gonna open fire. Doesn't matter whether we're with you or not."

Tom looks around. He's noticed a momentary pause in the shooting. He can see beyond the worst of the crash zone. It's clear. It's still a long way to the end of the bridge. Even then, they still need to get deep into Marin County to meet up with Jack's people. It's still a long way to safety, and a long way with nothing to hide behind. He can see people running, fleeing the gunfight.

He checks the abandoned cars nearby that haven't been caught up in the crash. Engines are still running. That means the keys are still inside. Only problem is, they're too far away to reach without being gunned down.

Nina lies flat and looks under the truck. "It's Simon and his people," she says.

"What are they doing?" Jack says.

She doesn't answer Jack. She looks at Tom. Her face is grim. "They're talking with Orlando and his team. It looks like they might be familiar with each other." She gets up off the ground. "We either need to kill them or find a way off this goddamn bridge."

Tom is still looking around. The closest vehicle to the right has nothing between it and them. It's a killing zone. It would also be a tight squeeze to get through the crash zone. Off to the left, in the southbound lane, there's a minivan idling. The way behind it is clear. The way to it, save for the barrier, is covered. It's further away, and it'll be a long run, but it's their better chance.

"We're gonna have to run," Tom says. "This time, we stick together."

47

Orlando had a close call in the van, when Rollins first opened up on them through the windshield. Stuart got through into the back before him. Orlando followed close behind. He heard the rifle open up. Eddie was standing. He was close, ready to move out. Too eager. Orlando grabbed him and twisted, using him as a shield. He felt Eddie's body vibrate as the bullets thudded into him. Orlando fell back, Eddie on top. The rest of the team were already lying flat in preparation. They didn't see what Orlando did. Didn't see him sacrifice Eddie for his own life.

His team can use Eddie's death as motivation. Orlando, for his part, feels nothing. He knew Eddie, Eddie answered to him, and now Eddie is dead. The circle of life. He's lost two men today, both because of Rollins, and he feels more for Rollins himself than he does for either of them. He craves vengeance, though not necessarily for his men, the same way the others will. No, he wants it for what Rollins and Nina have caused. The issues they have created, and the headache they have given him.

They're pinned down, now, with the Fielders. They're not going anywhere, not unless they want to risk sudden perforations from Orlando and his men's M4s. Plus, Simon and his people have arrived.

Orlando points toward the truck, talking to Simon. "They're currently concealing themselves behind that vehicle," he says. "With you here, we have the numbers to keep them pinned and simultaneously flank them. We have them now. There's no escape."

Simon looks around, taking in the rest of the team, as well as the death and destruction on the bridge. He wipes sweat from his brow. He's in over his head, and he knows it. "What about –" He has to clear his throat to continue. "What about the senator and his family?"

Orlando feels Stuart's eyes upon him, waiting to see how he responds. Harris and Corey are nearby, M4's pointing toward the truck, ready to open fire should any of their targets present themselves.

"Rollins and Perry still have them," Orlando says. "At this point, we have no way of knowing if they're still alive or not. If I'm honest, it doesn't look good right now. In their desperation, trapped like this, they may have already killed the family."

Simon swallows. He looks back at his people. The woman, Christie Llewellyn, looks sick. "Bastards," she mutters.

"If you and your people keep them pinned, my team can flank them, deal with them once and for all, put this whole nightmare to rest. The Fielder family have the best chance if *we're* the ones getting the drop on them all. If they're still alive, that is."

Simon looks up, away from the bridge, into the sky. Orlando knows what he's looking at. He can hear it, too. The chopper he called in is approaching.

He also hears sirens. They're coming from the south, from San Francisco, but they're still a way off. There's time enough for them to finish here.

"Is that a helicopter?" Simon says.

"The media?" Christie says.

"Don't worry about it," Orlando says. "It's ours, but forget about it. We can't wait for it to get here. We need to act now. Do you understand?"

Simon tears his eyes away. He manages an uncertain nod. "More cops are coming," he says. "I can hear them. Shouldn't we wait for them to get here?" Simon is concerned. He didn't expect things to get this far. He didn't expect to reach a crash site on the Golden Gate Bridge and see so many dead bodies strewn upon the road. He thought they'd corner Rollins and Nina somewhere quiet, do them there. He never expected it to get to this level. He never thought he'd have to 'rescue' a senator and his family.

Orlando slaps him. Simon blinks. The cops behind him seize up, shocked. Christie glares. Orlando thinks he can hear her growl. "We don't have time for you to shit your pants," Orlando says. "We need to do this *now*. The Fielder family can't afford for us to wait."

Before Orlando can further impress the importance of immediate action, before Simon has a chance to respond, Corey calls out. "They're moving!" He opens fire and Harris soon joins him. Stuart moves up beside them. Simon and the other cops pull out their handguns.

Orlando watches. He sees Rollins and Nina returning fire

as they run between vehicles, firing back when they're able. They keep the Fielder family between them, covering them.

Orlando clenches his jaw. He looks at Simon and the cops. They've seen the same thing he has. Simon is holding out a hand to the others to keep them from shooting, his eyes narrowed, his gun lowered. He turns to Orlando. "What are your people doing?" he says. "The family are alive. Nina is *keeping* them alive! She's covering them. They both are. What's happening here?"

Orlando doesn't have time for this. He guns down Simon. The cop drops to the ground in a burst of blood.

Christie reacts first. She fires back. Two rounds hit Orlando in the vest, close together, near his heart. Orlando stumbles back but doesn't go down. Stuart has spun at the nearby shooting. He turns his rifle on the cops, blasting them. "You good?" he says to Orlando.

Orlando spits out the corner of his mouth. The cops were a waste of time. They've *cost* them time, and gained them nothing in return. The helicopter is getting closer. Corey and Harris have ceased shooting. They're looking back to see what he says.

"Cops are coming," Orlando says. "We need to end this before they get here."

48

At a pause in the shooting, Tom hears the helicopter approaching. He glances toward it, a quick look. He can't afford to take his eyes away from what he's doing for too long. It's an Mi-17, dark green in colour. There's no way to tell whom it's here for, but Tom doesn't plan on waiting around to find out.

He saw Orlando and his people gun down the cops. Saw how Orlando stumbled back, shot in the vest. Nina saw it, too. She looked at Tom, wide-eyed. They didn't understand what was happening, but there was nothing they could do for them. They needed use the distraction to their advantage.

They get to the minivan in the southbound lane and jump inside. Tom gets behind the wheel. Like before, Nina is beside him and the Fielder family are in the back. Before they can close the doors, he's turning the vehicle around. He floors the pedal, speeding down the bridge in the wrong lane. There's nothing coming. People at the end have pulled up and prevented anyone else from getting on.

Tom starts blaring the horn. He doesn't slow as he approaches. People scatter for their cars, desperate to get them out of the way before the speeding madman can reach them.

"There's a pretty solid barrier all the way down, separating these roads," Nina says, bracing herself against the door and the dash. "How are we going to navigate that?"

"We'd better hope people get out of the way," Tom says.

"There's gaps between the barrier when we're off the bridge," Jack says, leaning forward. "That's probably not *as* solid, right?"

"I've seen people go through them," Nina says. "The cars would get pretty messed up, though."

"Well, this isn't our car," Tom says. "Apologies to the owner, but if it has to get damaged, then so be it."

"Could we separate them?" Jack says. "The barriers, I mean. Could we pull a pin or something?"

Nina nods. "Yeah, yeah, we can do that. Get ourselves into the proper lane. It's clear on that side."

The gathering at the end of the bridge has parted, people having pulled aside, thinking that they're escaping from the crash and whatever else is happening on the bridge – which they are. They probably just don't realise that the passengers of this vehicle were an integral part of the gunfight.

Tom wants to look in the mirror, to see what the helicopter is doing, but he can't. He needs to focus on the road, and only the road.

Tom pulls the minivan to the right, close to the barrier. Nina jumps out and Jack follows her. They pull connecting pins from the barriers and push them aside, wide enough for the minivan to pull through. Tom does, and then they push the barrier back into place to keep anyone from following with ease. When they're back inside, Tom starts driving again. The road ahead of them is clear. On the other side, the southbound lanes are gridlocked as far as they can see.

"Do you have directions?" Tom says to Jack.

"Keep going straight for now," Jack says, wiping sweat from his mouth. There's dirt on his hands from working at the pins, and it leaves a smudge on his lips and his cheek. "I'll tell you when there's a turn."

49

Orlando sees Rollins and the others escape. His men all look to him. The cops are drawing closer.

"What do we do?" Stuart says.

"They're heading for Marin County," Corey says. "And they're going fast. If I don't get to my laptop right now we're gonna lose them."

"We could follow them in the chopper," Stuart says.

"Depends on where they go," Corey says. "And hasn't *this* already caused enough mess?" He gestures to the bridge. "We're already gonna struggle to explain this away. We ride a chopper around Marin County and try to mow down a minivan carrying a senator and his family, how do we spin that? It's getting late but it might as well be broad daylight. We're not operating in the shadows here anymore."

Orlando doesn't answer. Tony, the helicopter pilot, contacts him on his radio. Orlando doesn't respond immediately. The sirens are getting closer. "I think it's too late to explain anything away at this point," he says. He motions to Stuart and Corey. "Go keep the cops at bay."

They don't question him. They follow commands. They do as he says. As they open fire on the approaching cruisers, causing them to swerve and hit their brakes, Orlando pulls out the radio. "Pick us up," he says.

"From where?" the pilot says. "It's wild down there. We can't land on the bridge."

"Then throw us down a rope," Orlando says. He puts the radio away. Harris is looking back at him, thumbs through his vest. "Get the computers out of the van," Orlando says. "And then blow it."

Harris grins, then nods. As he runs off to the van, Orlando speaks to Stuart and Corey through their earpieces. The chopper is hovering above them, unrolling a rope ladder down to them. "Harris is blowing the van. We're out of here."

Orlando starts climbing the ladder, swaying with the motion of the hovering chopper. It gets louder as he ascends, deafening. He looks back, continuing to climb. Stuart and Corey continue to lay down suppressing fire. The front three cruisers are decimated. Orlando spots a couple of dead uniforms, lying bloodied on the road. The rest of them are sheltering behind their vehicles, taking poorly aimed potshots.

Harris is out of the van. He has the two laptops. He throws a couple of grenades inside and then runs for the ladder. The van blows. Throwing the grenades into the van wasn't an effort to destroy the van entirely. It'll destroy a lot of evidence present, though, and mangle Eddie's body. It'll give forensics something to keep them busy while Orlando and the rest of the survivors extricate themselves from this shitshow situation.

As Harris climbs, Stuart and Corey start making their way to the ladder. Orlando reaches the top and climbs inside. The co-pilot hands him a headset.

"Where we going?" Chet, the co-pilot, says once Orlando has it on.

"Anywhere but here," he says. He takes a seat and straps himself in, opening and closing his fists. He grits his teeth until his jaw aches. He switches channels on the headset and calls Hanley.

Hanley sounds exasperated when he answers. "What's going on out there?" he says. "Where are you? What's that noise?"

"We're getting out," Orlando says.

"Are you in a helicopter?"

"This whole thing has gone south. Rollins was the wrong man to use. Nina Perry wasn't any slouch, either. I hold up my hands and admit we made a mistake."

Harris gets aboard the chopper. He straps himself in, looking at Orlando, seeing that he's talking.

Hanley is breathing hard. "Where does this leave me?" he says finally. "Jack is still alive. *Everyone* that matters is still fucking breathing. We were promised a lot of money to deal with this problem." Orlando can imagine him pacing, sweating, running his hands back through his hair and tugging at his collar. "This can be traced back to us. It can be traced back to *me*. Do you understand how serious this is? We should have pulled the damn plug the second Rollins and the woman got away."

"We did all we could, but when a mission is a failure, it's a failure," Orlando says.

"Damn it, Orlando, what do we *do*?"

Orlando runs his tongue around the inside of his mouth. There's a bitter, burning taste in his throat. Stuart is next onto the chopper, and Corey is soon behind him. Corey brings up the rope as the chopper veers to the right, leaving the bridge.

"I'll tell you what I'm going to do," Orlando says, thinking of the payday they're not going to see. "When this all dies down, I'm going to kill Rollins. This is personal for me, now. I'm going to track him down, and then I'm going to follow him. I'm going to always be with him. And then, when he least suspects it, I'm going to tear his fucking spine out."

"That's all well and good, but I doubt I'll ever receive the satisfaction of hearing about it while I'm rotting in a prison cell."

"Mm," Orlando says. "If Rollins and Nina were able to figure out who the target was, they're probably going to figure out *why*, especially if they're with Fielder. And if that's the case, they're going to work it out sooner than you're expecting. If you've got any sense, you should start moving. Kiss your old life goodbye. You need to disappear."

Even over the noise of the chopper, Orlando can hear Hanley grinding his teeth. "Come and get me," he says.

"Come get you?" Orlando repeats.

"That's what I said, isn't it? Come and get me."

"You're still in Nevada?"

"I'm at home. You're in a chopper, right? What's that, a couple of hours? Damn it, I pay you. You work for *me*. Come and get me."

Orlando switches channel, talks to the pilot. "We need to go to Nevada," he says. "You got the fuel for that?"

"Nevada?" the pilot says. "Yeah, we've got the fuel for it.

We'll have to refuel when we get there, but I know a place. You got an address?"

Orlando relays it to him, then gets back on to Hanley. "We're on our way. You've got two hours. Pack your shit and be ready for us."

50

LC Security are based out of Los Angeles, but they have a safehouse in Marin County. Jack directs Tom to it. It's on the side of a hill, the nearest neighbour two miles away.

Tom has made sure that Orlando and his team have not been following them. His eyes have checked on the mirrors regularly, and Nina has been watching, too. They've made sure to check the sky, but the only helicopters they've seen have been flying toward the bridge. News choppers, presumably. No one has followed them through Marin County.

"Do you want to tell us why you think they were coming after you?" Nina says, looking back at the senator.

"When we get to the safehouse," Jack says. "I just need to know that my family are safe first. Then I'll tell you everything I know. Lee has said he's coming down personally. Eight of his men were killed back at Sea Cliff. He won't take that lightly."

"Lee?" Nina says.

"Lee Cobb," Jack says. "He's head of LC Security. He's an

ex-Navy Seal. Most of his people are either ex-military or ex-cops."

"I didn't think senators had security details," Nina says.

Jack looks at his family. "Ordinarily not..." he says. "Look, can we talk at the safehouse?" He doesn't want to say too much in front of his wife and child. Doesn't want to scare them. Nina understands. She doesn't push.

Tom continues to drive. Jack surprises him by addressing him. "I have to say something about you, Rollins."

Tom glances up at the mirror. "What's that?"

"I'm familiar with you already. I don't just mean from the news today. I mean I'd already heard about you. Senator Seth Goldberg is a friend of mine."

"Senator Goldberg," Nina says, thinking out loud. "Texas, right? Very progressive. Works a lot on green reform bills, renewable energy, that kind of thing."

"That's him. Rollins saved his life in Dallas," Jack says.

Nina's eyes widen. "The attempted bombing," she says. "I remember that. It could have been worse than today if it had actually gone ahead."

"Rollins here stopped it," Jack says.

"Wait a minute, wait a minute," Nina says. "That was you? How come you never said?"

"It never came up," Tom says.

"Saved Seth's life, and his family," Jack says. "Not to mention everyone else who was there that day. Seth speaks very highly of you, Rollins. After you've done the same for me, I can see why. When I heard your name on the news in association with the bombing, I wasn't sure I was hearing right after everything Seth has told me. But sure enough, the more reports I saw, the more it became clear that you were the same guy that he talks about. I haven't had a chance to speak to him yet today. He's likely had a lot on his mind, as have I."

"Then that means we have another friend who can back us up, right?" Nina says. "Help explain that today had nothing to do with us."

"I'm sure Seth will be more than happy to help. The news from today has probably shaken him more than anyone else. He'll be relieved to hear the truth."

It's dark when they reach the safehouse. Tom approaches slowly. A security light is on outside, and there are three cars parked close to the house. It's a big house, and it's secluded. There are cameras on the outside, covering all approaches. Bushes line the property, obscuring the downstairs windows.

There are also men clad in black hiding in the greenery that lines the dirt road leading to the home. Tom stops the car.

"What's wrong?" Jack says.

"There's people in the bushes," Tom says.

"Lee's men, surely?"

"Do we want to take that risk?" Tom says.

Nina leans an AR15 toward him. Without making any sudden movements, Tom reaches over and grips the handle, keeping his trigger finger outside of the guard.

The front door of the house opens and a man steps out. He's tall, and broad across. Blond hair in a crewcut. He wears dark slacks and a light-blue shirt tucked in. His build is tight and muscular.

"That's Lee," Jack says.

Lee Cobb leaves the house and steps past the bushes onto the dirt road, hands raised. He continues to approach. Tom rolls down his window. Lee is grinning. "You've seen the men in the bushes?"

Tom nods.

"I'm impressed. We can't be too careful. I have men all over the area. Though I suppose if you've made it this far with a whole city and a specialist team after you, it shouldn't come as too much of a shock that you made them." He holds out a hand. "Lee Cobb. Thank you for getting the senator and his family to us."

Tom shakes his hand. "Tom Rollins. I'm sorry for the men you've lost."

Lee's face darkens, turns grim. "I'm going to have to make some difficult phone calls." Lee looks into the minivan, taking in everyone present. "Keep the van going and head inside," he says. "I'll follow you in."

Tom rolls down the rest of the road slowly, eyeing the men in the bushes as he goes. He sees the whites of their eyes as they stare back at him. They're probably unhappy that he saw them.

Tom and Nina wait by the door. Lauren pauses on her way past them. She's carrying Joel. She looks each of them in the eyes. "Thank you," she says. Her expression is earnest. She looks like she wants to hug them both, but she refrains. "Thank you for saving my son – for saving all of us. If it wasn't for you..."

Nina places a hand on her shoulder and leads her into the house. Lauren's eyes are glassy, close to tears. It's been a draining day for all of them. Her adrenaline is wearing off now, and she's no doubt exhausted.

Jack and Lee join Tom at the door. They go inside together. There are four other men present, dressed similarly to Lee. Two of them lead Lauren and Joel upstairs to a room. Lee makes quick introductions to his men, and then leads Tom, Nina, and Jack through to the kitchen. He has a tech team of his own gathered around the table, locked in and typing away.

"Before we go any further," Tom says, "we've spent all day wondering why the blame for a bombing was placed on us. We need answers."

Jack nods. "Of course," he says. He sighs and runs his hands down his face. "I suppose I should start with Lee here. Like you said back while we were driving, Nina, ordinarily senators are not assigned security details, unless their lives are in imminent, clear danger. My life was not in *clear* danger, and so I had to hire LC Security off my own back."

"Because of Hanley?" Nina says.

"Because of him," Jack says, his face twisting. "Though I never thought he'd go so far as this... Lee and his men were for peace of mind. I was aware of Bob's private team. I didn't know if they existed or not, but most of us have heard the stories. I wasn't taking any chances, not when I have Lauren and Joel. I can't afford to be careless."

"Why did you stay in San Francisco after the bombing today?" Nina says.

"I wasn't targeted directly. The bombing was downtown, far from our vacation home. And when there's a problem in a city you love, you can't just flee. What kind of a message does that send? We stayed, and carried on as normal. We needed to project strength for the city. To be with them in the face of adversity. To show that San Francisco would not be crippled, would not be fearful in the face of what happened."

"Why does Hanley dislike you specifically?" Tom says.

Jack sighs. "That's going to take some telling."

"Feels like for the first time today, we have the time."

Jack takes a deep breath, marshalling his thoughts. He

looks between Tom and Nina. "Are either of you familiar with Wilbur Magnusson?"

"No," Tom says.

"The name sounds familiar," Nina says. "I can't think why."

"He's the CEO and founder of WilburForce. They manufacture weapons."

"That must be how I've heard his name," Nina says.

Jack nods. "He's been mentioned in the news in the past. He's not in it regularly, but he's still a public figure and his name crops up from time to time. They've been in business for more than two decades now, making the standard fare you would expect – shells, bullets, missiles, all that kind of thing. The last few years, however, they've been delving deeper into AI-led weaponry."

"What kind of things?" Tom says. "Drones? Missiles?"

Jack nods. "Both of those, yes, as well as anti-aircraft rocket launchers, and more besides. But those aren't the weapons we need to be concerned about right now. Those aren't the weapons that have caused all of this." Jack clears his throat. When he continues, it almost feels like he's changing the subject, moving onto a more conversational topic. "Have you ever seen those AI dogs?"

"I've seen them," Nina says.

"Have you seen the videos of them with flamethrowers mounted on their backs? Or with missiles mounted, or machine guns?"

"Yes," Nina says. "Is that WilburForce?"

"No. WilburForce have made something worse. They've taken the basic premise of the dogs, and they've shrunk them down, made them lighter, sleeker, faster, focused, and more deadly. They've called them Wolverines."

"And do these Wolverines have weaponry mounted on their backs?" Tom says.

"Not yet, but it's probably just a matter of time," Jack says. "They're hunter-killers, supposed to be silent. Sent to get in and get out. No loud weaponry. Instead, they're armed with retractable blades. Their handler is elsewhere, out of danger, feeds them the target via an image loaded into a tablet – and that's it. The Wolverines attack. And that's the problem. Well, actually, that's one of multiple problems. In initial testing, simulations were run. They were tasked to eliminate specific targets. The human operator could override them and choose not to destroy a target for whatever reason. Except, the Wolverines decided the human operators were an obstacle to their mission, and they killed them. Some modifications have been made to their programming since, and that in turn has opened a new can of worms. When the Wolverines are set off, they don't stop. They're not relaying back to their controller to check in if what they're doing is okay. Rather than relay to their handler, or waste time turning around and killing them, they just act, completely autonomous. Nothing can stop them until they reach the target. They kill without discretion, bulldozing through bodies until they've fulfilled their task."

"How do you know about this?" Nina says.

"Because I don't trust Hanley, or anything he's involved in, I've had reporters and private investigators look into every business he's been taking kickbacks from. This, with Wilbur-Force, has been the most concerning."

"Have the Wolverines been field-tested?" Tom says.

"Not yet," Jack says. "I've been blocking it as best I can, talking others round to do the same, making them aware of what's happening. Seth Goldberg is with me on this.

What we do know is, the Wolverines have only been tested in a controlled environment, and they tear through everything."

"It sounds like they're still prototypes."

"That's what I think, too. But WilburForce is continuing to push them. They want them incorporated into the US military. They want them sent overseas on black ops missions, to eliminate enemies of our country."

"I'm not saying you're wrong," Tom says, "but you object to that?"

"I object to what the Wolverines are capable of," Jack says. "Let's use a hypothetical situation. Say there's a Middle Eastern terrorist, and we've been tracking them, and finally we get a hit on them in some marketplace. A Wolverine is deployed. It heads directly for the target, in a straight line, and nothing can stop it. Men, women, and children – it doesn't care. All they are is an obstacle. They're just in the way. And let's say it's not an open space like a marketplace. Let's say it's an apartment building. Same damn problem. Anyone it passes in the hall, it will attack. And yet all WilburForce can think about is the bottom line. They don't care that the Wolverines aren't ready. They just want the contracts. Once they have the money, nothing else matters to them.

"As far as I'm concerned, the Wolverines are too brutal, too mindless to be put out in the field. It's just a matter of time before weapons like these are banned under the Geneva Convention. I can't in good conscience allow our government to permit a weapon like this. I couldn't sleep at night if I allowed this to pass through."

"And Senator Hanley is a supporter," Tom says.

"Senator Hanley is on the WilburForce payroll," Jack

says. "He's effectively one of their biggest lobbyists, though he won't admit it and it can't be proven."

"So now you need to prove Hanley's involvement," Nina says. "You need to prove what he's done today."

"It's already in motion," Lee says. He's leaning against the counter, arms folded. "Before you got here, I contacted some of my people in Nevada. They're on their way to Hanley as we speak."

"And what are they going to do when they reach him?" Tom says. "You're not cops. You can't arrest him."

"He needs to be punished for what he's done," Jack says. "But first we need to be able to *prove* what he's done. I know Bob. He's no martyr. He just wants to get rich. If we talk to him, he'll admit to everything. Once he talks, A, he'll go to prison, and B, there's no chance WilburForce will ever get another contract with the US government again after coming at one of its senators, not to mention all the other death and destruction they've caused in the course of their endeavour."

"I get what you're saying," Nina says, "but if Cobb's men here take Senator Hanley, that's kidnapping."

"He came after my family," Jack says.

"I get that, but you're going to struggle to build a case if you gain your information through coercion."

"He's hardly going to cry about kidnapping after the number of deaths he's caused today," Lee says. "With everything that will be levelled against him, one singular protest from him is gonna be like spit in the ocean."

Nina holds up her hands. "Look, I'm hardly on his side – far from it – but despite everything, we need to keep level heads here. I'm just playing devil's advocate."

Tom cuts everyone off before they can say anything else.

"We should wait until Cobb's men are bringing him in before we argue about this any further," he says. "Orlando knows we have you. Knows we got you clear. We linked you to them via Hanley. They're likely to do the same. It stands to reason that they'll be in regular contact with each other. He's definitely in Nevada now, not DC?"

"We were already monitoring his movements before today," Lee says. "He's in Nevada."

"Whereabouts in Nevada is his home?"

Jack answers. He doesn't have to think about it, and it's clear he's been keeping up with LC Security's monitoring of Hanley's whereabouts. "Just outside Henderson."

"That's not too far from California, is it?"

"It's not a million miles away, no."

"Orlando and his team escaped in a helicopter," Tom says. "If Hanley is in Nevada, if he's in Henderson, that's not very far for them to go by chopper. They could be nearly there by now, if they're not already."

"I've got my people here trying to track their chopper down," Lee says, motioning toward the men on the computers sitting at the kitchen table. He straightens and reaches for his cell phone. "I'll place some calls. I've got other friends who might be able to help us track them." He heads out of the room, dialling.

"That chopper isn't going to have logged its route," Nina says.

Tom nods. "True, but there's always other ways to track them. Scanners, sky reports. I'm sure they'll be thorough."

Jack stands in the centre of the kitchen, balling his fists. He looks between Tom and Nina. "What if they *have* reached him?" he says. "What if they all get away?"

"You'd best hope Lee's men are able to find them while

they're airborne," Tom says. "Otherwise, it's going to take me a long time to track them down."

Jack looks at him. "You're going after them?"

"Of course I am," Tom says. "They tried to kill us. They tried to blame us for what happened today. They killed a lot of people, and they planned on killing a lot more. I won't let them get away with that. It might take a while, but no matter where they go, I'll find them."

51

Senator Bob Hanley's ranch-style mansion is in Clark County, Nevada, on the outskirts of the city of Henderson. He has no neighbours. It's easy for the helicopter pilots to land in his grounds.

"How far away is your refuel spot?" Orlando says to the pilot, leaning through into the front but speaking into the headset. The rotors are still running. They don't plan on being here for long.

"Forty miles north-east," the pilot says. The pilots, Tony and Chet, work for Orlando. He hadn't expected to need them for the San Francisco mission, but no matter where the team goes he always has them on standby. There always needs to be an alternative exit plan, as today has proven.

"Will it take long to get there?"

"Not long at all."

"Good."

Stuart looks toward the mansion, holding onto his M4. The mansion is well lit. It doesn't give the appearance of having an owner who is about to flee. Stuart turns back to Orlando. "There's no sign of him."

"I'll go get him," Orlando says. "Corey, with me."

They leave the chopper, taking their M4s with them. They take off their headsets but they're still wearing their earpieces. If Stuart or Harris need to contact them they still can.

Orlando and Corey approach the house with caution at a light jog, sweeping the area to make sure no one is about to pop out and surprise them. Orlando calls Hanley. He answers.

"I'm in my office," Hanley says, sounding harried. "I'm nearly done."

"We're coming in," Orlando says.

"You know where to find me." Hanley hangs up.

"Anything to worry about?" Corey says.

"He's just being a slow son of a bitch," Orlando says. "But still, stay alert."

The bottom floor of the rear of the mansion is all glass, affording a view of the rocky desert expanse beyond. Orlando can see clear through the house. The fire is roaring in the lounge, though it's not a cold night. There's no one to be seen. They enter through the rear. The door is locked but Orlando smashes a window with the butt of his rifle and they walk straight through. He's not concerned about the damage. Hanley has bigger issues right now, and he's probably going to have to leave this house behind permanently. If he didn't want a window smashed, he shouldn't have left his doors locked.

They make their way through the mansion and go upstairs, heading to the rear, to Hanley's office. Corey has never been inside before, but Orlando knows his way around. He remains alert, but he sees no sign of anything to worry about. He reaches the office and enters without knocking.

Hanley is emptying his wall safe into a bag. It's full of cash, jewellery (mostly watches), and documents. Orlando recognises some of the documents. He and his team compiled them. They contain details of blackmail and corruption among other senators and senior government officials. Hanley is obviously looking to force some hands and call in some favours down the line.

Hanley gives a start as they enter, looking them both over. "Jesus Christ," he mutters, zipping his bag closed. "You nearly gave me a heart attack. You don't knock?"

"You've had two hours to get ready," Orlando says. "You should be good to go by now. You should've been out there on the grounds waiting for us."

"Yeah, well, I had a lot I needed to do." He tilts his chin toward Corey. "Why don't you send your man to go and gather my bags and take them out to the chopper. They're down next to the front door."

Orlando gives Corey a nod. Corey holds out his hand for the bag Hanley is holding, but he turns his body away and keeps a tight grip on it.

"This one stays with me," he says.

Corey shrugs and leaves the room, heading downstairs to get the rest of the bags.

When he's gone, Hanley turns on Orlando, his eyes wide and fiery, bulging out of his skull. "This is a real mess you've got me into here, Orlando."

"I've heard this already," Orlando says.

"And you're gonna hear it again. Do you understand

what we have to lose if they figure out what's happening here? It's not just the money – it's our *lives*."

Orlando looks back at Hanley, his own eyes steely and calm. "There's no time for this," he says. "We need to leave. If I'm right and they've worked out who we are, if they made their way to Fielder, then they've probably worked out who *you* are."

"How are they going to get here from San Francisco in time?" Hanley says. "Did *they* have a helicopter? And if they call the cops, so what? It's all just theory and conjecture right now. There's no proof."

"Then why are you ready to run with us?"

"To create some breathing space. I need to see where the chips fall, to see the lay of the land. I can't fix a mess if I'm caught right in the middle of it." Hanley leans on the edge of his desk. He's calmer now. He's more confident in himself. He wants to berate Orlando, and he wants to be able to take his time about it.

Hanley raises a finger, wagging it at Orlando. "I'm giving serious consideration as to whether I maintain your contract," he says. "You're supposed to be the best, but what you've done today is *far* from be the best. In fact, today you've gone on like the group of borderline criminals you really are. You picked the wrong man. You were unable to adapt and overcome the various obstacles he created. You –"

Orlando steps forward, backing him down. "If you keep that finger pointing at me, I'll break it off and stick it up your fat ass."

Hanley quickly lowers his hand.

"I'd be very careful about how you talk to me," Orlando says. "If you don't want to keep me and my team on contract, then what's stopping me from cleaning up one mess right here? *You.* You know who we are, and you know where we could go. That's information I could make sure doesn't get out."

Hanley swallows. He's pale. "Now, uh, let's not be hasty," he says. "Emotions are running high, that's all. I didn't mean any offence –"

Orlando holds up a hand to silence him. Stuart is contacting him on the earpiece.

"We have incoming," Stuart says. "Coming toward the front gate."

"You expecting anybody?" Orlando says to Hanley. "And don't lie to me."

Hanley shakes his head vigorously. "No, no one," he says.

"Pulling up to the front gate," Orlando says.

Hanley looks back at his desk, at his laptop. "I have cameras," he says.

They move around the desk so they can see the laptop screen. Hanley brings up the footage at the front gate. They see a vehicle approaching.

"I don't recognise it," Hanley says.

Orlando keeps watching. The car doesn't pull up to the intercom. Instead, it stops at the gate and four men jump out. They're all in black. They're moving fast. One of them has a blowtorch. He starts cutting through the lock on the gate. While he does this, another smashes the cameras and the feed goes dead.

Hanley is panicking. "I don't know them," he says.

"I'd guessed as much," Orlando says.

Hanley is shaking now. "They're not cops," he says. "Who are they? Who sent them?"

Orlando shrugs. "How should I know?"

"Shit! You need to get me out of here, Orlando. Don't let them take me."

"You're singing a very different tune to the one you were putting out just a few minutes ago."

"Listen, I'm sorry. I was just worked up, that's all. I'm sorry. Get me out of here, Orlando. That's why you came here in the first place, right?"

"Uh-huh," Orlando says. He readies his M4. "Let's go." He starts walking out of the mansion, Hanley following close behind, holding tight to his bag of money and documents. Orlando gets on the radio. "How's it looking out there?"

"They're through the gate," Stuart says. "But we're in position. What do you want us to do?"

"Deal with them," Orlando says. "I'm taking Hanley to the helicopter. We'll meet you all there."

As they reach the smashed window, they hear gunfire erupt at the front of the house, at the gate. Hanley looks at his broken window and all of the shattered glass, but he knows better than to say anything about it.

The gunfight is short. By the time they're halfway to the still-running chopper, it's already over. Orlando radios through again before the rotating blades can deafen him. "Status report?"

"All dead," Stuart says. "No casualties on our side. We're making our way to you now."

"You recognise them?"

"Never seen them before."

"Any form of ID?"

"Corey has checked them. Nothing. But he's taken pictures of their faces to look into later."

Orlando and Hanley reach the chopper and climb inside. Looking out across Hanley's acreage, toward the house, he sees his men making their way toward them at a jog. Orlando puts on the headset. He addresses the pilot. "Let's go get your fuel."

Tony looks back at him. "Where to after that?"

Orlando looks at Hanley. He's wearing his own headset now. He's heard the question. "Do you have a preference?" Orlando says. "Run for the hills, or is there further business to attend to before we split?"

The other members of the team are climbing into the chopper. They're ready to go.

"We need to go and see Magnusson," Hanley says. He swallows. He takes a deep breath. It's clear he doesn't want to go, but it needs to be done. "He has to be informed."

52

Tom and Nina are in the living room of the safehouse, finally resting, finally catching their breath. They're heavily bandaged, their various injuries tended to by Lee's men.

Finally with a spare moment to think, Tom finds his thoughts drifting to Cindy. Mostly, he feels concern. He wasn't able to get in touch with her, and she's never gotten back to him. He would have expected to hear from her by now, one way or another. She'd find a way to get in touch. Tom doesn't believe for a second that she'd think him responsible for today's events. She knows him better than that. So instead, he worries about her. It crosses his mind that she could be in trouble.

Before he can pursue this line of thought further, Lee Cobb comes into the room and Tom's attention is drawn back to the present. Jack Fielder follows. Lee's face is grim. His jaw is clenched tight.

It's late. It's dark outside. Lauren and Joel have managed to fall asleep in a room upstairs, both of them sharing a bed.

Tom has a feeling that the peace that has settled is about to come tumbling down.

Jack bites his bottom lip. "We've just got word," he says. "The team Lee sent to get Bob have all been killed."

"By who?" Nina says, sitting forward. "By Orlando?"

"We don't know for sure," Lee says, forcing himself to speak, spitting out the words. "But we can guess. The timing would work out for their chopper to have reached him."

"Have you had any luck finding it yet?" Tom says.

Lee shakes his head. "Still working on it."

"How many were in the team?"

"Four," Lee says. "Four good men." Lee is glowering. He's angry. Like the rest of them, this is personal for him now. By Tom's count, he's lost ten men to Orlando and his team.

"If Bob gets away..." Jack begins. He doesn't finish. They all know what he's thinking. If Senator Hanley gets away, they have no way of proving any of this, not really. If he gets away, then they all escape justice. If he gets away, then who knows when or where they might surface next.

Tom will find them, no matter where they go. But he's aware that if the trail runs cold, it could take a long time to track them down. He can be patient, but it could still take longer than he'd like. He looks at Jack. "Any idea where he might have gone? Anywhere you know he goes on vacation, any friends he might have far afield? Anything at all?"

Jack thinks, but he shakes his head. "We were never exactly on friendly terms," he says. "I tried to avoid him as best I could. I didn't *want* to talk to him. I didn't want to be anywhere near him. I had no interest in his personal life."

"Nothing you overheard?" Nina says.

"I'm regretting it now, but I didn't *want* to know more about him than I already did. I already knew enough – his connections to WilburForce, the rumours of his private black ops team. That was as much as I needed to know."

Tom looks at Lee. "How confident are you that your people are going to find that chopper?"

"I've sent out messages, and I've got every tech in my employ working on it. In the past, they've found more with less information than we have now."

"Fairly confident, then?" Nina says.

"I make no guarantees," Lee says. "But I have hope that we'll know where they're going within a couple of hours. If not... Well, then my confidence in finding them any time soon will begin to fade."

Lee and Jack leave the room, heading back through to the kitchen. Nina gets up and paces. She stretches out her arms and yawns.

"Why don't you go sleep?" Tom says. "I'm sure there's a room free somewhere. This is a big place for a safehouse."

Nina shakes her head. "No way," she says. "I'm staying right here, same as you, and for the same reasons. I'm seeing this thing through. If they get a hit, I want to know about it. If they find where they're going and head to intercept, I'm going with, same as you. I'm not resting until this is over."

53

The home of Wilbur Magnusson is similar to Hanley's in that his mansion has no neighbours. Other than that, they're both very different buildings. Hanley's is ranch style, but Wilbur's is big and boxy, very modern. The helicopter lands in his grounds. This time, they kill the engine. They don't know how long they're going to be here for.

"Sit tight," Orlando says. "Same as at Hanley's – keep an eye on the surrounding area, just in case. Get in touch if you see anything you don't like."

Stuart nods.

Orlando and Hanley head up to the house while the rest of the team disperse and spread out across the grounds, disappearing into the darkness. The mansion is bigger than Hanley's. It's also not surrounded by desert. Instead, there are rolling hills, dotted with California redwoods. The house is lit up, security lights illuminating it like a beacon, and also giving an idea of the sheer size of it. The exterior is all sheer walls and thin windows. It looks like it might have been constructed out of box containers. The house itself covers roughly three acres of land.

There's a hut with security at the main gate, and guards patrolling the ground. Hanley called ahead, let Wilbur know they were coming. His guards were alerted to their arrival, and told not to interfere with them.

Hanley is carrying his bag of money and documents still. He looks around while they cross the grounds, like he expects an ambush. Orlando is carrying his M4 again, keeping it close.

"Wilbur told us to go to the front door," Hanley says. He swallows. He's sweating. He's nervous about this meeting. Orlando looks down and sees that his hands are shaking, despite how tightly they squeeze the handle of the bag. "He said we'll be let straight in and escorted up to his office."

Orlando grunts. They cross the front of the mansion and go to the main entrance. Orlando notices how some of the guards are gathered to one side, close to the gatehouse, watching them.

Hanley doesn't get a chance to knock on the door. It opens as they approach. An older man dressed in a suit is waiting for them. Orlando wonders if he's the butler. The man motions them inside. "Mr. Magnusson is expecting you," he says, eyeing Orlando's M4, then turns and leads them through the house without remarking upon the weapon. They don't go upstairs. Wilbur's office is on the ground floor, toward the back. Orlando reckons he probably saw them land and cross the grounds from in there.

The office is a large, wood-panelled room, completely at odds with the exterior of the house. It feels instead like the inside of an Alaskan hunting cabin. There's an expansive fireplace running along the wall on the right, and mounted animal heads adorn the walls. A stuffed bear stands in the corner, behind Wilbur's grand desk. Wilbur is sitting there, watching them as they enter and take it all in, his fingers tented in front of his mouth. Once they're situated, the butler turns and leaves without a word, closing the door on his way out.

Wilbur takes his time talking. Even sitting, it's clear that he's a tall man. Thin, too. His hair is in a fashionable cut and slicked back. He's in his forties, but it's clear he tries hard to make himself look younger.

There are two chairs in front of his desk, but Orlando and Hanley do not sit. Wilbur breathes in deep, un-tenting his fingers and slowing rising to his feet. "Well," he says as he comes around the front. He perches on the edge of the varnished mahogany, hands clasped in his lap. "It seems we have a disaster on our hands, doesn't it, gentlemen?" He doesn't speak with any discernible accent.

"Mr. Magnusson," Hanley says, "I – *we* – we came here to apologise. We understand that things haven't gone exactly according to plan..."

Wilbur snorts. "That's an understatement, wouldn't you say?" He stares at Hanley. Hanley clamps his mouth shut. "I paid you an awful lot of money in advance to deal with Senator Fielder. There was the promise of so much more. So what I want right now is for you to explain to me why I haven't received a return on my hefty investment."

"There was a man," Hanley says, "Rollins, and a cop with him –"

"I've been following the news," Wilbur says. "I know all

about your fall guys. I've witnessed your failures play out in real time."

"Rollins ruined our plans," Hanley says.

Orlando is silent. He watches the exchange taking place, hands resting on his M4.

"Then it sounds like you needed firmer plans," Wilbur says. He looks at Orlando now. "Do you have anything to say for yourself? I heard promising things about you and your team."

"Often things will go your way," Orlando says, "and sometimes, rarely, they don't. Rollins was underestimated. I take responsibility for that."

"Uh-huh. How good are you usually?" Wilbur says. "Hanley here was singing your praises. Told me I had nothing to worry about, despite my concerns that you're all a bunch of military criminals. He promised me that everything was in hand."

"We're the best," Orlando says without hesitation. "Today was a blip."

Wilbur grins. "Even the best can have off days, isn't that right?"

Orlando shrugs one shoulder.

"Mr. Magnusson, the reason we came here –" Hanley says.

"More bad news?" Wilbur says, turning back to Bob.

Hanley shrinks under his gaze. He tells him of Orlando's theory, and of the men who turned up to his own home in Nevada, potentially proving him right.

"And you think this could all be linked back to me?" Wilbur says.

"I don't know," Hanley says. "Maybe. If Jack Fielder had

men sent to my home, then he's going to suspect you for sure. He'll probably have some kind of idea as to what this is all about."

Wilbur doesn't say anything for a while. He's thinking this over. "Perhaps you should have alerted me to this while you were en route."

"It was hard to relay too much information while we were in the helicopter," Hanley says.

Wilbur takes a deep breath, still thinking things over. "Well," he says, raising his eyes. "If Senator Fielder *has* worked out what's happening, I suppose we can kiss goodbye to any hope of securing that military contract. All of this has been for naught."

"If Jack has worked out what's happening," Hanley says, "we have bigger problems than contracts for AI animals."

"I'm very aware. After what's happened in San Francisco, we stand to lose everything." Wilbur pushes himself off the desk and takes a couple of steps, still thinking. "This is a very dire situation we find ourselves in."

"May I make a suggestion?" Orlando says.

Both men look toward him.

"Let's not hang around any longer to see how things play out," he says. "We leave now, flee overseas – somewhere with no US extradition. For you, Mr. Magnusson, starting over will be easy. You have the means. You take the Wolverines to a country that *will* buy them – and I'm sure there's plenty of them out there that won't worry about the moral quandary your machines have caused Senator Fielder. It won't take long before you're back in a house as big as this one. Possibly bigger, in fact." Orlando can see from the look on Wilbur's face that he likes this idea.

Wilbur smiles. "Not bad," he says. He points at Orlando. "Despite your failures today, I think I like you."

"I'm pleased to hear it."

"What kind of guarantees can you make that the issues you've had today won't happen again?"

Orlando shrugs. "Everyone has a bad day. My team and I learn from ours."

Wilbur claps. "Excellent. That's a good answer."

Orlando suddenly feels like he's in an interview.

"How many men do you have left?" Wilbur says.

"Three," Orlando says.

"And you trust them?"

Orlando nods.

"Have any of you ever been to Bolivia, Orlando?" Wilbur says.

Orlando grins, remembering. "Yes," he says. "Many times."

"He's been there for me," Hanley says.

"And I've been when I was still on Uncle Sam's dime," Orlando says.

"I have a lot of contacts in Bolivia," Wilbur says, ignoring Hanley. "A lot of friends who can take good care of me. Get me back on my feet. Put me in touch with other governments and *their* militaries. Militaries run by *real* men. Men of class and taste who understand a good thing when it's staring them right in the face. A good thing like the Wolverines."

Orlando understands. "And there's no extradition treaty with Bolivia."

Wilbur snaps his fingers and points at Orlando. "Bingo," he says. "I'm going to need security while I get myself set up. Some men who can stick close, and who I can trust. Who can train up some of the locals, make them elite, make sure *they're* loyal, too. Are you and your team capable of that, Orlando?"

"Yes," Orlando says. "But what about your guards outside?"

Wilbur waves a dismissive hand. "House security, nothing more. They've never been out in the field. Most of them are ex-cons. Street level. There's nothing special about them. They're not trained."

"What are you getting at here?" Hanley says, his head cocked, suspicious.

Again, Wilbur ignores him. He looks only at Orlando. "Are you up to the task?"

"Are you offering me a job?" Orlando says.

"Now, hey –" Hanley says.

Wilbur cuts him off. "I could be," he says. "Today has been an abject failure, but I've heard stories of your past exploits. I know you're more than capable. Are you interested in a change of scene?" His eyes flicker toward Hanley now. "A change of employer?"

"I guess that would depend," Orlando says before Hanley can continue protesting.

"On what?" Wilbur says.

"Salary, of course," Orlando says.

Hanley looks between them both, eyes bugging. He's concerned about what he's hearing.

Wilbur flicks his head toward Hanley. "Double the amount you're getting from him."

"Then consider me newly employed," Orlando says.

"And your team?"

"I speak for them."

Wilbur claps his hands together again. "Splendid," he says.

Hanley stammers. "Will the two of you just slow down and hear me out one second? Where do I fit into all of this?"

"That's a good question, senator," Wilbur says. He speaks to Orlando. "Your first task as my new employee... I need a problem cleared up."

"What's the problem?" Orlando says.

He covers his mouth with his hand, then gestures theatrically toward Hanley and, in a stage whisper, says, "The senator problem."

"No, wait –" Hanley says.

Orlando pulls out his handgun. He doesn't want to make as much noise as the M4 will cause. He shoots Hanley twice through the head. Hanley falls flat to the ground.

"If we weren't about to leave," Wilbur says, "I'd be very disappointed about the mess that blood is making of the rug."

The butler pokes his head into the office. He takes in the scene before him, his face dispassionate, then looks at Wilbur. "Sir?" he says.

"You can take the rest of the night off," he says. "In fact, consider yourself on an indefinite vacation. When I get settled I'll be in touch, and you can come meet us there."

"Very good, sir," the butler says, then slips out of the house, closing the door behind him.

"Your butler," Orlando says, turning to Wilbur. "British?"

"No," Wilbur says. "Just miserable. What's in Bob's bag?"

"Money," Orlando says. "And some blackmail records you might be interested in."

"Will I indeed? Grab it, we'll take it with." He starts leaving his office. Orlando grabs the bag, tearing it out of Hanley's dead hands, and then follows. "I just need to grab a few things," Wilbur says, "and then we'll be on our way. Is your chopper fuelled?"

"Yes, but it's not going to get us to Bolivia."

"We don't need it to get us that far. Just to one of my factories. It's not far. I need to get the Wolverines, and their blueprints – perhaps blueprints for a few other items that may be of interest. And then, from there, to my private jet. And *then* Bolivia."

54

When Tom next sees Lee Cobb, he's no longer in slacks and a shirt. Instead, he's dressed in all-black, similar to Orlando and his men. He wears a tactical vest and pads. He's ready to head out into the field.

Tom and Nina had become aware of a flurry of activity in the house. It wasn't loud or invasive, not enough to wake Lauren and Joel, but Tom heard how a lot of the men were suddenly heading to and fro down the hall, and up and down the stairs. He's not surprised to see that Lee has changed into what he's wearing.

"You've got something?" Nina says when he enters.

Jack is close behind him. His clothes have not changed.

"We got a hit on them," Lee says. "One of my contacts got word of an Mi-17 refuelling at a Nevada airstrip. Same one that was spotted hovering over the Golden Gate Bridge. My techs were able to get a track on it from there and we've been following it since."

"Where's it going?" Tom says.

"Well, first it came back to California. Went to the home of Wilbur Magnusson."

"As we suspected," Jack says, his tone bitter.

Lee nods. "But they're airborne again. I've sent some men out there to check it out, but I doubt they're going to find them there."

"Where's the helicopter going now?" Nina says. "Any idea?"

"I assume you have some kind of idea," Tom says, looking Lee over. "Judging by the change of clothing."

"There's no guarantee," Lee says, "but we've plotted the trajectory of their route. And right now it looks like they're heading for northern California. Santa Rosa, in fact."

"What's in Santa Rosa?" Nina says.

"It's not what's *in* Santa Rosa," Lee says. "It's what's *near* it. A WilburForce factory."

"Beyond that, they must be planning on escaping," Jack says. "But they obviously aren't going to leave empty-handed. Who knows what they could take with them from that factory? They'll have the blueprints for God knows how many kinds of weapon."

"Do you think they'll take the Wolverines?" Nina says. "This is what this has all been about, right? It would make sense for them to take them."

"I dread to think about it," Jack says.

"I don't plan on letting them get away," Lee says. "No matter what they're taking. But we're going to have to move fast. I have a couple of choppers of my own, and they're currently on their way here as we speak."

"What about the police?" Nina says.

"We've already talked about this," Lee says.

"Yes, but if it's a question of speed then surely the local PD can get there before us."

"And for what?" Lee says. "What are we going to tell them? Right now they still think the two of *you* are responsible for what happened today. We don't have the time to persuade them otherwise. This falls to *us*. They came at us hard, and now we have to do the same to them. We don't have time for anything else."

"Even if you were able to talk the cops round," Tom says, "they'd go in with sirens blaring. Scare them off. Spook them straight back into the skies. And then we'll need to start this process all over again."

Jack checks the time. "How long until the choppers arrive?"

"Less than five minutes," Lee says. "If we leave then and head straight for Santa Rosa, we should arrive just after them, cut them off there. If they're fast and airborne before we can land, we'll at least have them in our sights. We can give chase from there, and do our best to gently persuade them to land." Tom is sure the gentle persuasion will involve warning gunfire and radioed threats.

Jack starts to leave the room. "I need to go and wake Lauren and Joel," he says. "I don't want them getting scared when they land." He turns and a moment later they hear him running up the stairs.

"I'm coming with," Tom says to Lee.

Lee nods. "I figured as much. I've read your history, Rollins. I know your training, and I know what you're capable of. There's some spare tactical gear and weaponry in the spare room upstairs, end of the hall, door on the right. You'll need to get changed right now."

"I'm coming too," Nina says.

Lee is a little more reticent this time. "You're a cop, right? What kind of training have you had?"

"Weapons and tactics," Nina says.

"I can vouch for her," Tom says. "And we don't know what we're heading into. They could be meeting with backup. You're going to need more bodies."

There isn't much time for debate. Lee nods. "Fine," he says. "Go with Rollins. There won't be tactical gear that fits exactly, but it should only be a little baggy on you. Nothing that'll get in your way."

Tom and Nina leave the living room and head upstairs at a run. As they make their way to the room at the end of the hall, passing the room where Jack speaks softly to his family, they hear the approaching choppers waking the night.

55

There's a helipad at the rear of the Santa Rosa factory. The factory runs twenty-four hours. The Mi-17 lands and Orlando and his team get out with Wilbur Magnusson and walk with him to the factory. Tony and Chet stay with the chopper. The rotors are still, but they're ready to take off as soon as everyone returns. Wilbur's private jet is at an airstrip not far from the factory. They leave here, they go there, and then on to Bolivia. Tony and Chet will be staying behind. They're not coming to Bolivia. Tonight is their final flight with the team.

Orlando and the rest have their M4s still. Orlando questioned if it would spook the workers.

"Take a lot more than some guns to scare them," Wilbur said. "They won't even bat an eye."

As they reach the entrance, Orlando signals to Corey and Harris to stay outside, on guard. He wants Stuart inside with him.

The factory is alive with the sound of grinding, pounding

machines. As they cross the work floor, flanking Wilbur, Orlando sees that he was right – no one so much as looks up as they pass through. As it's late, the factory isn't overflowing with staff. A few dozen at most. Not exactly a skeleton crew but certainly less than it's capable of utilising.

Wilbur leads them up a flight of stairs to the gangway and along the corridor to an office. His name is stencilled on the door. He pulls out a key to get inside. He goes straight to a filing cabinet in the corner.

"Blueprints," he says. "Everything is in print. I don't run the risk of anyone hacking in and stealing my models. And with that in mind, we'll take one of the Wolverines as proof of what it's capable of. The rest we'll destroy. We don't want anyone else getting their hands on them."

"What are you gonna tell the workers out there?" Stuart says, nodding his head back toward the work floor.

Wilbur shrugs. "I'm not going to tell them anything. They can find out that they're jobless in due course. I'm sure it won't take long."

Corey speaks to Orlando in his ear piece. "Sir, we've potentially got a situation."

Orlando frowns. "What is it?"

"Two choppers have just landed in the distance – I'd say about two klicks away."

"You're sure?"

"They came in lights off, but we spotted them. Heard them, too. The fact they descended in darkness, and that they've landed so far away –"

"It's not a good sign," Orlando says, working out where he was going. "Got it. Stay alert and keep me updated if anything else happens." Orlando turns to Wilbur. Stuart has already heard. He tells Wilbur what's happening.

"And they're coming here?" Wilbur says.

"No sign yet, but where else are they gonna go?" Orlando says. "There's nothing else around here for miles. The same people that turned up at Hanley's mansion, this could be them again."

"I thought you killed them."

"Same organisation, different members."

"Whoever they are, seems like they've got funding behind them," Stuart says. "And bodies. They turn up in Nevada, and now here?" He whistles through his teeth. "If they've turned up in two choppers, that means we're outnumbered. We don't know what kind of choppers they were, neither, so we have no idea what kind of bodies they were carrying. We need to get out of here right now. We need to go."

"They see us leave, they're just going to follow again," Orlando says. "All the way to the airstrip."

"They won't have the fuel to follow to Bolivia."

"You think they're going to follow at a safe distance?"

"Now wait just a moment, gentlemen," Wilbur says. "You're concerned that there's a team coming for us. That's understandable. You don't know who they are, nor who sent them. That concerns you."

"If I had to guess, I'd say they have something to do with Senator Fielder," Orlando says. "There was a security detail at his vacation home. After everything we've been up to today, these people didn't start coming after us until after we made contact with Fielder and killed those men."

"So he potentially has a security detail," Wilbur says. "Do I look concerned?"

Orlando has to admit that Wilbur does not.

"Would you like to know why? Because whoever they

are, and whoever sent them, if they're coming after *us*, *here*, in *my* factory – well, that's the biggest mistake they could have possibly made." He grins. "I haven't destroyed the Wolverines yet. You must have heard so much about them by now. Would you like to see what they're capable of?"

56

Tom and Nina ride in the chopper with Lee Cobb and three of his men. The second chopper carries six more members of his team. Everyone is dressed in black tactical gear – vests and pads, night vision goggles – and armed with AR15 assault rifles and Sig Sauer P365 handguns, as well as a couple of M67 grenades. The grenades make Tom think of Harris and the way he's been stroking the ones on the front of his vest every time he's seen him. Tom keeps his own grenades far away from the front of his vest. Harris is clearly a psychopath. What he's done today, with his Semtex, is more than enough proof of that.

"We're going down," Lee speaks into the headset, the radio signal reaching the men in the second chopper, too. "Chopper one, my men with me, on point. Chopper two, bring up the rear. Rollins and Nina, the two of you in the centre. Today has proven that you're both more than capable of handling yourselves, but I know my men and what they can do. If shit goes down, I need to know I can rely on the man to my right and the man to my left, not two unproven commodities."

"Roger that," Tom says. He understands.

The chopper descends. Through the open side door, Tom can see the factory in the distance. They know it runs twenty-four hours. They know there'll be workers inside. Civilians. Three members of chopper two are tasked with getting them to safety, and then to secure the outside area. Tom and Nina are to assist them. The rest will be going after Orlando and Hanley, and potentially Wilbur Magnusson, too.

The chopper lands. Lee is on his feet. "Let's go, people. Move, move, move."

He hops out and the others follow him. Tom and Nina are last out. Lee's team consists of ten men, including him. Twelve, including Tom and Nina. They get into position. They have a lot of ground to cover on foot. NVGs are activated. They start running.

They cover the first klick, and then Tom hears a whirring sound cutting through the air. It's above them. It's slight at first, and then grows to a buzz. Others have heard the same thing. They look up.

"Shit," someone to Tom's left says. "Drones! They know we're here!"

"They're heading for the choppers!" Lee says. "Bring them down!"

While they raise their rifles and start firing, attempting to down the drones before they can reach the choppers, Lee gets back on the radio. "Pilots, out! Incoming! Incoming!"

The drones make contact. The two choppers erupt, lighting up the night. Tom turns off the NVG. The pilots don't respond on the radio. They weren't fast enough.

"*Shit*," Lee says. "Press on," he says. "They know we're coming so take extra care. Let's move."

They resume running. They're not far from the factory now. Up ahead, through the dark, Tom sees movement. It's low to the ground, and fast – too fast to be a person.

"Cobb," he says. "There's more coming."

They're almost close enough to make out, now. Three of them. Tom has never seen them before, but after what he's been told it doesn't take him long to figure out what the oncoming creatures are.

The Wolverines have been unleashed.

57

The Wolverines hit them like a hurricane. One of Lee's men is dead before any of the rest realise what's happening. A Wolverine cuts him down at the ankles, and another slices his throat. There's a squirt of blood, and his scream gargles in his throat.

Then, the third Wolverine gets behind the group, burying its blades into the knees of a man at the rear. It launches itself at his throat, and Tom is able to get a good look at a Wolverine for the first time, lit up in his NVG. They're low to the ground, and about two feet long. Their hides are armoured, a darkened metal that is no doubt bulletproof. Tom would guess it to be titanium, or steel. Their blades pop out from beneath their armour, at their joints – their shoulders and their knees, and from under their chins. Their heads are rounded and blunt, much like an actual wolverine.

Gunfire erupts, but the Wolverines are fast. Too fast. The bullets that do make contact don't do enough damage. The bullets bounce off their carapace. They're too fast and it's too dark for Tom to see where their weak points may be.

Another of Lee's men is taken down. A Wolverine pounces, launching itself onto his chest. It doesn't attempt to pierce his vest, as if it knows it's going to struggle to get its blades to puncture through. Instead, it goes straight for his throat. The blade under its chin punches out, through his neck and the meat between his collarbone and trapezium. The man falls back and the Wolverine continues stabbing.

Tom grabs Nina. "We need to keep moving," he says. He grabs Lee and pushes him ahead. "If we stay here, we're all going to get cut down."

Lee fires at a Wolverine, but his bullets eat dirt as the robot barrels into another of his men.

"How do we kill these fucking things?" Lee says.

Tom doesn't have an answer. Not yet. He needs a better look at them. Needs to see where the gaps in their armour are. But there might not be time for that. Their best bet could be to stop their controller and try to shut them down that way.

"We need to get into the factory," Tom says. "It could be our only chance."

Lee watches the carnage as the Wolverines tear through his men. There's blood on his face, but it's not his. He manages to nod. He knows Tom's right. He gets on the radio. He talks into the speaker, contacting his still-living men through their ear pieces. "Run! Get away! We can't take them!"

Out of the dark, one of the Wolverines gets the drop on Nina. It sneaks around, diving at her and knocking her flat.

Out the corner of his eye, Tom sees it happen. He follows them down and jams his AR15 between them, pressing the barrel into the ground and raising the stock to keep the Wolverine away from stabbing her. Its blades jab in and out, trying to get at her. Tom pulls out his Sig Sauer and shoots it twice in the face, but the bullets have no effect. He sees where the blades protrude from the joints at its shoulder and he attempts to fire into the gap. Some of the armour comes loose.

"Tom!" Nina says. She's seen how his bullets have knocked the armour back. She passes him a grenade. She's pulled the pin out. Tom takes it from her, holding down the level in her place, and forces the grenade into the opening. He lifts the rifle higher and kicks the Wolverine in its armoured underbelly. It falls back. Nina scrambles away. The grenade goes off. The Wolverine whirs and clicks, but it's incapacitated. Its legs hang loose. After a moment, it lies immobile on the ground.

Tom and Nina start running to the factory. Lee follows them. He has three men with him. Three survivors that he's managed to drag away from the battle. The rest have either been killed by the Wolverines, or are being finished off by the remaining two robots.

"I see their chopper," Tom says as they draw closer to the factory. It's around the back. Its rotors are not running. The survivors run fast and don't look back, don't check to see if the Wolverines are in pursuit. They can't afford to slow. Can't afford to trip and fall. They need to press on. Forward is their only hope. "I'm gonna keep it grounded," Tom says. "We can't let them get away again."

"We'll see you inside," Lee says.

Nina sticks with Tom. They run around the back of the factory, to the helicopter. The two pilots have either been alerted to their approach, or saw them coming. They're outside, and they're armed and waiting. They open fire, and Tom and Nina return it. The pilots only have handguns. One of them goes straight down, strafed by Nina. The other dives in front of the chopper, taking cover. Tom and Nina communicate via hand signals. Nina stays where she is, dropping to a knee and keeping the chopper covered, and Tom goes right to get the drop on the pilot.

Tom moves slowly, crouching close to the ground so he can see under the chopper, too, in case the pilot tries to get underneath and shoot out their legs. He hears gunshots. The pilot is taking shots at Nina. Tom gets close to the front. He can see the pilot's body from under the chopper. He's in a crouch, twisting toward Nina's position. Tom looks around, checking the area, making sure no one – man or machine – is sneaking up, looking to get the drop on him in turn. There's no one around. There's no sign of the Wolverines, though the gunfire and sounds of dying down at the killing zone have silenced.

Sure that he's clear, Tom lowers himself slowly to his stomach, not making a sound, then sights the pilot. He lets loose a tight volley that buries itself in the pilot's ribs. He cries out and falls onto his side. Tom and Nina reach him at the same time. He's dead.

Tom pulls open the door to the cockpit and raises the AR15.

"Should we maybe leave it operational?" Nina says. "Our rides are blown. We might need this to get clear."

"We don't have a pilot," Tom says. "We deal with the present situation, and then we find another way back. We can't take a risk on them getting away again."

Nina nods and steps back. Tom fires into the cockpit,

filling the control panel and console with bullets, rendering it inoperable.

They turn back to the factory, and as they do so they hear an alarm sounding. Around the front, there's a flurry of activity. The workers inside are leaving, running, fleeing.

Lee radios them. "Rollins, Perry, come in. How are things there?"

"We're coming to you now," Tom says.

"The Wolverines have followed us in," Lee says. "They're tearing apart the factory workers."

"Shit," Nina says.

"We're on our way," Tom says.

58

There are security cameras dotted around the factory, inside and out. They're linked to the screens in Wilbur's office. Orlando watches the events outside as they unfold.

"They've taken out one of the Wolverines," Wilbur says, drawing his attention. It's hard to tell from his tone of voice if he's annoyed or impressed.

Orlando joins Wilbur behind his desk. He looks down at his tablet, seeing what the two remaining Wolverines see. Wilbur has no real control over them anymore. All he can do is watch. Rather than issue commands, he can only give suggestions. Whether the Wolverines listen to him or not is up to them. Orlando wouldn't like to be anywhere near these killing machines.

"Jesus," he mutters, watching them work.

"Beautiful, isn't it?" Wilbur says. "The way they move, the way they strike. The way they kill." He shakes his head. "Magnificent beasts. I don't know if you know this about me, Orlando, but I hunt –"

Orlando is distracted from his story. Something on the security cameras has caught his eye. He hurries back to the bank of screens. "Fuck," he says. "*Fuck*." He watches as Rollins and Nina kill his pilots, Tony and Chet, and then Rollins shoots up the inside of the helicopter cockpit. "Goddamnit!"

Wilbur is watching, too. "Don't worry about the chopper," he says. "We can drive to the airstrip. It isn't far."

"Getting to the airstrip isn't what's bothering me," he says, jabbing a vicious finger toward the screen. "It's these two. They've been the biggest pain in my ass all damn day."

"They'll be dead soon."

"I want them dead *now*."

Wilbur grins. "I've gotten their faces from the security footage. The rest of the survivors, too. I've inputted them into the Wolverines. Marked them as priority targets."

"But will they listen?" Orlando says. Ideally, he wants to kill Rollins and Nina himself, but being able to witness them die through a Wolverine POV will suffice.

An alarm sounds. Orlando looks at Wilbur. Wilbur is checking the factory's cameras. Orlando does the same. He sees what has happened. "The robots are killing your workers," he says.

"Mm," Wilbur says, grunting. "They're trying to get to the men who've broken into the factory."

Orlando frowns. "What if they come here? What if those men reach us and the Wolverines are right behind them? Are they going to attack us, too?"

Wilbur taps the tablet. "We had issues in the testing stage with them attacking their controllers, but we've corrected them now."

Orlando thinks he understands. "They won't attack the controller anymore," he says. "And I hope that goes for anyone immediately near them, too."

Wilbur clears his throat. "Not exactly," he says. "There's a failsafe now where if they try to attack their handler, there's a destruct option on the tablet. I press that, they blow." Wilbur turns the tablet to show him the option on the top right of the screen, bright red.

"What if you hit it by accident while they're in the field?"

"Nothing – they need to be within twelve feet. Gives the handler enough time and space to know if their own life is in danger from the Wolverine."

Orlando doesn't like the risk involved, but it's better than nothing. He turns and watches the screens. Sees how the Wolverines cut through the workers, piercing through limbs to bring them down, then puncturing ribs, stomachs, throats, and, in one instance, an eye. The work floor is covered in blood and dead bodies. The workers who haven't been impaled are fleeing from the factory.

"Where are the team?" Orlando says. "I don't see them."

"They're getting the workers out," Wilbur says, grinning like he finds this funny.

"So they're outside?"

"The front of the building."

Orlando looks through the screens. He sees them now, waving people on, aiding them in their escape. He spots Rollins and Nina, too, running to join the others. Orlando speaks into his radio, contacting his men. "Targets are at the front of the building," he says. "Prepare to engage. And whatever you do, stay far away from the fucking Wolverines. They don't care who they shred."

Orlando gets acknowledgements from his surviving men, then hears Wilbur say, in a very small voice, “Oh.”

“What is it?” Orlando goes to him.

“The Wolverines,” he says. He scratches his cheek, alarmed at what he’s viewing. “They’re following the workers out of the factory. They’re chasing them.”

59

Tom, Nina, Lee, and the surviving three members of Lee's team shepherd the factory workers away from the building and the Wolverines, guiding them away from the burning choppers, too. There's nothing for them down there.

"The Wolverines are already inside," Lee says to Tom. "And they're going wild. Orlando and his men will be inside, too. Hanley and Wilbur Magnusson will presumably be hiding out in Wilbur's office. We're heading into a real viper's nest here."

"Orlando and his team look like they're at as much risk as we are," Tom says. "Like Jack said, the Wolverines don't care who they kill."

As if the machines hear him talking about them, they burst from the front of the factory. Tom and the others tense, raising their rifles, preparing to go against them once again, but the Wolverines don't attack them. The team aren't directly in the Wolverines' line of sight. Instead, they're chasing the workers.

Lee looks at the factory, then after the Wolverines and the fleeing people. He points to two of his men. "Go after them," he says. "Do what you can. They're going to slaughter those people. We have to try and help."

The two men's faces are grim, but they know he's right. Without a word, they turn and they give chase to the Wolverines.

Tom, Nina, Lee, and his remaining team member ready themselves and then head inside the factory, rifles raised. Tom checks his magazine before setting off, then replaces it with a fresh one. They pass through a reception area, then enter the work floor. The smell of blood and death is thick here. There are bodies strewn everywhere. They raise their rifles and scan the area, sweeping the floor and the upper levels.

"We split," Lee says. "Rollins, you come with me. We'll take the east of the building. Nina, you're with Jones here. The two of you take the west. Stay in touch. We all need to be hyper-vigilant here."

Tom and Lee head to the east. The alarm is still blaring. The machinery is still running, though there's no one to tend to it. The deeper they get into the factory, the more deafening it is. It's important to remain alert. Tom keeps his rifle raised and his head on a swivel.

Then, the power dies.

The machinery falls silent, along with the alarm. The lights go out. They're alone in the silence and the dark.

Lee doesn't say a word, but he and Tom both pull their NVGs back on. They know Nina and Jones will have done the same. They step lightly. Tom checks the area for security cameras, looking to see if they're being watched. He saw some out on the work floor, but they promptly moved away from them. There aren't any here. He checks in the darkened corners lit up in hues of green through his goggles.

As they approach a corridor, making their way to a flight of stairs at the rear of the factory, a man emerges at the end and opens fire on them with his M4. Tom and Lee scatter, diving for cover. Tom shelters behind a pallet. He doesn't know what's inside the boxes stacked up inside it. The shooter clearly doesn't, either, as he doesn't fire at Tom, knowing there could be explosives packed within. Lee, however, is behind some machinery, and the attacker keeps him pinned as he approaches. Tom glances back. Their assailant is also wearing NVGs. Tom can make out his long hair and beard. It's Harris Elkin.

Gunfire comes from the gangway above, sweeping the ground, aimed at both Lee and Tom. They scatter in different directions, getting clear. Tom dives behind machinery and hears bullets ricochet off it. He doesn't see where Lee goes. Doesn't make out who the overhead shooter is, either.

Both shooters stay on Tom. Harris advances upon his cover while the shooter above strafes the wall above Tom's head to keep him from firing back. Tom stays low. He catches glimpses of Harris coming, but when he's not in view Tom can't hear his approach. The gunfire is too loud.

The shooter overhead pauses to reload. As Tom attempts to fire back, Harris opens up on his position and Tom ducks back into cover. He's pinned. He imagines Harris readying one of those grenades that he's so fond of from the front of his vest. Imagines him rolling it across the ground, toward Tom's position. When that moment comes, Tom has two options – either dive out of cover and get shot, or stay where he is and get blown up. Neither is appealing.

Before he has to make that impossible choice, however, he hears AR15 gunfire. Lee has returned. He fires upward, toward the shooter on the gangway. As the shooter falls back into cover and Lee pursues, Tom dives from cover. He heads straight for Harris. Harris is momentarily distracted by Lee. He spins as Tom charges and manages to bring up his M4, jabbing the stock at Tom's chest. It knocks Tom back a step, but he's already swinging his own rifle, smacking the stock across Harris's jaw.

Both men drop their rifles with the blows. Harris spits blood. Tom advances. He throws a punch, but Harris is able to parry. He lashes out with a kick in return, but Tom lowers his elbow to keep it from driving into his ribs and shrugs it off. Harris swings and Tom ducks. Harris catches him with a kick to the vest, knocking him back. Tom's spine reverberates against a railing. Harris pulls his knife and lunges forward as he stabs it downward, aiming for Tom's face.

Tom spins to the side and Harris's blade glances off the railing. Tom slams his left elbow across the bridge of Harris's nose, breaking and bloodying it. He's close, though, and Harris manages to latch his left hand onto the back of Tom's neck, squeezing tight and pulling him in close. He brings up the knife, the tip of the blade pointing toward Tom's right eye. Tom wraps his right hand around Harris's wrist, keeping the knife from coming closer. He braces himself with his left hand gripping the top of Harris's tactical vest. His neck strains as he's trying to break free of Harris's grip.

"Orlando wanted the honour," Harris says, speaking through blood-flecked teeth. "But he'll just have to be satisfied with your head."

The two men are locked together in a stalemate, each as strong as the other, knowing that to weaken is to die.

Tom's eyes flicker to the two grenades on the front of Harris's vest. "Your bombs killed a lot of people today," he says.

"It was my best work," Harris says. He manages to grin. "And no one will ever know."

Tom keeps his left hand on the vest, but he slides it down, toward the grenades. "All those people you killed today, you need to feel a fraction of what they felt." Tom reaches the grenade. Harris senses the change in pressure from his hand. "This is a stupid fucking place to keep your grenades," Tom says, and he pulls a pin.

Harris panics. He lets go of Tom's neck and reaches for his chest. Tom lets go of his wrist holding the knife. He doesn't need to keep it at bay anymore. He turns and dives. Harris doesn't have enough time to get the grenade off his vest. It's going to explode, and when it does, it's going to set off the other one, too.

Tom gets behind the machinery where he earlier took cover as Harris goes boom.

He hears impact as Harris's body hits the wall. Tom steps out from behind the cover. Everything is green through the NVG, but it's clear that the wet smear on the wall where Harris made contact is blood. He lies in a heap on the ground. Tom rolls him over with the tip of his boot. His front is a gaping hole where the grenades have blown through him. His face is gone. What's left of his hair is a matted mess.

Tom hears screaming from deeper inside the factory, on the west side, where Nina and Jones went. It's a man's scream.

Tom grabs his fallen AR15, as well as Harris's M4, and runs toward the sound.

60

The Wolverines have returned. They're covered in blood. It drips from their armour.

Nina runs.

The two men Lee sent after them, they must be dead. Most of the factory workers, they'll be dead too, bodies strewn in pieces across the parking lot, unless the two men were able to buy them enough time to get away.

Jones is dead.

The Wolverines didn't come storming back in to the factory. They didn't announce their presence with a lot of noise. Instead, they were sneaky. Stealthy. Nina and Jones never saw them coming, until Jones was knocked to the ground and the Wolverine's blades punctured his face and neck.

Nina fired upon it, emptying the magazine, but there was no point. Jones was already dead, the sound of his scream ringing in her ears and echoing throughout the factory, along with the running gunfire she's heard, and the explosion that went off a moment before. She didn't hang around. She dumped the empty AR15 and she ran.

One of the Wolverines stuck with her. The other split off, heading elsewhere. One is more than enough. As Nina runs, she sees her life flashing before her eyes.

She doesn't give up. She pushes herself harder. A man emerges from the darkened corridor she flees down, his M4 raised, and Nina briefly recognises him as Corey Crewe. He sees her running as fast as she can and he doesn't fire. He realises she's running from something. He turns on the Wolverine.

"Oh, *shit*!" He opens fire, but the Wolverine pounces upon him.

Corey hits the ground, but his finger is locked on the trigger. He fires until the M4 is empty, spraying bullets around the factory. Nina dives into the nearest room, slamming the door shut behind her. She breathes hard while she looks around. She's in a storage room. Rocket launchers are stacked in racks, covering every inch of the walls. She takes a closer look at them. She's not well-versed in rocket launchers, but it's no kind she's ever seen before. She doubts Tom, or Lee, or any of Lee's men have, either. It's hard to tell their colour through the NVG, but peering out from under them and leaning close she thinks they're khaki. They're long and sleek, bigger than an RPG but smaller than an anti-tank rocket launcher. They're printed with the WilburForce logo, a W and an F with an arrow splitting the two letters, and there's a screen and pad built-in on the top of the launchers. From what Jack told them, Nina guesses that, like a lot of WilburForce weaponry, it is AI-led. The pad must be for punching in information about the target.

Before Nina can investigate further, something slams

against the door from the outside. The wood is already splintering near the base. It's the Wolverine. Nina looks around. At the far end of the room, there's another door. Nina runs through it, and finds herself in another storage area. This time, however, there are no more doors. She's cornered.

She looks at what this room holds, hoping there could be something to help there. This room, stacked similarly to the launchers, contains the missiles. They're short and sleek, the ends of them slightly bigger where the explosives are stored.

Nina can hear the Wolverine burst through into the previous room. It almost instantly attacks the next door when it realises she isn't present.

Nina is trapped. She doesn't have long until the Wolverine is in here with her. She pulls out her Sig Sauer, but knows it isn't going to do her much good. If she's going to die, she's going down fighting. She won't give it, or the men behind it, the satisfaction of lying down and letting it kill her.

The bottom of the door splinters. The Wolverine charges it, over and over, inexhaustible, unyielding. Nina backs up into the corner of the room opposite the door, handgun raised and steady, both arms outstretched. All she can hope now is that maybe its armour has taken some damage. That maybe it's no longer as impenetrable as it once was, and her bullets might get inside and do some actual damage.

This is her only hope. The alternative, and the reality, is that in less than a minute she's going to be dead.

The door continues to splinter. She can see its face beginning to poke through. If it was an animal, it would sniff at the hole, bite at it. It would attempt to squeeze through now. But it's not. It's programmed smarter than that. It doesn't check if it can fit. Doesn't inspect the damage it's done so far. It'll keep charging until it bursts through, and even then it will only stop long enough to see where Nina is.

Her shoulder knocks against the rack. The missiles briefly jostle together. Nina picks one up, feeling its weight. It's lighter than she expected. Still holding it, she stares at the rattling door. She wonders if it could be of any use. It could do more damage than any of her bullets.

As the thought crosses her mind, the Wolverine bursts through.

Nina doesn't stay where she is. She starts moving, launching herself to her feet and firing upon the Wolverine, the impact of the bullets keeping it at bay as she runs closer to it, the missile in her left hand. When she reaches it, she drives the thinner end of the missile into the Wolverine, in the space between its head and shoulder joints. She wedges it in, pushing it in deep and tight. The Wolverine struggles to move. The missile slows it down. Its knife attempts to pop at its shoulder with the missile, but it blunts itself against the explosive.

Seeing how the missile slows it, Nina dives toward the damaged door, throwing it open. What's left of its base knocks the Wolverine to one side. Nina starts running again. As she goes, she checks her magazine. She has three bullets left. She needs to hit the missile, to blow the Wolverine from inside.

She hears the Wolverine following behind, but slower than before. Nina stops and drops to a knee in the doorway of the rocket launcher storage. She takes aim. Her first shot bounces off the Wolverine's head. Her second hits the ground in front of it. She has one bullet remaining. The Wolverine is getting closer. If she misses this time, the

Wolverine still has enough movement left in it to catch and kill her.

She holds her breath. She ignores everything else. She focusses only on her aim, and the missile, the bulbous tip that contains the explosives.

She shoots.

The bullet is on target. Nina throws herself to the side, out of the doorframe. The missile explodes, blowing the Wolverine apart.

Nina waits until the explosion has died down, and then she peers inside. The Wolverine is gone, parts of it scattered and embedded in the walls and ceiling. She lets out a long breath of relief, and then Tom contacts her through her earpiece.

61

Tom finds Jones dead, but there's no sign of Nina. There's no sign of Lee, either, though he can hear gunfire still resounding throughout the factory.

Tom doesn't rush into anything. He keeps the AR15 raised and proceeds with caution, Harris's M4 slung over his shoulder.

He finds Lee. He's still alive, but he's bleeding, sitting sheltered on the ground in a storeroom doorway. His left hand is clamped to his right trapezium. "Nearly fucking got me," he says through gritted teeth.

Tom kneels beside him, continuing to look out, prepared for an ambush. "It looks like they got you good enough," Tom says. "Gunshot?"

"I'm still breathing," Lee says. "And yeah."

"Any idea where they are?"

"Gangway," Lee says. "Two of them. Orlando Higgs and Stuart Lynch. I got a good enough look at them both."

"See anyone else?"

Lee shakes his head.

"What about the Wolverines?"

"Not here, but the sneaky bastards could be anywhere."

There's an explosion from the north-east of the factory. Tom gets on the radio. "Nina?" he says. "Was that you? If you're able to speak, come in."

Nina is breathing hard when she responds. "That was me," she says. "Managed to take down one of the Wolverines, but I'm out of ammo. Although…" She pauses. "There's something here that might be useable."

"Whatever it is, grab it and then find somewhere close to your position and take cover. We're on our way to you now, but we're not the only ones who would've heard that explosion."

"Corey is down," Nina says. "Wolverine got him."

Tom adjusts his mental tally. That just leaves Orlando and Stuart, and maybe Hanley and Wilbur.

Lee starts to push himself up. "Go on ahead," he says. "I'll slow you down like this, but I can catch you up."

Tom nods. He makes his way through the factory, heading north-east, toward the explosion. He looks ahead and he looks up, checking for anyone hiding out on the gangway.

Gunfire erupts up ahead of him, coming down. One of them is on the gangway, lying flat. Tom throws himself behind a wall, the bullets thudding into it. He lies low and returns fire, his bullets rattling off the metal railing.

Then, as he's behind cover, he hears screaming.

Tom looks out. The man on the gangway is being attacked by the remaining Wolverine. There's more gunfire, but it's not aimed at him. He looks up and sees Orlando firing upon the Wolverine. He's shouting something, but Tom can't make it out. When he sees his bullets can't save

Stuart, he turns and runs. Tom jumps back to his feet and heads for the stairs up to the gangway. He cuts Orlando off at the pass, throwing himself into him.

Orlando hits the wall, but he braces himself against Tom. “Are you fucking crazy?” he says. “That thing is coming! It’ll kill us both!”

Tom grins. “It’ll certainly kill you,” he says. “After I throw you to it.”

Orlando starts speaking, but he’s not talking to Tom. “Wilbur, hit the destruct,” he says. “It’s coming this way. It’s already killed Stuart. Hit the destruct.”

Tom tilts his head. He doesn’t hear anything. It’s clear Orlando doesn’t, either. “Wilbur!” he shouts now. “Hit the fucking destruct! What do you mean it’s out of range? Damn it, get your ass out here!”

“I don’t think he’ll get here fast enough,” Tom says.

They hear the Wolverine’s approaching steps coming along the gangway, nearing them from around the corner.

Orlando struggles. He attempts to headbutt Tom, but Tom easily avoids it. He brings up his knee and drives it into Tom’s ribcage, loosening Tom’s grip a little. He manages to raise a leg enough to kick Tom, knocking him back toward the stairs. Tom, however, keeps hold of him. They fall back and tumble down the steps together. They hit the ground hard, but neither of them is stunned. They’re promptly back up to their feet. Tom has dropped his AR15 in the fall, and Orlando lost his M4 when Tom tackled him to the wall. Tom pulls the M4 from his back forward but Orlando saw it and was prepared. He dives forward and grabs the barrel, forcing it away from him.

The Wolverine is at the top of the stairs. Tom and Orlando exchange glances. Orlando lets go and Tom fires upon the Wolverine, driving it back. When it's stunned, Orlando drives a fist into Tom's right kidney from behind. Tom drops the M4 and falls to a knee, but, despite the pain, the fall is a feint. He sweeps his leg out wide and takes Orlando down. Orlando lands on his face, bloodying his nose on the ground. Tom looks back over his shoulder and sees the Wolverine preparing to launch itself at him. He falls flat on his back in anticipation of its dive. When it does, he kicks it back into the stairs. It lands on its back and struggles to right itself.

Orlando is back on his feet, trying to run. Tom dives for his legs and catches one of them, grabbing it by the shin and bringing him back down. Tom mounts him, pinning him, and punches Orlando across the face with rights and lefts, cutting and swelling his cheeks and lips.

While he punches, Orlando reaches for his knife. He pulls it out, but Tom saw the movements of his arm. He stands and stomps down on the hand holding the knife, crushing it between his boot and the ground, hearing finger bones break. Orlando cries out.

There's gunfire, but Tom looks and sees that Lee has arrived, and he's firing upon the Wolverine. It's managed to right itself, and was attempting to sneak up on Tom.

Tom steps away from Orlando and reaches down for the dropped M4. He hears running footsteps on the gangway overhead. "Orlando!" the new arrival calls. Tom has seen this man before, but only in a picture shown to him by Lee on the chopper here. Wilbur Magnusson.

Wilbur is carrying a tablet. He takes in the scene before him.

And then something interesting happens. Tom and Lee

both see it. The Wolverine looks toward Wilbur. It sees the tablet in his hands.

It charges for him up the stairs.

Wilbur panics. He sees the Wolverine coming, and he turns and runs.

"We need to get him," Lee says.

Tom looks back at Orlando. He's prone on the ground, his face bloodied, his broken hand clutched to his chest. Tom turns and runs up the stairs, following Wilbur and the Wolverine. Tom remembers what Jack Fielder said about how the Wolverines were attacking their own handlers. Clearly the issue has not been resolved. Tom saw the way the Wolverine zeroed in on the tablet. How it began chasing Wilbur when it realised what he was holding.

He thinks, too, of what Orlando was saying to Wilbur when Tom had him pinned against the wall, waiting for the Wolverine's arrival. He told him to hit "the destruct". Tom wonders if it's something to do with the tablet. A failsafe, should the Wolverines turn against their handler. A self-destruct button. Presumably Wilbur hasn't hit it yet in his panic. He's running back to wherever he's been hiding out, to get himself safe and secure before he finally pushes the button. Tom wonders if Hanley is there, too. So far, there hasn't been any sign of him.

Lee follows him up the steps and along the gangway, but he moves slower, blood from his trapezium wound covering his neck and the side of his face, and dripping down his arm.

The gangway leads to a corridor lined with offices. Tom can see Wilbur's running figure up ahead. He reaches for an office door, but as he does so, the Wolverine charges his legs. It slashes the back of his right calf. Wilbur falls forward into the office, but as he does so he drops the tablet. Tom accelerates and scoops it up. The Wolverine has turned. It lunges forward, blades protruding, but Tom steps back, lifting his legs and avoiding the blades.

"Tom, move!" Lee calls from down the corridor behind him.

Tom leaps to his left and Lee fires at the Wolverine with his Sig Sauer. His bullets bounce off it, but the Wolverine backs up, shielding itself. Tom motions for Lee to stop firing, then steps forward and kicks the Wolverine into the office with Wilbur. Tom slams the door shut.

Lee catches him up, leaning against the wall to catch his breath. From inside the office, they hear screams. They look down at the tablet. On the screen, it shows the Wolverine's POV. Without hesitation, it has attacked its maker. They watch as its blades jab in and out of Wilbur's torso, ripping through him. The blood spills from him, and the blades go so deep his insides begin to hang out. He's still screaming. He's not dead yet. Tom notes that there is no sign of Hanley inside the office.

"Orlando said something about a destruct button," Tom says. He holds up the tablet. "It must be on here somewhere."

They inspect the tablet together while the Wolverine is preoccupied. There aren't many options on the screen. He spots the red touch button in the top right of the screen. It's marked as 'Failsafe'. Tom presses it.

The Wolverine explodes.

"Jesus," Lee says, the office rattling and the door almost blown from its hinges. "A little warning next time."

Tom enters the office, handgun raised. It's clear. Wilbur and the Wolverine are both dead, and there's barely anything left of either of them.

"No Hanley," Lee says, leaning against the doorframe.

Tom shakes his head. "Not here."

Before either of them can say anything else, they hear Nina in their earpieces. "Tom, you still alive?"

"I'm here," Tom says.

"I heard the gunfire and made my way to your position," she says. "Orlando is running. I saw him leave the front of the building."

"Why didn't you stop him?" Lee says.

"Because he's not going to get away," Nina says. "But I want him to run first, same way he made us run all of today."

"What do you mean?" Lee says.

"Come here and I'll show you."

62

Orlando is dazed, but he runs, his broken right hand held close to his chest.

Blood drips from his swollen face. He spits it out the corner of his mouth while he goes, stumbling along. His head throbs from the beating Rollins gave him.

Rollins was a mistake. They shouldn't have ever gone anywhere near him. The problem was, he was a perfect choice for their scapegoat – *too* perfect, perhaps. Orlando underestimated him. He expected an ex-Army grunt of limited skills. A homeless soldier meandering across the country from state to state. The perfect fall guy for their plans. They should have paid closer attention to the redacted sections of Rollins's file. Orlando won't make the same mistake again. Next time, he'll be ready for Rollins and everything he is.

First, he needs to get clear. Needs to regroup. Needs to *heal*. When he does, he'll come back stronger. He'll strike directly at Rollins, and make him pay for everything he has cost him today. He'll get Nina, too, but he doesn't see her as of great concern. She's a cop, and she'll return to her duty, and she'll be kept busy. Rollins is a loose cannon. He's not beholden to anyone or anywhere. He moves freely. He can devote all of his time to tracking Orlando down if he wants to. Orlando needs to make sure he gets Rollins before Rollins can get him.

He gets clear of the factory, running toward the parking lot. He passes the slaughtered bodies on the way. The aftermath of the Wolverines. For machines, they were incredibly bloodthirsty. This is the kind of situation Orlando will be sure to stay very clear of in the future. This will be the last time he has anything to do with fucking robot attack dogs.

Orlando pauses next to the corpse of one of the dead factory workers. With his unbroken hand, he pats down his pant pockets until he finds keys. Car keys. He presses the lock and hears the beeping of a disarmed alarm. He looks around, following the sound, and sees a white Honda, its signal lights flashing. Orlando goes to it. He glances back toward the factory. He sees three people at the entrance. They're not chasing him. They're just watching him. Like they're letting him get away.

Or attempt to.

Orlando doesn't have many other options open to him. He gets into the Honda and starts the engine. He has to use his left hand to do everything. The car is an automatic, which makes driving easier at least. He pulls out of the space, looking up at the mirror toward the factory. The three are still there. Orlando doesn't like it. He puts his foot down.

63

Tom drapes Lee's arm over his shoulder to assist him out of the factory. They find Nina waiting for them outside. She's carrying a rocket launcher. It isn't any brand Tom has seen before.

Nina points across the grounds, toward the parking lot. "There he goes," she says.

Tom watches Orlando running. He's hurt, and clutching his broken hand to himself. They watch him pat down a dead body and take its keys.

"I assume that's why you've let him run?" Lee says, nodding at the rocket launcher.

Nina doesn't respond. She just smiles. It's answer enough.

Orlando looks back at them. He hesitates, only briefly, and then continues running toward the car he's taken the keys for.

Nina holds the rocket launcher out to Tom. "Do you want the honour? I've never fired one of these before."

Lee takes his arm from Tom's shoulder's and leans

against the wall. Tom takes the rocket launcher from Nina. He looks it over. He taps the screen on top. "What's this do?"

"I don't know," Nina says. "Probably some kind of AI-targeting bullshit, but I've looked it over and I think you can still operate the launcher manually, too."

"Now, that I can do," Tom says.

Orlando starts the Honda. He pulls away from the parking space. He doesn't turn on the lights, perhaps thinking it'll make him harder to see in the dark. The Honda, however, is white, and easy to make out. Tom targets it. The launcher has no sight, presumably because of the input on top. Tom has to go old school, by eye alone.

The Honda is drawing closer to the parking lot's exit. Tom squeezes the trigger. The missile flies toward the Honda. It connects with the trunk and explodes, touching off the gas tank. The car erupts into a fireball, then flips forward and lands on its roof.

Tom drops the rocket launcher, pulls his Sig Sauer, and he and Nina approach the fiery wreckage for a closer look. Lee stays behind, propping himself against the wall. He's weak, and getting weaker.

Tom and Nina get closer to the Honda. They feel the heat emanating from it. Orlando has not attempted to crawl clear. Tom doubts he's able. The whole vehicle is in flames. They crouch down to see better.

They spot Orlando through the windshield. He's burning. He's already dead.

64

After the battle at the WilburForce factory, Lee got on the radio and called in a helicopter to come and pick them up, and told them to bring a medic for himself. Tom and Nina took turns keeping pressure on his wound until the chopper arrived.

A full day has passed since then. A full day of Tom and Nina not being chased. A day to rest and recover.

They went back to the safe house with the Fielder family. Jack gave them his sincere thanks for what they did for him and his family. Lee was taken to a medical facility for his wound, taken to see a doctor he trusts and keeps on retainer.

Tom and Nina didn't stay at the house. It was still dark, and they were tired, but they drove back to San Francisco. They drove back to Nina's home. Just to be safe, they made sure it was clear. That there was no one watching in the street. There wasn't. They set up empty glass bottles, stringing them around the door handles so that if anyone tried to get in they'd hear. Once that was secure, they collapsed into bed.

Tom slept for twelve hours straight. Nina is out for eighteen. Tom has been monitoring the news.

"Anything about us?" Nina says, sitting beside him on the sofa when she finally awakes. She's showered, and she smells clean and fresh.

"Plenty," Tom says.

Senator Jack Fielder held a press conference early this morning. It doesn't take long for it to replay on the news and for Nina to see it for herself. Jack explains the events of yesterday. Explains who was truly behind the attacks, and what they were attempting to accomplish. He tells of WilburForce, and the Wolverines. He reveals everything. There is heavily censored footage shown of the aftermath of the WilburForce factory near Santa Rosa, and the names of all the dead workers are listed.

And, most importantly for Tom and Nina, he vindicates their innocence. Throughout the news reports it's repeated, over and over, that they were not responsible. It runs along a banner across the bottom of the screen.

"Have you heard from your station yet?" Tom says.

"Not yet," Nina says. "I've checked my phone and there's plenty of missed calls and messages, but nothing from Bayview Heights. I'll get in touch with them, but I'm not in a rush. Right now, we've earned this rest." Nina goes through to the kitchen to get a drink. It's late evening. The sky is dusky.

"Surprised there aren't any news vans outside your home," Tom says, peering out the window.

"Probably don't expect us to be here," Nina says, coming back and sipping water from a refrigerated bottle. She's brought one for Tom, too. "Has there been any news on Senator Hanley?" she says, handing the bottle over.

"Dead," Tom says.

Nina sits back down, raising her eyebrows. "Yeah? When?"

"Cops went to Wilbur Magnusson's house. They found Hanley there, shot."

"Shit," Nina says. "Any idea what went down?"

Tom shrugs. "No," he says. "But at this point, it doesn't really matter anymore." He motions toward the TV. "The reports have been cycling all day, so you'll see it for yourself soon enough, but I'll tell you now. WilburForce factories across the country have all been shut down. The contents seized. Obviously Wilbur is dead, but there's still a board of directors, and Jack says he's going to make sure the whole organisation is dismantled. There's no chance of them getting any kind of military contracts going forward."

"Anything said about the Wolverines?"

"They're gonna ban them," Tom says. "It's gonna have to go through all the necessary stages, but after yesterday, and last night, and all the factory workers they killed, there's no possibility they're ever going to allow mass production of them. They're too dangerous. Wouldn't surprise me if the blueprints have already been destroyed."

They sit in silence for a while, watching the news cycle.

A while passes before Nina speaks again. "So, what now?"

"Well, right now, I'm going to rest," Tom says. "Yesterday was a very long day, for both of us. But next, I'm going to leave San Francisco. There's going to be a lot of journalists, and a lot of questions from cops and government officials, too, and I'm not interested in wasting my time with that. We proved we weren't responsible, we stopped what Hanley's team had planned and more besides. It's time for me to leave."

Nina nods like she expected this to be his answer. "I figured as much," she says.

"You?"

"Well, I'm gonna field all those questions from journalists, and fellow cops, and government officials," she says with a grin. "And I'll take all the photographs with Senator Fielder where we shake hands and smile for the camera. But don't worry, all the way through, I'll be sure to say plenty of good things about you."

"Appreciate it."

"But before that, I'll go and see Liz, and thank her *profusely* for everything she did for us. And then pay her back for any damages incurred during said help. And I suppose I should go and visit Dante, too, and see if he managed to free himself." Nina pauses, then adds, "But I'm not in a rush to do that. I'm sure he's fine."

"That covers what's next," Tom says. "What about *now*?"

Nina smiles at him. "You know, before we were picked up yesterday morning, I remember we'd spent a damn fine evening together. It would be a shame if that was the epilogue we put on things between us."

"You're right," Tom says. "But do you think anyone's going to be doing an open mic tonight, after everything that's happened?"

Nina laughs. She's leaning close to him. The news is still playing in the background, but they've heard it all already. They don't need to keep watching. They've taken onboard all of the important information. They're exonerated. They're no longer the most wanted people in America.

Tom kisses Nina, and then he takes her in his arms and carries her upstairs.

EPILOGUE

It's another day before Tom leaves Nina's place. He goes when she's not there, having left to visit Liz Farr and make sure she's okay, and to give her both of their thanks.

Tom borrowed a baseball cap from her. He walks back to his apartment, the cap pulled low to conceal his features. There's no guarantee that everyone has been informed of their innocence. When he reaches his street, he spots a news van parked down the road, watching the front. He goes around the back and sneaks inside.

It's clear that the place has been searched. The lock on the front door is broken. Cops, probably, but it could have been Orlando and his team while they were trying to find him and Nina. Tom is sure the landlord won't be happy with the broken door and the mess, but Tom won't be around to deal with the aftermath. He's leaving San Francisco right now. He doesn't know where he's going to go, but that's never stopped him before.

He finds his backpack where he stashed it at the rear of

the wardrobe. Either it was missed in the search, or whoever was looking didn't see anything important about it. Tom checks the inside. Everything is still present. His Beretta. His KA-BAR. A change of clothes. A folded and worn picture of Alejandra. His burner phones.

He checks them. He has missed calls from his father, and from his best friend, Zeke Greene, and from others he has become acquainted with over the years. No doubt they called after seeing the news. They won't have believed he was responsible, but they'll have called to check if he was all right, if he needed help. Tom will have to call them back.

But first, he sees a number of missed calls from Cindy Vaughan. Tom has wondered about her lack of response to his calls. He's worried about her, too, though not as much as he'd have ordinarily been able to. There was too much going on. Too many pressing matters at hand.

He calls her back. This time she answers, almost instantly.

"Tom?" she says.

"It's me," he says. "How've you been? I tried to call."

"I assumed those unrecognised numbers might have been you," Cindy says. "And I got your message. I saw the news. I saw the footage, too."

"That's why I was calling."

"Uh-huh – to help prove that footage was bullshit, right? It was good, I'll give them that, but I saw through it, and I didn't need to know you already to know you weren't responsible."

"I appreciate that. Is everything okay your end?"

There's a pause, and instantly Tom knows that everything is not. "Things are resolved there for you, right? I saw yesterday's news, too. And today's. They're calling you a hero.

It's not the first time. They've had people on proving that the footage was faked. So you don't need to hang around, right?"

"I'm not planning on it," Tom says. "Cindy, what's happening? Something's wrong. I can hear it in your voice."

"Yeah, something's pretty fucking wrong all right," Cindy says, her voice on the verge of hysterical laughter.

"What's happened?"

"Uh, I don't know if we can talk on the phone, Tom."

Tom understands. "I'm on my way," he says.

"You know where to find me."

Tom hangs up. He grabs his bag and he leaves the apartment. He goes out the back way again, and to his parked Ford. He keeps the baseball cap pulled low. The news van doesn't see him. He gets into the Ford and he sets off for Texas.

For Cindy.

ABOUT THE AUTHOR

Did you enjoy *Kill Switch*? Please consider leaving a review on Amazon to help other readers discover the book.

Paul Heatley left school at sixteen, and since then has held a variety of jobs including mechanic, carpet fitter, and bookshop assistant, but his passion has always been for writing. He writes mostly in the genres of crime fiction and thriller, and links to his other titles can be found on his website. He lives in the north east of England.

Want to connect with Paul? Visit him at his website.

www.PaulHeatley.com

ALSO BY PAUL HEATLEY

The Tom Rollins Thriller Series

Blood Line (Book 1)

Wrong Turn (Book 2)

Hard to Kill (Book 3)

Snow Burn (Book 4)

Road Kill (Book 5)

No Quarter (Book 6)

Hard Target (Book 7)

Last Stand (Book 8)

Blood Feud (Book 9)

Search and Destroy (Book 10)

Ghost Team (Book 11)

Full Throttle (Book 12)

Sudden Impact (Book 13)

Kill Switch (Book 14)

The Tom Rollins Box Set (Books 1 - 4)

Printed in Great Britain
by Amazon

47768454R00182